The Vampire of
the Val-de-Grâce

The Vampire of
the Val-de-Grâce

by
Léon Gozlan

translated, annotated and introduced by
Brian Stableford

A Black Coat Press Book

ISBN 978-1-61227-123-1. First Printing. November 2012. Published by Black Coat Press, an imprint of Hollywood Comics.com, LLC, P.O. Box 17270, Encino, CA 91416. All rights reserved. Except for review purposes, no part of this book may be reproduced or transmitted in any form or by any means, electronic or mechanical, including photocopying, recording, or by any information storage and retrieval system, without permission in writing from the publisher. The stories and characters depicted in this novel are entirely fictional. Printed in the United States of America.

TABLE OF CONTENTS

Introduction 7
ANOTHER SOUL SOLD TO THE DEVIL 17
THE VAMPIRE OF THE VAL-DE-GRÂCE 45

Introduction

Le Vampire du Val-de-Grâce by Léon Gozlan, here translated as *The Vampire of the Val-de-Grâce*, was originally published in book form in Paris by E. Dentu in 1861. The second story, included as a makeweight, "Encore une âme vendue au diable," here translated as "Another Soul Sold to the Devil," first appeared as a two-part serial in the *Bulletin de l'ami des arts* in 1844.

Le Vampire du Val-de-Grâce comprised one volume of a two-volume set collectively entitled *Le Faubourg mystérieux* [The Mysterious Neighborhood]. The set comprises a series of tales narrated by the same character, Monsieur Morel, an aged male nurse in a sanitarium in the Faubourg Saint-Denis. The other volume contains the slightly shorter novel "La Folle du no. 16" [The Madwoman in No. 16] and the short story "Le Portefeuille de maroquin noir" [The Black Morocco-Leather Wallet]. Judging by appearances, the series was probably first published as a sequence of *feuilletons* in a periodical, but I have not been able to locate those original versions, if they exist.

As Monsieur Morel observes in his preamble, one sometimes looks for the fantastic in the wrong place, and *Le Vampire du Val-de-Grâce* and "Encore une âme vendue au diable" are both, in essence, stories about looking for the fantastic in the wrong place: the world of objective events rather than the world of the human imagination. The novel is primarily a horror story, while the short story is a comedy, but, like many *feuilletons* of

the two distinct periods in which they were written—
before and after the revolution of 1848 and the coup
d'état of 1851—they also try to be other things as else as
well, in the hope of engaging all reading tastes. "Encore
une âme vendue au diable" is also an apologue, a flip-
pant but not entirely casual *conte philosophique*. *Le
Vampire du Val-de-Grâce*, being longer, has scope to be
even more ambitious; it is also a love story, a mystery, a
comedy and, at least marginally, a scientific romance.
Perhaps, as a result, both stories are a trifle confused, but
that very confusion is productive of more than mere ec-
centricity. *Le Vampire du Val-de-Grâce* is a story unique
in its excess and its bizarre absurdity, and that gives it a
certain precious verve as well as a certain capacity to
make the jaw drop.

Léon Gozlan (1803-1866) was a writer fond of oc-
casional excess, who was not entirely a stranger to extreme experiences himself. In the brief memoir he wrote
of Gozlan, Eugène de Mirecourt records the actual incident that Gozlan used as the launching-pad for the best
and most bizarre of all his novels, *Les Émotions de
Polydore Marasquin* (1857; tr. as *The Emotions of
Polydore Marasquin, A Man Among the Monkeys* and
Monkey Island), which tells the story of a castaway on
an island prolifically inhabited by dangerously intelligent apes. As a young man wanting to follow in his father's footsteps as a successful entrepreneur, Gozlan had
charted a ship to take a cargo of champagne to the African colonies. The trouble that he ran into when the bottles had all been smashed in a violent storm and the ship
had to make a forced landing on an unknown shore, was
not as ludicrously bizarre as Polydore Marasquin's adventure among the apes, but it was fantastic and horrify-
ing nevertheless, and nearly cost him his life—at least in

the way that Gozlan told the story to his friends in Paris, when he had decided that the life of a writer was preferable to that of an adventurer.

It is, of course, entirely possible that Gozlan's anecdotal account of being trapped by an African horde and having to fight his way out, using his rifle as a club, after failing to placate his captors by giving them all his gunpowder and bullets, was slightly exaggerated, as travelers' tales often are, but it was not as exaggerated as the second-hand versions of the tale that were peddled in Paris, growing as they spread. The rumor finally assumed such proportions that Gozlan was said to have murdered his ship's captain and turned pirate—and the true measure of the man is that, according to Mirecourt, when this suggestion was put to him, he simply shrugged his shoulders and pointed out that the storyteller had forgotten to add the necessary detail that, after having killed the captain, he had eaten him.

That was not the kind of additional detail that Gozlan was ever likely to overlook in his own works, as *Le Vampire du Val-de-Grâce* eventually proves, in some style. Although no modern reader is likely to be unable to penetrate the mystery element of the novel's plot as soon as it is formulated, the point of the story is not the mere revelation of that solution, but the extra detail piled upon it in the climactic chapters, which do not hesitate to go over the top and keep on going, ever further into the wilderness of absurdity. Although the principal substance of the story is clearly descended from the *romans noirs* produced in France in imitation of German and English "Gothic novels" in the early decades of the century, it obviously belongs to a later and more sophisticated period, in which it had been generally realized that horror and farce are closely akin, and that there is considerable narrative currency to be gained from dancing on the thin tightrope that separates the two.

Insofar as it makes use of the vampire folklore originally introduced to France in Dom Augustine Calmet's *Dissertations sur les apparitions des anges, des démons et sur les revenants et vampires de Hongrie, de Bohème, de Moravie et Silesie* (1746; tr. as *The Phantom World*) and repopularized by the oft-reprinted *Infernaliana* (1822), incorrectly attributed to Charles Nodier, *Le Vampire du Val-de-Grâce*, belongs to the cynical and somewhat tongue-in-cheek tradition of Pierre-Alexis Ponson du Terrail's *La Baronne trépassée* (1853)[1] and Paul Féval's *Le Chevalier Ténèbre* (1860)[2], which teasingly refuse explicitly to confirm or deny the real existence of vampires, but play extravagantly with the idea, while merrily exploiting the sinister fascination and appeal of anecdotes of that sort.

Modern readers are, of course, thoroughly accustomed to horror-comedy of various shades of ambiguity, but in Gozlan's day such hybridization was still relatively new, and ripe for innovative literary exploitation. No matter how fantastic *Le Vampire du Val-de-Grâce* ultimately becomes, however, it remains based on real terror and real experience; the one fate that all his characters somehow contrive to avoid—that of actually falling prey to the cholera epidemic that ravaged Paris in 1849— Gozlan suffered, and although he did not die of the disease (and managed to avoid the various crazy treatments that were then applied in cases thought to be desperate),

---

[1] tr. as *The Vampire and the Devil's Son*, Black Coat Press, ISBN 978-1-932983-55-5.
[2] tr. as *Knightshade*. Black Coat Press, ISBN 978-0-9740711-4-5.

it scared him sufficiently to drive him out of Paris following his recovery, in order to seek temporary refuge in Brussels. There is an echo of that real terror in the construction of the novel's climax, just as there had been an echo of Gozlan's actual experience in Africa in his account of Polydore Marasquin's tribulations, and just as there is a measure of real conviction and feeling in the conscientiously peculiar anticlimax of "Encore une âme vendue au diable."

The manifest element of scientific romance in *Le Vampire du Val-de-Grâce* is restrained, in that it refers not to a speculative discovery that might be made in the future, but to the rediscovery, albeit in a somewhat exaggerated form, of an invention supposedly made in the past. Modern readers might think the subject of embalming a rather odd choice for a speculative novel, but it must be remembered that our thorough familiarity with the practice is relatively new. Not only had the art not been mastered in 1861, but its potential still remained inestimable. If Dr. Kanali's hopes for his method seem exaggerated, it is worth considering the subsidiary use of the same theme in Hippolyte Mettais' *L'An 5865* (1865)[3], which imagines a future society in which the practices of interment and cremation are regarded as repulsively primitive, and civilized societies use improved embalming techniques to keep all their dead permanently available for contemplation, after the fashion of Jeremy Bentham—and, at a later date, Lenin.

In Dr. Kanali's view, in fact, competent embalming is merely a significant step on the road to resurrection, a long-term project in which he is playing the role of a

---

[3] tr. as *The Year 5865*, Black Coat Press, ISBN 978-1-61227-100-2.

modern alchemist rather than a physician—but that too seemed not entirely impossible in 1861, when alchemical dreams still had a certain currency, in aspiration as well as anecdote. That element of the plot is its clearest echo of the work of Honoré de Balzac, whom Gozlan had once served as secretary, and about whom he wrote three memoirs, most famously *Balzac en pantoufles* (1856; tr. as *Balzac in Slippers*). It is arguable, however, that the more intriguing aspect of scientific romance in the novel is the attitude of its narrator and the story's construction as a psychological "case study."

The three stories making up *Le Faubourg mystérieux* are by no means the first psychological case-study stories ever written, but they are among the earliest substantial examples of the subgenre reflecting the emergent attitude that refined attitudes to madness in the course of the nineteenth century and embedded it securely in a clinical context. They appeared in book form in the same year as Oliver Wendell Holmes' classic *Elsie Venner* (1861) and two years before William Gilbert's *Shirley Hall Asylum* (1863), the most notable early collection of such stories published in Victorian England. The most notable nineteenth-century French example, "Soeur Marthe" by "Charles Epheyre" (Charles Richet) did not appear until 1890. Seen as a contribution to that subgenre, *Le Vampire du Val-de-Grâce* is perhaps less interesting than "La Folle du no. 16," venturing too far into the fantastic to be considered as a plausible account of psychological distress, let alone a typical one, but that does not distract from the particular tone of Monsieur Morel's positivist analysis and studious approach, which, although not intended to be taken entirely seriously, are a significant aspect of the narrative and its manner of considering its themes.

As is typical of *feuilletons* of the period, *Le Vampire du Val-de-Grâce* is rather repetitive, in the interests of reminding readers forced to absorb the story over a period of weeks what has gone before, and—equally typically—was not revised for book publication in such a way as to remove repetitions unnecessary in that context. It helps to remember, in suffering such mild annoyances, that writers routinely made such serials up as they went along, never knowing whether they might suddenly receive orders to cut the story short or expand it indefinitely. They often indulged in blatant padding if they ran short of inspiration, but rarely did so quite as blatantly as Gozlan does the entirely gratuitous Montmartre-set passage in *Le Vampire du Val-de-Grâce*, into which he drops a short play that has nothing whatsoever to do with the plot. The play is not without an interest of its own, however, in terms of its somewhat *avant-gardist* method; it is, in effect, a radio play written three generations before there was any such thing as radio.

Like most 19th century writers, Gozlan began his career as a poet, arriving in Paris in 1828 from Marseilles with the manuscripts of his early verses. Like his peers, however—and with the assistance of his fellow-Marseillais Joseph Méry—he soon switched to journalism, which offered the only real hope of making a living from his pen at the time. Although he was fortunate enough to start more-or-less at the top, working for *Le Figaro*, and later the *Revue de Paris*, even that career proved difficult, and although he branched out into novels with some success in the 1840s, the work he did for Balzac at that time must have provided him with a useful steady supplement. Gozlan probably did not achieve any substantial financial security until he began writing plays in considerable quantities, eventually becoming one of the leading Parisian producers of dramas and comedies in the early days of the Second Empire—but that too must have had its tribulations, especially during the direly difficult years following the 1848 Revolution and Louis-Napoléon's coup.

Like Méry, but unlike many of his other literary friends and acquaintances, Gozlan was indifferent to the Revolution; Mirecourt records with some amazement that Gozlan never seemed unduly bitter about the fact that Louis-Philippe appeared to loathe him, and routinely struck his name off any list of candidates for honors offered for his approval, but that he was equally unmoved when wooed by Republicans. By virtue of being politically uncommitted, he was able to stay in Paris and keep working during the awkward interval of turmoil, but he must have had a difficult time; it is not entirely surprising, therefore, that he would take time out in 1861, while writing a novel set in 1849, to reminisce about the tribulations that men of his stripe had to endure even before he came down with cholera, nor that he should take the opportunity to publish a play that he would never have been able to put on the stage, in 1849, 1861, or any other phase of his career, because it was simply too eccentric. It would, at any rate, be a trifle inappropriate to hold the self-indulgence against him.

It is worth noting, too, that Gozlan's talent for the baroque stayed with him to the end, and beyond. He had regarded himself throughout his life as Jewish, like his highly successful father, and had been regarded as Jewish by everyone who knew him, but when his funeral was in the process of being conducted by a rabbi, one of his relatives on his mother's side appeared waving a certificate of Christian baptism, referring to a ceremony apparently carried out in his infancy—thus bringing the funeral to an abrupt halt and requiring a substitution of clergy and place of interment. Gozlan was in no position to laugh about it, but he would surely have appreciated the irony of having gone through his entire life without ever knowing that he was a Christian. He would not, however, have said that one couldn't have made it up; he knew better than that, and in his career as a literary artist had long regarded himself, albeit in a less spectacular manner than Mandanne, as another soul sold to the Devil.

This translation of *Le Vampire du Val-de-Grâce* has been taken from the version of the 1861 Dentu edition reproduced on the Bibliothèque Nationale's *gallica* website. The translation of "Encore une âme vendue au diable" is taken from the 1844 volume of the *Bulletin de l'ami des arts* reproduced on the same website.

Brian Stableford

ANOTHER SOUL SOLD TO THE DEVIL

I

"It's strange! It's distressing! It's enough to make one throw oneself in the Seine, or to poison oneself with the rest of the Chinese vermilion in the bottom of that bladder," the young artist Mandanne said to himself, miserable, haggard, crazed and desperate, as he gazed with convulsions of rage at a painting set in front of him. "Me, refused by the jury! Refused! Yes, refused, in the most odious fashion possible."

He plunged his clenched fists into his pockets, stamping on the parquet, to the point of making his plaster casts and skeletons tremble in every corner of the studio. "What, then, does one have to do?" he murmured. I consulted my friends while I was working on my painting; I listened to all their criticisms, welcomed all their advice, and retouched my subject bit by bit, in a thousand different places—everywhere, in sum. The composition, design and colors have been redone relentlessly—and after all that trouble, care, late nights and time, a refusal! Tomorrow, the newspapers will publish my defeat and my shame—the newspapers, those consolers who enlarge wounds with the intention of healing them. Tomorrow, the stepfather of the woman I was to marry will send me away, and my landlord will tell me to get out of his house, under the pretext of repair and decoration; tomorrow, my porter will say to me: 'What do you expect?' Tomorrow…but tomorrow, I shall be dead."

Mandanne fell silent momentarily in order to concentrate his dolor on his refused painting, a painting forty feet in circumference, encased in a magnificent frame, representing the most poetically beautiful mythological theme: *Time Discovering Truth.*

"Yes," he went on, with a new bitterness, the time to discover, one say soon, the truth of my merit, my talent, the charm of my work; but I shall no longer be alive, I shall be with all the great persecuted artists, with..." At this point Mandanne recited a long litany of the martyrs of art, and was not consoled.

"Let's be done with it," he added, going to the far end of the studio to look for one of those poor painter's inkwells in which there is everything but ink. He succeeded nevertheless in tracing a few lines on a piece of paper on which there was the beginning of a caricature: *I die innocent, and after my death I want my painting of* Time Discovering Truth *to be given to Champigneulles, my birthplace.*

Then he picked up his hat in order to go and drown himself opposite the Louvre, a few meters from the monument where he had been refused. He was very fond of the place.

"One more look at my work," he said to himself—and he paused, tears in his eyes, a few paces away from the painting proscribed by the warrant of the members of the Institut. The sun, as it set, cut diagonally through the cage of his studio and illuminated the only two figures in his vast canvas. The effect of the light, as usual, lent considerable value to the painter's subject—a charm that it does not always have in reality. The setting sun is a flatterer.

The veil that Time, suspended in mid-air, was lifting seemed delightfully light, and Truth was rendered with a great seduction of color. To Mandanne, everything seemed perfect, incomparable and sublime: the head of Time, his gray beard, his knock-kneed legs, fading backwards into the clouds, and the face of Truth, her colors, her hands and her expression. Raphael had passed that way, but a Raphael enriched by three centuries of progress, humanitarian ideas and a thousand other improvements.

Mandanne choked with despair as he drowned himself thus in his superiority, before going to drown himself in the Seine opposite the Louvre.

"There would be reason enough to give oneself to the devil a thousand times over," he exclaimed, as he opened the door of his studio, "if the Devil existed—but he no longer exists..."

At this point, Mandanne was about to proffer a horrible blasphemy, and that is doubtless what brought forth, violently, the individual with whom he found himself face to face as he extended his leg toward the first step of the staircase.

"I beg your pardon," said a man dressed in a black velvet overcoat and wearing furry gloves, "but I exist."

"Are you...?"

"I'm him."

"That's implausible," said Mandanne.

"I don't deny it. But what is plausible? Is it plausible that one would drown oneself for a painting?"

"Do you think it's bad too?"

"I don't say that; I don't say anything. You wanted me; I've come. I can only prove to you that I exist be giving you evidence of my power. Speak!"

"Make all the members of the jury die of apoplexy right away, and I'll believe you."

"What good would that do you?"

"None, in fact; my painting would still have been refused."

"Ask me for a useful impossibility, and you'll see."

"All right! That my painting of *Time Discovering Truth* should be transformed instantly, that its subject should be changed, and that, having been taken before the jury, it has been accepted."

"That's child's play. Your soul's worth more."

"You want me to sell my soul, then?"

"Since you don't believe in me, what risk is there in signing the pact?"

"It's just that you're unsettling me..."

"Hurry up, young man; I have a deal to make with a minister before ten o'clock this evening, and another with a young woman before midnight. My minutes are precious."

Mandanne went pale.

"But if I accept," he stammered, "will I at least have a good place at the Salon?"

"The best."

"You assure me?"

"You'll have the king's corner, when he's painted with the Garde Nationale..."

"You're tempting me."

"That's my trade—and not only will you obtain the most favorable place in the gallery of the Salon, but you'll have eulogies in all the newspapers, you'll be awarded the croix d'honneur, you'll have commissions, you'll give audiences to the director of the Beaux-Arts—in sum, you'll have everything that you desire."

"It's agreed, then," said Mandanne, who had become accustomed to the Devil, as one becomes accustomed to the Garde Nationale, "that our pact will last throughout my life, that you won't have the right to limit it."

"It's agreed—but as soon as your final hour sounds, I'll be there to take your soul."

"But what will you do with it?"

"Ah—that's my secret!"

"Bah!" said Mandanne, after a few moments' hesitation. "I might as well be burned for one thing as another!" He extended his hand to the Devil, who had the prudence to withdraw his own, and cried: "I accept!"

"You swear to be mine?" the tempter said to him.

"I swear."

"Raise your eyes," the Devil said to him then, "and look."

Mandanne looked.

He was at the Salon, in the midst of three or four thousand people, who, at close range and from afar—from every distance—had their eyes fixed upon a magnificent portrait in oils representing the wife of a famous notary. The portrait was signed "Mandanne."

II

And this is what people around him were saying:

"Has a better resemblance ever been seen? What fire! What originality! What vigor! What relief! It's as beautiful as the portrait of François I by Titian, or that of the old pensioner by Van Dyck."

"Leave off!" murmured young people coiffed in red caps. "Titian and Van Dyck aren't worthy to wipe Mandanne's brushes."

Mandanne blushed; justice was being rendered to him.

"And when one thinks," they added, "that an artist like him isn't decorated, while bushels of crosses and ells of ribbon are thrown at chapel daubers whose only merit is knowing how to wait every day for twenty years in the corridors of the ministry for the director of the Beaux-Arts to pass by, in order to kiss his boots."

The opinion of serious people was, extraordinarily, in perfect accord with that of those young hotheads—not that they disparaged Van Dyck and Titian to raise up Mandanne, but they all agreed that nothing as gripping had been seen in painting since those old masters.

"Don't you think, though," Mandanne hazarded to say, with a timidity that still reflected the modesty of his former obscurity, "that the forehead is a little too much in the light?"

"It's your eyes that aren't sufficiently in it," a red cap immediately replied to him.

"Let's help Monsieur to see a little better," added another cap, lifting Mandanne three feet off the floor.

"To the lantern!" shouted a third. "There's no lack of light there!"

So, for having risked a very feeble criticism of himself, Mandanne was about to pass through one of the Louvre's large windows, and perhaps fall into the same river in which he had wanted to drown himself a few hours before.

The danger was not, however, without charm for him; he would gladly have thanked his murderers if they had permitted him to speak, but they were strangling him; all that he could do, in that situation, was smile at them. He would doubtless have died asphyxiated if an energetic flood coming from the door had not caused a powerful diversion among the group of frantic admirers in the midst of whom the glorious and unfortunate Mandanne was choking.

That undulation brought admirers of a more elevated sphere before Mandanne's painting. Members of the four academies could be distinguished, officers of the king's household and that of the princes, and, in their midst, the Minister of the Interior—who, after having congratulated, embraced and introduced Mandanne to the ambassadors associated with that ovation, awarded him with his own hand the Civil and Military Order of the Légion d'honneur.

One can easily imagine the astonishment of the two or three hundred pupils seeing the great artist Mandanne honored in that fashion, in the person of the man of whom they had almost made a victim. A singularity worthy of note is that none of them, suddenly changing his opinion of the merits of the recompensed painter, said: "Another donkey decorated while so many illustrious artists, such as Trillebardou, Chantefouille and the great Crapoussin, are neglected!" Mandanne was deemed pure, although fortunate. He was carried around the gallery three times, and applauded like a bad tragedy.

The happiness of his first day of glory was not to stop there. On returning home, he found two letters, one large and square, the other oblong and perfumed. He opened the latter first, for he was not yet thirty, and read:

Monsieur,
Renown has borne your name into the depths of my boudoir; if you do not think me unworthy of your brushes, come to my home, the Hôtel d'Armainville in the Rue de la Ferme, before noon tomorrow. You will find a

model as docile—I dare not sway beautiful—as you de-
sire.

    Your admirer,

                    Comtesse Burgos.

"I'll begin with the Comtesse," Mandanne murmured. "Where shall I end up? Let's see what the second
letter contains."

Again, he read.

Monsieur,

    *I am instructed to tell you that Monsieur le Ministre
de l'intérieur grants you a gratification of 20,000 francs
from the funds of the Beaux-Arts. You may present yourself to the Treasury to collect your check.*

"It appears," said Mandanne, whose wit had not yet
been eroded by prosperity, "that my soul is of the finest
quality."

Those who might have been tempted to set the perfectly true, though seemingly fantastic, story of
Mandanne in the present era will immediately have realized their error on seeing a Minister of the Interior recognize, reward and decorate merit. No allusion to the
present time is possible; the remuneratory fact is sufficient proof of that.

Mandanne placed the letter from the Ministry of the
Interior under his head and the note from Comtesse Burgos over his heart, and did not get a wink of sleep.

No one will be astonished to hear that he expected
at any moment to see the Devil come into his room, in
order to obtain an account of the day's complete success,
but the Devil did not appear. As a gallant man, a man
who knows how to behave, he has no need of grati-

tude—and besides, as you shall see in the continuation of the story, if you take the trouble to read it, he is only in the habit of showing himself when his presence is violently desired.

III

Finally, dawn broke, and it had never seemed rosier or more cheerful to Mandanne's eyes. Among all the wishes that he had been permitted to formulate, that of being considerably more handsome, for example, in order not to run any risk of displeasing Comtesse Burgos, had never crossed his mind, no man having the desire to be other than he is, even with the opportunity of being better. On the point the devil has no bargain to conclude.

When Mandanne had shaved, arranged his hair and dressed in the latest fashion, as one used to say in the good old days, and had put a hundred francs in gold coins in each of his pockets, he went...to the home of the Comtesse Burgos? Not at all! For an artist, you ought to know, there is something more seductive and more irresistible than the love of beauty, than the lure of curiosity, even than hunger or duty: it is the need to know what is being said about one in the newspapers, which he pretends he never reads. Reading-rooms, as everyone knows, only survive on the profits brought in by those who never go there, most notably men of letters, painters, députés, actors and all though who have dealing with the great dark individual known as the public.

People talk about the joys of the seventh heaven, but the seventh heaven is a mere attic compared with the exceptional voluptuousness of an artist reading his eulogy while drinking his morning coffee. The gilded carvings of the café, the moldings, the arabesques and guilloched cornices, seem to his fascinated gaze to be a reflection of the Alhambra; the bread is ambrosia, the fatty cutlet exhales the perfume of all the meadows in Brittany, and even the lady at the counter is a nymph reminiscent of mythology.

Mandanne experienced that poetic and dreamlike sensation, and a thousand others, as he savored his eulogy in the headlines and columns of the newspapers. One said: *The Salon is as execrable this year as it was last year; without the masterpiece of masterpieces, the miraculous portrait by the celebrated Mandanne, it would definitely be necessary to close it and put the keys under the door.*

A painter is always secretly flattered, in the depths of his soul, to hear it said that the Salon is pitiful while he is praised. Everyone thinks that he is an exception—and in the final count, the Louvre is hideous and sublime at the same time.

Another paper expressed its opinion of our artist in these terms: *We heard a rumor that Monsieur Mandanne's painting had been refused. The jury has not yet sunk so low, thank Heaven. Not only has Monsieur Mandanne's famous painting not been refused, but it is exciting everyone's admiration; it is one of those marvels that appears in the arts from time to time in order to prove to jealous nations that France still holds the scepter, and is still the classical terrain of genius. It is always to her that it is necessary to turn in matters of taste, intelligence and superiority.*

When the café's waiter came to give Mandanne change due on a twenty-franc piece for the price of breakfast, Mandanne said: "Keep it."

The waiter thought: *The man's mad!*—but he kept the sixteen francs anyway.

He was going out drunk with glory, in order to go to the Hôtel d'Armainville to the home of Comtesse Burgos, when his hand fell on a wretched little newspaper edited by one of that barefoot legion who live on theater tickets while waiting to obtain a ticket to the hospital. Mandanne scanned it indifferently, his hand on the café's brass doorknob. One line stopped him—a line that as the blade of a dagger.

Yes, it read, *we agree with the immense majority of connoisseurs and the public that Mandanne is a great, sublime portrait-painter, but we are waiting for a historical painting. Until then, we shall reserve the compliment of our admiration of Monsieur Mandanne's talent.*

That petty criticism, in a ridiculously obscure paper—was it even a criticism? that observation, rather; that simple reflection born of a extreme benevolence—caused Mandanne more pain than the thousands of compliments he had gathered over breakfast had given him pleasure.

"Oh, I'm not a painter of history! But who isn't a painter of history? I shall be one when I want to be. They reproach me for not painting history..."

The word *history* returned to Mandanne's lips three or four thousand times before he arrived at the Comtesse's house, which he eventually reached, and where he was received by two liveried domestics.

"Madame la Comtesse is not seeing anyone today."

"But I'm Monsieur Mandanne."

"That's different," one of the domestics replied, begging the artist to accompany him to Madame la Comtesse's apartment.

Treading carpets as thick and soft as lawns, Mandanne spent ten minutes going through vast drawing-rooms decorated with a luxury redolent with an utterly royal silence. Finally, the amplitude of the rooms diminished, each one becoming smaller than the next, but always more exquisitely ornamented, until he reached the Comtesse's boudoir.

The domestic retired respectfully.

Although it was March, the Comtesse de Burgos was clad in light muslin—so light that when she raised herself up on her elbow to greet Mandanne, the latter glimpsed the blue nuance of her silk stockings through the vaporous fabric of the Oriental robe. A Greek bonnet surmounted by a golden acorn, Chinese slippers, and shoes veritably worthy of a fairy-tale completed her delightfully eccentric costume.

The Comtesse's costume naturally indicated the mild temperature that reigned in her boudoir, an atmosphere lightly charged with the perfume of hothouse flowers, and the emanations of sachets that could be seen scattered on lemonwood shelves.

"Is this pose suitable for you?" the Comtesse asked him, without giving the artist the time that was normally wasted in gazing at the whites of his eyes, his black hair and his ruddy ears the first time people saw him.

She had negligently thrown one leg over the other, set her bonnet aside and fastened a rose between the graceful shell of her ear and the gilded tangle of her beautiful blonde hair.

"You can admire me when you've painted me," she told Mandanne, who seemed to be devoting an ecstatic slowness to placing his canvas on the easel.

I didn't imagine the Comtesse like this, Mandanne thought. *How beautiful she is! How resplendent! How marvelous!*

"Your hair is slightly untidy, Madame."

"There!" she said, passing her fingers through her hair with the insouciance of a schoolboy. She was then Aida! She was the Orient! She was Spain! She was the beautiful Comtesse Burgos!

In a more emotional voice, Mandanne said: "Your arms slightly more exposed, if you please."

"You'd prefer this?" she said, pushing her long gauze sleeves back toward her neck, and then added: "So be it! It's not too bad."

Already, an astonishing resemblance a gliding beneath the trembling fingers of the painter, and as if without his being conscious of it, a delicate but emphatic, and minutely exact sketch, was delimited by the softest and warmest colors. The Comtesse de Burgos seemed to be emerging from the depths of a cloud and gradually setting herself before Mandanne's eyes, who thought himself less the author that the witness of his work.

Intoxicated by his talent, and intoxicated by his model, Mandanne said once more to Comtesse Burgos, in a more emotional voice: "Your shoulders a little less hidden, Madame."

Scarcely had he expressed this wish that the Comtesse, laughing, threw off the diaphanous fabric wrapped around her neck, and her bosom, as white as a dove in flight, and her shoulders were exposed in all their dazzling firmness to the eyes of our artist—or, we ought to say, our lover. His mind was no longer on the painting; it was soaring around his model in decreasing spirals of fire; his hand alone, distracted and agitated, never ceased to cover the canvas with a thousand enchanted layers.

And he said to himself: *A young woman who receives me in a boudoir, in a transparent muslin skirt and a Greek bonnet, which she takes off for me, and lays her arms and shoulders bare in such unusually obliging manner, must be in love with me.*

So, quitting his easel and hurling himself at the Comtesse's feet like a madman, Mandanne exclaimed: "Madame, the work of my mind is complete; that of my heart is beginning."

"Before replying to you," said the Comtesse, with an expression that as noble without ceasing to be jovial, "I want to see my portrait. If you don't have talent, I'll have my domestics throw you out; if you have an extraordinary amount..."

"Look, Madame," Mandanne replied, with conscientious conceit.

"It's sublime!" cried the Comtesse de Burgos, who added: "I'm sorry, Monsieur, not to respond to the love of a man of genius like yourself, but if I had had the weakness to love an artist, I would have wanted him to be both a great painter and a great sculptor, like Michelangelo, Puget and a few others."

It would be difficult to dismiss a passion with greater delicacy and good taste.

As she bid Mandanne farewell, the Comtesse slipped ten thousand-franc banknotes into his hand.

The Devil—take note, you who might one day have dealings with him—only ever gives you what you ask of him, and you'll agree that that's already a great deal. Mandanne had not asked him worldly enjoyment, and he had completely failed to obtain it in his interview with the Comtesse de Burgos. He would have known, otherwise, that the more elevated a person is in dignity, and the more use she makes of a casual manner and familiarity with those she believes to be her inferiors, the more certain it is that, at the moment that you fall at her feet, she will crush you. Imperious creole women display themselves nakedly to their slaves.

IV

Mandanne had no sooner gone home than he said to himself, in a truly unjust fit of rage against the Devil: "Is it for that, then, that I've sold him my soul? To remain a painter of portraits, and not to be either a painter of history or a sculptor like Michelangelo or Puget?"

"You'll be both, my son," replied a voice that he already knew.

"But when?" Mandanne demanded.

"Right away. Get to work."

You will observe that it is the Devil's custom—and we are neither going to explain nor discuss it here—only to appear once in person. The times that follow are gradually diminishing manifestations of his individuality: soon he is a voice, as in this case, then a whisper in the ear, then an item of advice—and he ends up being no more than a abstract impulse. The latter transformations are the most dangerous, for they tend to make the purchased soul forget that it is prey to the evil spirit.

The year the followed was a series of unparalleled contentments for Mandanne. He painted history with the same success that he had painted portraits, and he produced pieces of sculpture as energetic as those created by Puget's chisel and as lifelike as those of Auguste Préault.

The beautiful Comtesse de Burgos, having no more reason to refuse her heart to Mandanne, gave him her hand. As it is the custom in Spain that the woman ennobles, Comtesse Burgos, who was Spanish, made a Comte

31

of her illustrious husband, who was no longer called anything but the Comte de Mandanne.

Happiness is a folly. Mandanne, as happy as a king, wanted to have a palace built according to his fantasy. He brought marbles from Greece and granite from Egypt, and employed them, with the rarest of taste, in the splendid habitation in which he took up residence.

When one possesses a palace, when one is a painter, at least one can have a studio worthy of a palace. Mandanne constructed one so great, so vast, that one could ride around it on horseback. It is inexplicable why painters, to whom silence is so necessary, generally acquire, as soon as they have a name, a determined penchant for noisy pleasures and soldierly fantasies; they become children again; they like drums, hunting horns, trumpets, rifles and yataghans. If they dared, they would demand to be addressed as "general." There is one, I believe, who adopts the title of major when abroad.

Mandanne surpassed everything previously seen in that kind of mania. In the morning, clad in an equerry's boots, he mounted a bay horse, in the evening a chestnut mare, and often painted in a cabriolet with a groom who stood behind him on the bracket-eat holding his palette. His studio permitted that kind of painting, about which there was much talk in society. That was not all; as soon as one went into his home, a drum-roll and a volley of rifle-shots was heard, and it was not rare for a canon to resound in the antechamber in the middle of a conversation, to announce the visit of some important individual.

The newspapers made fun of these puerile extravagances, but it is as well to say here—and we beg the reader to remember it—that Mandanne had passed from reputation to renown, and from renown to celebrity; he no longer read the newspapers, although he got them all, in contrast to his early years when he had read them all but did not receive any. What would the papers have told him? Did he not have more glory than all other painters put together? What price was refused for his works? He had no time to read, when Prussia was appealing to him loudly, when Russia had commissioned twenty fifty-foot paintings, when England had sent him a thousand pounds sterling to beg him to think about her in his spare time.

If you are wondering what role the Comtesse Burgos as playing in that Olympian festival, the answer is that she was handed down to posterity every day in different guises—which is to say that she posed for her husband, sometimes modeling as a virgin and sometimes as a bacchante; one say she lent her smooth shoulders to Venus, on another her charming face was recognizable in the midst of a group at a public drinking-fountain.

She also received frequent notes composed along the following lines: *Madame, I have seen your divine torso in Brest, in a public square, beneath the cupola of a fountain; I have come to Paris expressly to assure myself that the original is as beautiful as the copy.* On other occasions there were different notes written in these terms: *I saw you this morning, naked, beneath the features of a divine statuette. Would it be permissible for me, Madame, to see clad that which, for modesty's sake, I dare not buy?*

In sum, Mandanne squandered her so wantonly, as an image, as an allegory and as an emblem, that one day, one of his colleagues stole her from him as a reality. To conjure her up in his tearful eyes, he went from fountain to fountain, contemplating the voluptuous deltoids, femurs and torsos that he had sculpted in her image.

His anguish did not last long, although he promised himself a striking vengeance. How many women, in any case, wanted to console him! Painters are in a privileged position with regard to being loved. All women flatter themselves with the thought of being models in their eyes, and—unlike poets and novelists—they never have any need to spread wit around incessantly; they are loved gratis.

Mandanne was, therefore, loved, and loved by women of the highest society. The wives of ministers adored him simultaneously; one, in order not to name her, was the wife of the Minister of the Interior; another was the wife of the Minister of Commerce.

That double intrigue was not without its storms; those two powerful women became rivals, and then it was not a matter of which one would kill the other but of which one would most effectively dishonor the other. They both succeeded, as we shall see, and by means in which the devil lost nothing—for it's only fair not to forget him in all of this.

Twenty excellent artists had offered themselves as candidates to paint the interior of an immense church that had just been completed—to no one's great contentment, because no one wanted to see it finished. Those who had gained by it were locksmiths, roofers, gilders and, above all, the entrepreneurs who stole from all the more-or-less rascally suppliers. The twenty artists in question were perfectly worthy of painting the church in question; all of them had given proof of it, and all of them had the advantage over Mandanne of having already decorated basilicas and chapels.

Mandanne prevailed over them, however, and was given sole responsibility for covering a league of walls and two leagues of ceilings with all sorts of subjects taken from the Bible—which he had never opened. The wife of the Minister of the Interior wanted it thus. There was murmuring on high and mockery down below; people were scandalized, but the wind of fortune was blowing Mandanne's way, and he triumphed over the universal mockery.

One person who was visibly mortified and jealous was the wife of the Minister of Commerce, indignant at not having, like her rival, a basilica to give to Mandanne to paint. She could not, however, lie down under the impact of that defeat. She summoned wit to her aid, which is better than anger in matters of vengeance. Her boudoir was to be decorated. What did she do? She employed so much seduction on Mandanne that she persuaded him to paint portraits of her rival on every wall of her boudoir, in all the least conjugal actions of life.

Unfortunately, the wife of the Minister of the Interior was open to this vengeance in the style of Bussy-Rabutin.[4] Here she was seen in the Bois de Boulogne, riding in a calèche with the Marquis de D***; there she was supposedly taking the waters at Bagnères, but the bath-attendant was recognizable as another even older lover. As she also had the habit of finding employment for all her lovers whose reign had ended, there was much

---

[4] Roger de Rabutin, Comte de Bussy (1618-1693) was exiled from the French court in 1659, allegedly for attending an orgy, and allegedly amused himself and his mistress while in exile by composing a scurrilous "amorous history of the French," which committed to manuscript all the scandalous gossip to which he was party. It was said to have been circulated in that form, and perhaps embellished by other hands, thus confirming his exile and disrepute. His published memoirs are not without a certain scurrility, but we can only speculate as to how much smuttier the unpublished text might have been.

laughter at the sight of a medallion in the background of which she was seen distributing crosses, certificates and nominations to an innumerable crowd standing on the steps of her house.

When the boudoir was finished—and Mandanne had painted it with the finesse, wit and superiority whose secret you know. The wife of the Minister of Commerce hosted a soirée to which everyone illustrious in diplomacy and the arts was invited. You can imagine how the boudoir, open to initiates, was visited with curiosity, commented on malignly, and how much astonishment it caused, when rumor of it spread, to the court and everywhere else.

The rival was thunderstruck at first, but soon rallied, in order to say to Mandanne's face: "You've played an odious, infamous trick on me, but love is often nothing but a tissue of treason, cowardice and knavery. Your crime arises from the fact that you love my rival more than me. Tomorrow you might perhaps change your mind—but in the meantime, Monsieur, you have to do something for me today, and if you don't like it, I'll take back all the work that you've been commissioned to do on the church, under the pretext that you're incapable of carrying it out. I'll precipitate you morally from the height of your scaffolding..."

Mandanne waited, before replying, for the spirit from which he took advice on such occasions to appear to him.

"Speak, Madame," he said, finally. "I'm listening."

The Devil advised him to accept what had been proposed to him.

"My rival is beautiful," she began by saying. "Very beautiful."

"As are you, Madame."

"I know. That being acknowledged, listen to me."

"Yes, Madame."

"On the immense walls of the church that, thanks to me, you've been commissioned to paint, you doubtless propose to treat subjects borrowed from the Old and New Testaments?"

"I shall not employ any others."

"Among these religious scenes, women will often be depicted who are famous for their piety, their faith, their devotion or their martyrdom. They are seen dying of thirst in deserts, under torture by fire rather than allowing the slightest stain on their chastity."

"Yes, Madame."

"Well, I want all those women to have the greatest possible resemblance of face, body and appearance to my rival; in brief, I want everyone to exclaim, on seeing each of those saints: 'But it's Madame ***! It's her!' Do you understand?"

"But Madame, all Paris will utter a cry of indignation."

"You mean a burst of laughter. Anyway, the consequences of your work don't concern you. So, choose: no church to paint, or paint it as I've told you."

"But Madame, at least guarantee me impunity after my fearful boldness, for all Paris knows full well that your rival is no saint, and that her chastity..."

"I can only see one way of shielding you from her husband's vengeance, and that's to have you appointed as an ambassador."

"I suppose so," said Mandanne, with the most admirable aplomb—and he had, indeed, been dreaming for some time about the political glory of Rubens, who really was an ambassador.

V

The vengeance was carried out to the letter; the features of the rival of the Minister of the Interior's wife were reproduced in all the faces of the female saints painted in the church, and they will remain there forever to for the edification of the faithful. Thus, she is the one people adore in praying at the feet of all the virgins who decorate that famous basilica.

After that escapade, about which future memoirs will be much more explicit than us, Mandanne was obliged to think about realizing his desire to be an ambassador. In fact, nothing else remained for him to desire: as a member of the Institut, painter of the king and commander of almost every order, what other ambition could excite him, except that of being one of the most important individuals of his era after the king?

People certainly said: "But it's ridiculous for Monsieur le Comte de Mandanne to want to become a statesman, when he is, after all, merely an artist! How will he be able to preserve and defend the interests of a great kingdom, when he has only every lived in salons and his studio, having never been seriously occupied in anything but training horses and courting women?"

"I tell you that I shall be an ambassador," he replied to everyone, "or I shall deprive France of the glare of my genius. I shall no longer paint for her."

As it was truly impossible to grant him what he wanted with the stubbornness of a bad-tempered child, Mandanne went to Germany, where he avenged himself, as he had promised, by painting the small number of victories that the latter nation had won over France. That gesture alone proved how worthy he was to be an ambassador.

Like all the men of genius to whom he lost nothing in enjoyment of life and self-regard, he believed himself to be persecuted, and on that basis he persecuted all his colleagues. Those who did not paint according to his theory were certain of never obtaining any employment or achieving any distinction. He said, however, that his greatest pleasure was to surround himself with young people and live in the utmost simplicity. His joy was flowers, he claimed, and his only sensuality hearing the flute played. An honest man!

It was in Germany that hazard caused him to encounter his wife, the beautiful Comtesse de Burgos, and her lover. If there was ever a man who ought to have forgiven a sin, it was assuredly him, whose entire life had been nothing but one long infidelity, but le lacked that indulgence. As his wife's lover, as we have said, was a painter, and also enjoyed some consideration, although far from being able to oppose his, Mandanne abandoned himself entirely to the impulsion of his anger.

Loved by a young heir presumptive, he used his influence to have his wife's lover arrested, tried and sentenced to horrible labor in the mines, and, by a rather witty refinement of cruelty, contrived that he be employed in extracting from the bowels of the earth the blue mineral to which Prussia has given its name. He found a diabolical pleasure in painting with the color that he owed to the effects of his vengeance. He composed several paintings which he signed: *Painted by me with the color extracted from the mines by my wife's lover.*

We have reached the most brilliant and the most decisive epoch in Mandanne's life. A favorite of the prince, he lived with him on the footing of a familiarity so extraordinary that he shared his amusements and his pleasures, ate at his table and no longer wanted to paint except for him. But if happiness, as we have said, is a folly, grandeur is a vertigo; Mandanne experienced it. Intoxicated by his high position, one day when the prince was debating a matter of the history of art with him at table, Mandanne forgot himself so far as to say: "Have Vasari's work[5] brought in—ring!"

At that order, given to the prince as if he were his domestic, the latter threw a napkin in his face. Mandanne fainted.

He was dead; an attack of apoplexy had killed him. His supreme hour had sounded; the Devil had taken his soul.

VI

When he woke up, Mandanne, who did not know whether he had really lived or merely dreamed, found himself in Paris, in his mansard, in front of his gigantic refused painting, *Time Discovering Truth*.

One thing, however, told him that what he had experienced had not been a dream, and that was that he was fifty years old; he had wrinkles; white hair covered his temples, and his famous painting had become blanched and yellowed.

"So I haven't been the foremost painter of my era?" he asked one of his colleagues, however—who shook his head sadly, as one replies to a madman who asks you for an account of the past. "What! I haven't been the lover, and then the husband, of the beautiful Comtesse Burgos?

---

[5] Giorgio Vasari's *Le Vite de'più excelenti pittori, scultori, ed architettori* (1550; expanded 1568; tr. as *The Lives of the most Eminent Painters, Sculptors and Architects*).

Nor have I been commander of all the orders, favorite of the royal prince of Germany, the fortunate lover of the two loveliest women of my epoch?"

"It's possible, my friend," his colleague replied, "but it's necessary to work."

Mandanne sight, and stationed himself in front of his easel. Instead of the broad and tempestuous verve, the impetuosity that once he had not even had to direct, however, he felt the restraint of prudence, the embarrassment of doubt; he dared not take any risks. He did not draw a curve without wondering whether it was well-designed. Wanting, like all timid minds, to have a foot in all theories, he applied himself to reproducing all of them. And how willing he was to listen to all advice! How obedient to criticism he was! "It's necessary to draw," he said to himself, incessantly, "to draw, always to draw, and nothing but. Oh, the ancients—how they drew!"

That conduct, so opposed to what he had done before his death, had the result that he took two years to paint a portrait that was devoid of resemblance, and he spent five years relentlessly retouching his painting of *Time Discovering Truth*, which was refused six times at the Salon. He asked all the journalists for articles, and not one said anything about him.

Finally, when he was past sixty, still devoid of a name, a single commission or a single painting sold, he decided to go to America.

The only way he was able to make a living in America, was to stop in public squares or the middle of some Indian village and unroll his painting of *Time Discovering Truth*; someone would eventually give him a handful of rice, and he would go on.

Exhausted by fatigue, hunger and discouragement, he fell down one day in front of his painting with the intention of not getting up again. He was going to die.

A Frenchman was just passing by; that Frenchman, his compatriot, who was a man of considerable intelligence, since he was traveling in America in order not to read the speeches made in the Chambre des Députés, hastened to help Mandanne. He lifted him up, and reanimated the poor old man. Suddenly, he exclaimed: "Aren't you the famous Mandanne?"

"So I have been famous!" the moribund said. "It's not a lie, an error! I've had a studio as big as a palace! I've possessed a marble palace, horses, titles! I'm not mad, then? It's really me who sold his soul to the Devil."

When the Frenchman had restored some strength to Mandanne with an excellent diner, he said to him: "I can tell you that you haven't sold your soul to the Devil, although it's not entirely possible for me to assure you that you haven't had some mental aberration."

"Then that prosperity..."

"It's that very prosperity that has troubled your intelligence somewhat."

"But how is it that, although once famous, adored, borne into the clouds, I've fallen into this oblivion, this poverty, this dilapidation?"

"This is why: so long as you blindly obeyed the impulsion of your genius, so long as you only listened to yourself while you were working, without paying any heed to the world, uncaring about criticism, you rose up, you made progress, and you grew. People believed in you, praised you, rewarded you, made you a king; but from the day—unhappy day!—when you solicited advice, bent your ear and your knee, exaggerated the respect one owes to the past and yielded to criticism, you became a slave, you fell, and were passed over.

"The secret in the arts—why haven't you always understood this?—is to believe oneself infinitely superior to everyone else, and to have the useful common sense to declare oneself inferior to everyone else."

Criticism doesn't exist, then?"

"Undoubtedly it exists, just like the plague—but it's necessary to guard against its infection...just like the plague."

"But what about the Devil?"

"The Devil, my dear Mandanne, is our imagination."

THE VAMPIRE OF THE VAL-DE-GRÂCE

I

One often looks for the fantastic in places where it is not, and one then forgets to ask where it arises naturally, like grass in the plains of sand on the shores of the sea. The staff of sanitaria knew that a long time before the somber Prussian Hoffmann and the American Edgar Poe, who both deserve, for so many reasons, a place of honor in those establishments designed for the treatment of mental aberrations.

Where else in the world, in fact, gathers together in the same place so many varieties of maniacs, lunatics, dreamers, neuralgics, bizarre individuals, madwomen and madmen?—and madwomen and madmen of all species and all nuances: men mad with pride; women mad with love; men mad with ambition? And by virtue of a special privilege, sanitaria, the true fatherland of the fantastic, have the beginning and the end of all the insanities in the world. It is there that they are placed when there is still some hope of a cure; it is there that they are taken when their cure is not complete; whereas hospitals specializing in madness, like Bicêtre and Charenton, only receive the mentally ill when they have, so to speak, lost their classification number in life, when they no longer count, when there is no more to do than treat them as things and not as intelligences.

There will only be question here of human eccentricities and singularities, but of rare and precious singularities, which it would be difficult to offer as fireside tales during the most exciting winter evenings. That vanity is perhaps permissible to me. I do not create my stories; I offer them as they come to me. I am not an author, but a simple historiographer.

We are at the beginning of the year 1849, a year with a very jaundiced complexion. Cholera and political anarchy held sway; Paris was not a very cheerful place to reside, in spite of the comedies that certain legislators enacted every day.

In that era, therefore, which will be characterized more clearly in the course of the story, we see the arrival in Paris, on a warm day in May—and May 1849 was a very hot month—a foreign family composed of a father, mother and young daughter. It was the Kanali family.

The mother had come to seek treatment for a nervous affliction, the daughter for a chlorosis; the father was in very good health, but it seemed natural that he should accompany his wife and daughter into an establishment in which they were going to follow a rather long course of treatment. All three of them were accommodated here.

It was a strange time they had chosen to come here! The epidemic was taking on an apparent development that was not at all reassuring, and was still far from reaching its end; on the contrary, it was soon to extend to redoubtable proportions. Why, under such a threat, did these foreigners come to an establishment like ours, which had been obliged to put more than five hundred beds at the disposal of the sick? Why come here when their situation permitted them to take refuge elsewhere, at less expense and without exposing them to the dangers of such a residence? Did our great city not offer safer places, if they were absolutely obliged to remain in it for some time?

Besides which, the mother's malady, and that of the daughter, did not seem to me to be very grave—not sufficiently difficult to require treatment here and nowhere else. Salubrious country air, in particular, would have hastened their recovery. Never, it might be mentioned in passing, had the countryside been more beautiful, richer, and more apt to attract those who did not have the liberty to go any further from the nucleus of the epidemic.

The choice of our establishment by the family Kanali was, therefore, a veritable enigma for me—an enigma all the more obscure because our new lodgers visibly enjoyed a genuine ease, a well-being that authorized them to live where they pleased. I was entitled to be astonished by that determination, on the part of a family in which I saw a mother very susceptible, by virtue of her highly-strung nerves, to contracting all imaginable illnesses, and a young woman of such rare beauty that it was, so to speak, a crime to expose her to the risks of a scourge that has no pity on anyone—but I was even more astonished, if that were possible, when I learned that the Kanali family, before coming to us, had been resident in the Hôpital du Val-de-Grâce, where the malady had claimed, and was still claiming, as many victims as it had during its first appearance in 1832. That was veritably astounding. What was wrong with that family, who could cohabit with such peril?

That requires explanation. I shall provide it.

Monsieur Fabricius Kanali, the head of the family of that name, had obtained authorization, on the official recommendation of the Austrian government, to study the nature of the epidemic in Paris. His temerity had that medical and philosophical goal. It would be better to say that it had that pretext—I will reveal in due course the real motive for which he exposed himself, as well as his family, to the afflictions of an almost-inevitable disease, by lodging with them in our midst.

Dr. Kanali was an unusual man, and I believe that he merits our taking the trouble to pause, in passing, in order to describe him, albeit briefly. He was then about fifty years of age, but it was very easy to mistake his age, so rosy-cheeked and youthful did he seem sometimes, and so supple and lithe in his movements. I say *sometimes* because Fabricius Kanali, whom we sometimes called Dr. Kanali, changed character and expression with inconceivable rapidity. Sometimes he appeared cheerful, amusing, sprightly, full of zest and passion, making witty quips; at other times he was reflective and grave, slow in his gaze and his speech. He went with tempestuous violence from aphorisms to puns to the most amazing cock-and-bull stories—and he often concluded a Greek or Latin citation with a pirouette on his heels or an entrechat. The professor would suddenly depart from repose to become a clown; quitting the armchair where he was holding forth to bound on to the table like a charlatan in a public square.

It was not easy to tell what country Monsieur Kanali came from; he had no accent—neither English pronunciation, nor German, much less that Italian that it would have seemed most natural for him to have.

He dressed with care, but, for a serious man charged with a very serious mission, he was a little too fond, in my opinion, of bright and sprightly colors, suggestive of a provincial actor. I saw him wear waistcoats with yellow and white stripes, pearl-gray trousers and cravats of every spring-like shade. Because of that frivolity of costume, I often called him Doctor Lindor.[6] He was not annoyed by that; on the contrary, he encouraged the joke by singing: "I'm Lindor, of common birth!" But when he finished the song, he always took a large golden snuff-box from his pocket, on which the portrait of an old white-bearded scholar—Galen or Hippocrates—was visible, and solemnly took a pinch.

At other times, stopping in the middle of a scientific conversation, after having taken a pinch of tobacco, he would close his snuff-box abruptly with his elbow, after the grotesque fashion of a second-rate comic, and sing: *I have good tobacco in my snuff-box.*

In the beginning, these extraordinarily dissimilar habits surprised me to the point of making me doubt our guest's sanity; later, having got used to them, I paid much less attention to them. Besides, those eccentricities were explained to me by the individual's past—or, rather, pasts. Like the earth that bore him, of which he was kneaded like everyone else, he revealed, by means of his prismatic humor and character, various epochs of transition; he bore within him the traces of his primitive terrain and those of his tertiary train. His life had been clownish and reflective, studious and powdered. The inconsistent and variegated man described himself in those terms. He was fundamentally excellent by nature, generous and sympathetic, doubtless well-to-do, but allowing golden coins of bounty to slip through his cracks.

Madame Bela Kanali, much younger than her husband, was not at all similar in character. She was a calm

---

[6] There are several characters named Lindor in French literature, including two eponymous ones, but this reference is presumably to the Lindor in Pierre Lemonnier's comic opera *Le Maître en droit* (1760).

person, one of those women resigned to misfortune, thoughtful in temperament; to make her known at a stroke, she had one of those faces detached from a painting on wood by Memling or van Eyck, the master painters of saintly immobility, the great poets of ecstasy.

I shall now relate what happened during my first interview with the Kanalis, a few days after their installation in the sanitarium. Their domestic came to ask me to go up to the apartment they were occupying, at the western extremity of the large interior courtyard, in a corner of the building from which one could see the chestnut-trees and catalpas of several large gardens that have been entirely destroyed since the last upheavals that occurred when the new boulevards were opened. The three windows of the drawing-room in which they spent part of the day and all their evenings were open.

It was more than gloomy in the room; the lamps had been extinguished, doubtless to permit the discreet light of the moon, whose rise was truly magnificent that evening, to illuminate the drawing room alone. The noises of the house hardly every reached it. At other times I would have regarded it as the most agreeable place to reside—as was the rest of the apartment—but the epoch in which we were living altered its value completely. The infirmary was located directly opposite, and invalids were already populating it in large numbers. That long gallery, with its sinister façade, its uniformly white curtains and these casements that, when open, always allowed the sight in the background of a bed, the head of a patient or a nurse, did not present a very enviable horizon to the people lodged opposite, especially in 1849, when dramas of dolor were being completed and renewed at every moment behind the curtains.

We had, in all honesty, warned the Kanalis about the inconveniences of the location. The heard of the family had received the information in a very singular fashion; I will ever say that there was almost a satisfaction in the tone with which he replied. I was so surprised that the thought occurred to me—yes, it went back that far—that perhaps he had expressly arranged an accommodation facing the large infirmary.

Mademoiselle Marthe Kanali did not express any opinion when she was informed as to the neighbors she would have. Only her mother seemed troubled; a forceful frisson rather through her limbs; she paled all the way to her hands; but when the alarm had passed, she manifested a metallic calm, as if fatality had passed that way.

When I went into the drawing-room, Monsieur Kanali, clad in a white dimity jacket, was lying on the divan in the Oriental style, savoring a cigar. Happiness had never favored his digestion so well. The smoke that he was blowing out in long silvery spirals from his lazy lips, having played momentarily in the moonlight diagonally designed by the heavens on the parquet, faded away into the air, flocculating in little waves above the head of his daughter, who was sitting next to the window.

Mademoiselle Marthe had abandoned on her knees the book that she had been reading while the daylight permitted it. A bitter melancholy immobilized her visage, three-quarters lit by the star of amorous sorrows—and those two melancholies seemed, in fact, to be confiding matters of amour and regret to one another.

Mademoiselle Marthe Kanali combined in her features, and fused with considerable charm and originality, Italian pride, German solidity and French grace. The last nuance, to make use of an expression derived from the vocabulary of painters, *chilled* the other two, and poeticized them with an adorable harmony. Her dark eyes lit up a solidly pale face with a Southern vivacity, emphasizing the origin of her mother's father, an Italian from Dalmatia, and that of her mother, a Hungarian. Fabricius Kanali had cast a varnish of French grace over the whole.

It was obviously the suffering of love that had paled that lovely face, and the chlorosis that had come to reinforce the dullness of her pallor was nothing more than the suffering of repressed amour.

Marthe Kanali had to be in love—very much in love. We, who study all maladies—of which we are, so to speak, the turnkeys—also divine that gentle and dangerous malady, but we can never cure it, and never do. Yes, Marthe was in love; everything proclaimed it on her behalf: her hair, negligently disposed about her head; her head, inclined in the luminous vapor in which she was plunged; her neck, leaning toward the profound infinity that attracts all passion, because all passion is a vertigo drawing sufferers toward the abyss; and her hands, slackly abandoned on her knees.

She resembled her mother a great deal, but as the dawn resembles the evening twilight; there is no greater analogy, and no greater difference.

Madame Kanali owed her expression to a youth with no resemblance to her daughter's; she had habituated her life to aspirations other than love; her languor came from the depths of the soul and not the temporary disturbances of the heart. It was a very long meditation that had shadowed that forehead with gray hair long before time. Only the face remained young; the head had lived more than the face, because her thought was three times as old as her body. That thought was not one of those that real life wearies and bends over: it had searched other worlds, and brought back many doubts and fears, particularities only learned with time. That is why I speak of it with such certainty in anticipation.

I do not claim to have divined anything; the characteristics I am describing were familiar to me long before the pen for depicting them in the corner of a page. I am limiting myself to introducing the reader who is following me into the astonishment into which I entered myself in those first moments of my meeting with the members of the Kanali family.

Above the armchair in which Madame Kanali was sitting perched a bird, of which she seemed very fond. The bird was an owl, with yellow and melancholy eyes and a white beak terminated by a black point. A strange choice, such a bird! From time to time, the owl opened its wrinkled eyelids, and then its eyes of fire, surrounded by black circles, were unmasked—and its immobile gaze, red and lugubrious, stared into the gloom.

"Monsieur Morel," Madame Kanali said to me, with an accent slightly tinted with Italian, but sometimes a little more guttural than Italian, "I called you in order to ask you what time the sanitarium closes."

"It never closes, Madame."

My reply brought a great and painful annoyance to Madame Kanali's face.

"What? Never!" said Monsieur Kanali, for his part, sitting up.

"Let's be clear," I added, rapidly. "What I mean by that is that its doors remain open to all those who present themselves, at whatever hour of the night—but the gates are locked at ten o'clock, nine in winter."

"Good!" said Madame Kanali, slightly more reassured, and looking at the sky, where the moon was still rising, larger and brighter.

"Good!" said Monsieur Kanali, in a much less solemn tone: that of a good bourgeois who does not disdain locks. He resumed smoking.

"And once the gates are locked, no one can get in?" Madame Kanali continued her enquiry.

"No, Madame; no one can any longer get in without ringing the bell."

"Nor without identifying himself?"

"Nor without identifying himself."

Madame Kanali went on: "And not everyone who wishes to can enter, even by making himself known? It depends, does it not, Monsieur?"

"Of course, Madame, of course it depends..."

Mademoiselle Marthe smiled constantly, with an air of sight disdain, at all these questions addressed with various degrees of dread by her parents.

Madame Kanali resumed her inquisition: "And the walls that surround the house—are they very high? The exterior walls, that is?"

"Oh, yes, Madame—very high, I assure you."

"That's good to know," murmured Madame Kanali.

"Very good to know," repeated Monsieur Kanali, checking to see whether his cigar had gone out.

"However," Madame Kanali continued, "from those big trees that I can see from here, someone could jump over the top of the wall, and introduce himself by that means..."

"Madame, those trees, which seem to you to be so close because it's dark, are in reality some distance away, and I assure you once again that no thief, no matter how bold, would dare..."

"Oh, it's not thieves we fear," Madame Kanali interjected, with the same slowness of speech, and while a fearful expression ran through her eyes, above which the owl, for several minutes had been opening and closing its own eyes with a sinister gravity.

"With regard to thieves," Monsieur Kanali repeated, in his turn, "we have indeed no anxieties. Madame Kanali is right."

And Monsieur Kanali, without changing his horizontal pose, emitted a burst of laughter, followed by another puff of tobacco-smoke, which filled the apartment, and in the midst of which nothing could any longer be seen but the two fiery roundels that indicated the location of the eyes of the nocturnal bird.

II

Well, what do they fear, then, I wondered, *if it isn't thieves?*

After a period of reflection, during which I thought I had guessed, I continued in a low voice, placing myself as much as possible between Monsieur and Madame Kanali, speaking to both of them: "I don't think that lovers are in the habit of climbing over walls to get close to those they love."

"No, Monsieur Morel!" interjected Madame Kanali again, putting her hand forcefully on my arm and without lowering her voice—a precaution that I had thought it appropriate to make for fear of being overheard by her daughter—"It's not thieves and lovers that are to be feared, in these times of terrible proof that we're going through, by the will of God." Then, as if the gesture completed her thought, she looked at the dark row of windows of the large infirmary, where so many lives were being snuffed out in the midst of that darkness, so beautiful and limpid outside.

"Oh, my word, yes!" said Monsieur Kanali. "It is indeed lovers that it's necessary to fear. But we're alert, and if ever..."

"Fabricius!" Madame Kanali went on, solemnly. "You know full well that it's not them that are to be feared."

After letting these last words fall from her lips, Madame Kanali ran to embrace her daughter; with a surge of affection, she hugged her to her heart, the muffled palpitations of which I could hear.

During that effusion, the owl, perhaps jealous of that evidence of affection, which was not for itself, gave voice to its usual cry—the cry that is so unpleasant to hear emerging by night from some ruined monument: *crou! crou! crou!*—and the double speckled tuft on its head ruffled noisily, with strange feathery frictions.

While surrounding her daughter with a maternal embrace and caresses, Madame Kanali did not stop gazing at the pale walls of the infirmary. Her fear settled on one place after another, as if on one lighted lamp to another, behind the curtains.

What connection is there, I asked myself during that scene of tenderness and alarm, *between the fearful dread of that mother for her child—a dread to which I no longer know what motive to attribute, since it does not involve thieves or lovers—and that gallery of the dying in front of us?*

Mademoiselle Marthe sometimes looked at her mother, with an interest mingled with an obscure anxiety, and sometimes at her father, with a sentiment imprinted with resolute determination.

I was definitely beginning to sense a species of malaise, verging on fear, on the part of the three individuals—I might say four individuals, for the night-owl certainly counted as one of them, so important was the place it occupied in the Kanali family.

My presence having become unnecessary once I had assured them, as I had been able to do, as to the security of the sanitarium, I judged it appropriate to withdraw.

I left the apartment.

Monsieur Kanali followed me out. He stopped me a few steps from the door, and said to me, in such a way as not to be overheard by his wife or daughter: "You're not used to having guests like us in your house, I'll wager."

"I confess," I replied, "that at first sight you don't much resemble..."

"We don't resemble anyone," Monsieur Kanali interjected, with a serious expression—but suddenly corrected that serious statement by clapping me on the shoulder in a familiar manner. "We don't resemble anyone," he went on, "although we haven't the slightest intention of being eccentric. In life, however, there are origins, situations and events that give individuals incredible appearances. Have you ever gone into a theater after the play has begun? Yes? Well, you've seen around you people who were laughing or weeping as they listened to the play, while you didn't understand a word of it, and you were tempted to say: 'But these people are crazy to laugh or be moved by these things that make no sense!' Well, the life of every family is a drama or a comedy in progress; you don't understand that drama or comedy because, my dear Monsieur, you've come in a long time after the curtain has gone up. Everything about us seems to you to be incoherent, monstrous and extravagant. How I would like to redeem you from your error! If I were to explain to you what you don't know...but for the moment, pay no attention, my dear Monsieur Morel, to the slightly bizarre things you just heard inside. Let's talk rationally for a moment."

"Gladly, doctor."

"Let's not bother with the 'doctor,' I beg you."

"As you wish."

"You see to me to be a jolly fellow."

That beginning was original. "At present," I replied, slightly surprised by the epithet, "jolly fellows are at risk of losing their jollity completely in a matter of hours."

"No, no," Monsieur Kanali continued. "You have a good face."

"What? A good face?"

"Yes—a face admirably made for the theater: shiny little eyes, full of fire..."

"Everyone has them, from time to time," I said, with a certain irritation. "The description seems rather odd to me."

"You have a nose like a gimlet."

"Monsieur!" I exclaimed.

"Don't get upset! Noses like gimlets are excellent, precious. They inspire gaiety, expansion, joy; one laughs even before the mouth such noses crown has spoken. Tiercelin, the great actor, had a nose like a gimlet; Rébard, who recently died, had a nose like a gimlet—the finest gimlet-like nose that every embellished a face. And not only do you have a nose like a gimlet, but, like them, one of superb perfection! You have a ridiculously pointed chin."

"Permit me...permit me, Monsieur; this description..."

"You could have played Sainville and Arnal roles with an assured superiority."

"Well!" I said, forced to take it as a joke. "Are you trying to persuade me to become an actor?"

"Oh, Monsieur Morel—acting! Do you know anything in the world more excellent than performance? What an art! What a profession! I don't put any above that of the actor. The public! The stage! The sound of the orchestra! The emotion of seeing people listening to you, applauding you, loving you! I've seen Potier, I've seen Brunet, I've seen Baptiste; I've followed them; I've studied them. Well, I'd rather be Brunet or Potier than..."[7]

He stopped. Had he been about to inform me, at the end of his surge of enthusiasm, that he too had once been an actor? He resumed, in a less personal tone: "Are the theaters of Paris flourishing at present? It's nearly twenty years since I left France, and I'm no longer up to date..."

"I rarely go to the theater; my occupations keep me away. But I can assure you nevertheless, without any fear of being mistaken, that they're not getting rich, placed as they are between the political crisis from which we haven't yet emerged, and the epidemic crisis that we've just entered."

"The Palais-Royal, for existence, such a popular theater in my day?"

"I've heard it said that it's playing to empty halls."

"The Varietés?"

"Closed."

"The Vaudeville?"

"Its last director is running a café."

"And the Gymnase?"

"No better off than the others."

"I saw them in their heyday!"

---

[7] It is worth noting that the author uses the terms "*acteur*" and "*comédien*" as if they were synonymous, and that I have routinely translated the latter as "actor" because "comedian" has the wrong implication in English. All the actors whose names Kanali cites would have played dramatic roles as well as comic ones, but were all better known for the latter. The comparison that Kanali is drawing between famous *farceurs* he has known and Monsieur Morel thus offers a hint that perhaps Morel ought not to be taken as seriously, either as a psychologist or a narrator, as he wants to be.

"You must have gone to them very frequently back then, to take such a sincere interest in their fortunes?"

Monsieur Kanali replied in a discreet fashion: "Oh, very frequently! Looking upwards, addressing a sigh to the heavens that must have gone up to the topmost floor of the house, he added: "Oh, those were good times! Those were good times!"

I thought that I ought to respect the long silence with which he followed that expression of regret. Monsieur Kanali broke it abruptly with a question that had the effect on me of a cannon-shot fired next to one's ear when one least expects it.

"Can you tell me, Monsieur Morel," he asked, "where the gravediggers meet up after finishing work?"

I was nonplussed; I thought I had misunderstood the question.

He began again: "I'm asking you whether you know the location in Paris to which the gravediggers go to take their common meal."

This time, I had understood—but, because of the tone in which it had been asked and the subject about which we had just been talking, I took it as a joke, and only replied in a dilatory fashion: "I'll tell you later." And I started going downstairs.

Monsieur Kanali caught me up on the third step. "But I'm quite serious," he said, "in asking you that question."

What a diabolical man! I thought. *Why is he so keen to know where the gravediggers gather? What is this monstrous curiosity, this extravagant fantasy?*

"Do you have the intention of employing them on your own account?" I asked Monsieur Kanali.

"Perhaps, Monsieur Morel, perhaps—but not in the way that you mean."

"There aren't two ways of meaning it."

"Do you think so, Monsieur Morel?"

"For my part, I only know one. When one employs them, it's for..."

"Shush, Monsieur Morel, shush! Let's not darken the present; it's dark enough as it is. As for me..." Monsieur Kanali concluded by murmuring a refrain borrowed from Béranger: 'I'm alive, truly alive, very much alive!'[8] Come on, tell me where I can find the gentlemen in question. I have the greatest need and the greatest desire to see them."

I knew perfectly well where the 'gentlemen,' as Monsieur Kanali called them, gathered, but once again, still assuming that, in spite of his protestations, he was intent on joking and was making fun of me, I avoided his question, which remained devoid of any precise response.

You shall see, in due course, that he was not joking.

I confess, to the shame of my curiosity, that I was very keen to discover why the Kanali family had exchanged the pompous abode of the Val-de-Grâce—a veritable palace—for that of our sanitarium, a meager and bourgeois residence by comparison. There are princely apartments at the Val-de-Grâce, service worthy of a royal house, and an immense garden where one can stroll amid beautiful hornbeams trimmed in the fashion of those of Saint-Cloud, with view extending as far as they eye can reach in every direction. It passes like a bird in flight above the great city to soar, wings de-

---

[8] The line is from "Le Mort vivant" [The Living Corpse], one of many popular songs written by Pierre-Jean Béranger (1780-1857)

ployed, westwards over the woods of Meudon and Versailles, southwards over green and cheerful countryside.

What did that exchange, devoid of any plausible reason, hide? And take note that, in order to study the epidemic, Dr. Kanali had been much better placed at the Val-de-Grâce, where there were always two thousand invalids, than in our establishment, which was a long way from attaining that impressive figure.

It is probable that I would never have found out the reason that had caused him to preferred him to prefer one residence to the other had it not been for a hazard of circumstance, which I shall report.

A physician at the Val-de-Grâce, who had once been attached to the medical service of our establishment, came to pay us a visit one day. It was a good opportunity for me to satisfy my curiosity. The physician's name was Sainson.

I interrogated him, and my desire was satisfied beyond my expectations. Monsieur Sainson told me, in a low voice, that there had been "love and magic" in the motive that had obliged Dr. Kanali to leave the Val-de-Grâce suddenly one morning. Love and magic! That was more than enough to make an obscure medical orderly like me, unspoiled by the surprises of life, listen with all ears. Love and magic! I had never been to such a feast.

"Monsieur Kanali," Dr. Sainson told me, "with whose character you are now familiar, took care, on his arrival at the Val-de-Grâce—which was preceded by the finest recommendations from the great medical organizations of Vienna—to ingratiate himself with all the servants in the establishment. He's rich; he distributed little gifts in profusion and multiplied his largesse in all directions. The apartment in which he was lodged permitted him to receive guests, and he hosted dinners twice a week for his friends from outside, mostly consisting of foreign doctors who had come, like him, to study the epidemic, who were joined by the principal interns of the hospital.[9]

"These meetings offered all the more charm because the fear of contagion had broken all the established connections of intimacy with the outside world. That's the usual effect; people flee, isolating themselves, afraid of one another. If a few pleasant meeting-places remain, those who have the good fortune to be admitted to them and brought closer together, becoming equals, or more than that, and put into that party, which might at any moment be their last, everything precious that they have in their heart and mind, like a wager. That's why, at those perilous hours, imperishable friendships are formed between survivors, and alliances of souls more vivid than friendships. It has been observed that one never sees more marriages than in epochs that succeed great calamities of this sort.

---

[9] In French texts of this period, the dash signaling the opening of direct speech is only placed at the beginning of the first paragraph of the speech, and there is no signal to mark the end of the speech-act. It is thus unclear whether Dr. Sainson is speaking verbatim during the next few pages, or whether what he has told Monsieur Morel is being reported indirectly and paraphrased. I have opted for the former representation until part-way through the next chapter, because the text periodically employs "*vous*" as if a listener were actually being addressed, until a point in the narration comes at which there seems to be an explicit reversion to indirect reportage. Further confusion is added by the fact that it is difficult to believe that Sainson could be party to much of the information that Morel supposedly obtains from him.

"Among the guests at Dr. Fabricius Kanali's gatherings was a young intern who had been at the Val-de-Grâce for two years: an intelligent young man, carved like an Apollo: and like the Apollo of fable, he cultivated the arts in a superior manner—a good painter, a good musician, a good singer. His name was César Caseneuve. Caseneuve would have been perfect, save for one defect that I shall tell you about shortly—a very great defect, in his position.

"Mademoiselle Marthe had singled him out among all the external and internal French and foreign doctors admitted to her father's gatherings, and quite frankly, that passion was nothing very extraordinary, and nothing very criminal. She was eighteen, he was twenty-eight. Add to the attraction that young people of their ages exercise upon one another the privilege of being able to meet during this sad year of 1849.

"So, they fell in love, with all the affection that scarcely exists any more at the present moment. It was, so to speak, bequeathed to them by everything, to be shared by them alone. They subsequently recommenced the beautiful poem of love, which was born with the world and will only end with it. They went through that divine book by way of a strange and difficult path, on order, one could say, that it might seem more bitter and sweeter at the same time, and that each passage would be marked more memorably in the heart for having been traversed in the midst of dangers.

"Those dangers, for them, were Death in all its forms, since they lived in its domain. Unlike Boccaccio's young patricians and gracious Italian women during the plague in Florence, they did not have the egotistical joy of saying to one another: 'People are dying all around us, but we, life's fortunate privileged, are braving the danger behind several uncrossable rivers, and two or three dense forests, in the middle of a circle of flowers, birds, sunlight, bubbling springs, cool shade, salubrious perfumes and vivifying emanations.' No, they did not have the right to say that. Marthe and César Caseneuve loved one another with the abandon of the last hours, for each of those hours might, indeed, have been their last.

"You may judge for yourself whether the expression is exaggerated. In Dr. Kanali's study a kind of counter had been placed, which announced, by a chime, every death that occurred in the wards. Well, for merely two months, that sinister clock had been chiming every five minutes. The calculation is not difficult to make; nearly three hundred voids were produced every day at the Val-de-Grâce. Only great battles produce such a deficit, so frequently renewed.

"Monsieur Kanali, who had not failed to notice Caseneuve's liking for his daughter Marthe and his daughter's tender penchant for him, did not raise any obstacle to the mutual sympathy of the two young people. Far from it—he sought, on the contrary, to take every opportunity to make his home more agreeable to the young physician. He lavished attentions upon him based on a great cordiality—perhaps too great for the short time that they had known one another, although the doctor's expansive nature explains a great deal with respect to that excessive intimacy. The prospective father-in-law had already got under the slightly immature plumage of the friend of a matter of days.

"Madame Kanali put much less effort into attracting and retaining César, but without raising any opposition to the welcoming provisions her husband made in his regard. There was a conflict within her treatment of the young intern. It was, for instance, impossible for her to hide the suffering and apprehension that she felt when he arrived, when he came into the drawing-room—a painful impression that often extended as far as terror, and which sometimes obliged her to withdraw for a few minutes—but it was also rare for her, annoyed with herself for having behaved thus, not to seek thereafter, during dinner or the soirée, an opportunity to make the excellent young man forget the less-than-benevolent welcome.

"Unfortunately, it was always repeated. The next day and on the days that followed, there was the same terrible welcome, the same affable and cordial revisions. Is it necessary to conclude that Caseneuve reminded Madame Kanali of someone she abhorred, whom she dreaded, and that it was quite impossible for her to overcome the horror caused by that resemblance? That is what events will doubtless tell us."

III

"In the presence of these annoyances, to which he ended up no longer paying any attention, Caseneuve remained the most radiant lover on earth. The epidemic, which reduced the happy intern to rarely going out by day, and never by night, rendered his prison very gentle and very dear to him. For him, it would not have been merely the Val-de-Grâce, it would also have been the Val de Bonheur,[10] without the fault that I mentioned to you—a veritable imperfection, a real defect in a young man destined, like him, to exercise the profession of medicine.

"That fault was that César had a terrible fear of catching the redoubtable disease that was running riot, the disease that he was responsible for treating in others: a limitless, bottomless, indescribable fear. That fear wounded him, alarmed him, and terrified him. It gave him cold sweats, shivers and cerebral deliria, almost continuously.

"The mere name of the Indian epidemic—the epidemic that was filling the wards under his surveillance— paralyzed him from head to toe. At every moment he thought he had been infected, mortally afflicted and

---

[10] The name of the famous hospital can be translated in various ways, including "vale of mercy" and "vale of redemption," either of which would lend themselves to this play of words, where it is contrasted with "vale of joy" or "vale of happiness." It is worth bearing in mind, however, both here and in respect of subsequent episodes, that a *coup-de-grâce* is a death-blow.

doomed. The young man, who had fought with the energy of an old soldier during the month of June in the previous year, in the ranks of the valiant Garde Mobile, in the Place du Panthéon,[11] trembled like a leaf whenever it was necessary to approach the bed of an invalid.

"He had only stayed at the Val-de-Grâce when the epidemic erupted in its full violence because he had been forced to submit to that harsh obligation by a rich uncle on whom he depended. That uncle, a former army doctor, would not hear of his nephew being afraid of anything whatsoever. In spite of that, and even though César was due to be his heir, César would surely have ended up quitting his internship at the Val-de-Grâce and running away, if he had not made the acquaintance of Mademoiselle Marthe Kanali just when he was on the point of fleeing.

"When that love—a first love—penetrated the soul of César Caseneuve, although it had not exactly dispelled the fear, it had at least reduced the space that it occupied. There were even moments when he seemed to escape from the vertigo of that colossal fear—and God knows, the epidemic did not decrease around him! However, he waited with such great impatience for the night to return on which he was to go to Dr. Kanali's apartment that the days because less difficult to get through.

---

[11] During the June insurrection that followed the February Revolution in 1848, the Place du Panthéon, which was fortified with barricades by 1500 insurgents, was the site of one of the bloodiest battles, which took place on June 24. The Garde Mobile, a volunteer force hastily assembled by the new government to support the Garde Républicaine, assisted in that and other assaults.

"As soon as the night arrived, he ran there, and beside the young and charming Martha his terrors were forgotten. There were card games or games of chess, there was music, there was conversation about sciences, travels and literature, there was laughter; in sum, there was much amusement in Marthe's father's drawing-rooms—except that every night, at a given time, the laughter, the joyful chatter and the music suddenly stopped; the wagons were arriving.

"The interruption took place regularly, at eleven o'clock. As you know, it's at that rather late hour that the wagons do their work."

Monsieur Sainson made use of a specific term that designates a particular kind of long vehicle. I don't know why I shouldn't make use of the same term—which is to say, the word *tapissière*.[12] The function of these tapissières was to collect from all the hospitals in Paris a certain number of victims struck and carried off during the day by the pitiless breath of the epidemic.

"When the tapissières had unloaded their burden," he continued, "those guests who were not on duty resumed the momentarily-interrupted thread of their distractions, and stayed until daylight drinking punch or tea, or playing various card games.

"It was also then that Dr. Kanali spread around the waves of his verve and gaiety. He had constructed a little puppet-theater, of which he was simultaneously the director and the cast. He placed his dolls on the tips of his fingers, the exceptional thinness and intelligent suppleness you've doubtless observed, and made them speak

---

[12] A literal translation of this term, which normally refers to upholstery, would make no sense in English, and there does not seem to be a readily-comprehensible alternative.

on the stage of his theater with all the comic loquacity and exaggerated buffoonery of the Italian clowns he had had the opportunity to see and study in Italy. Any subject would do; people suggested them to him, and he improvised scenes that were often excellent, imitating the accents and gestures of the ridiculous actors and actresses he had heard marvelously.

"I was much less surprised by all those eccentricities later, when I found out—we all knew, eventually—that Kanali had once been an actor, under the name of Belleville. He'd been part of a troupe of French actors in Italy."

"What!" I exclaimed. "Dr. Fabricius—Monsieur Kanali—was once..." Astonishment choked the end of my sentence in the back of my throat.

"He had been a comic actor in a traveling troupe," Dr. Sainson went on, "but I won't dwell on that detail because I'm in haste to arrive at what you're doubtless most eager to know—which is to say, by virtue of what fatality of love and magic he had been forced to leave the Val-de-Grâce, in order to take up residence with you.

"I'll tell you how it happened—but it's necessary for that to listen to the story of little Colombe.

"Every morning, at four o'clock—five in winter—little Colombe Val-de-Grâce brought to the hospital little loaves of milk-bread that the hungry interns—which is to say, all of them—awaited impatiently. Since Dr. Kanali's gatherings had begun, the young portress had not failed to be introduced, with her little basket on her shoulder, into the middle of the drawing-room, where she had the joy of setting down her burden. People broke the bread standing up and devoured the delicious little loaves, still perfumed with the savory warmth of the oven, while chatting.

"Colombe Val-de-Grâce was an extremely remarkable girl, for her beauty and the elegance of her stature, in the fashion of the svelte caryatids of Jean Goujon, the Greek of Paris. She spread a blessing of grace and perfection around her. It would be necessary to go back to Raphael's *Fornarina*[13] to find anything as charming, as delicate and as sweetly beautiful as Colombe. She would have merited another Raphael modeling another Fornarina upon her. The double miracle of art and beauty would have been complete. That second Raphael has not appeared.

"Colombe owed her pretty name to the hazard of her birth, which had not been announced to the world beneath the gilded paneling of the Louvre, nor the silk curtains of Versailles. One winter night, some frozen leather-workers who were passing through the Faubourg Saint-Jacques observed, huddled beneath the gate of the Val-de-Grâce, a woman who was writhing, groaning and suffering mightily. They asked the cause of her complaints, and a few minutes later they rang the bell, rudely, had the gate opened, and carried the young woman into one of the wards. They were just in time; at that very moment a pretty little girl came into the world—a poor child who would have been destined, but for the providential help that she received, to die of cold on the icy paving-stones of the street.

"They took care of the child, as well as the mother, but the latter astonished everyone when, three days later, she clandestinely quit her bed and disappeared, leaving the infant to whoever cared to take responsibility for her. As you can imagine, the child was not sent away; she

---

[13] *La Fornarina* means "female baker"—hence the connection with the baker's assistant Colombe [Dove].

stayed where she had arrived. As for the fugitive, no one paid any heed to her beyond the curiosity and surprise of such an observation; no one bothered to run after a mother who cared so little for her daughter.

"A few days later, the child of the street, the orphan of the gate, was baptized in the name of Colombe Val-de-Grâce, because her mother had identified herself as a birdseed-seller when she had been asked for information about herself. From the nourishment of birds, one leapt, by natural analogy, to the name of a bird, and settled on that of Colombe for the child's name. Nothing was simpler thereafter than to add to the winged name in question that of Val-de-Grâce, which constituted thereafter a family name—and what a family! Val-de-Grâce!

"The baptized Colombe Val-de-Grâce grew up as desired beneath her blonde hair, living in the hospital exactly as she would have lived in her father's house. She came and went as she pleased through the courtyards, the linen-room, the chapel, the corridors, the wards and the garden. At first she was like a little green and pink caterpillar dragging herself around in the sunlight, without yet having the strength to walk; then she was like a fluttering butterfly, appearing and disappearing everywhere instantaneously. That nobody's child became, over the years, everybody's child, adored by all. The nurses taught her to read, the interns to write and the consultants to dance. Her dancing did not always have a sacred character, or the purest correctness, but Colombe was never more graceful than when she danced and fluttered in the style of the popular dance-halls of the barrières. People allowed themselves to feel a veritable gaiety before the deliberate poses of that little five-year-old fairy. As I said, everyone adored her.

"Her happiness grew with her; on feast-days she was given either a little pink headscarf, or a pretty tarlatan dress, or coral earrings, or an embroidered Nancy collar. When she had made her first communion at the church of Saint-Étienne-du-Mont, the curé demanded, with sound common sense, that she adopt a profession outside the Val-de-Grâce, or that she be give a job to do within the establishment, the profession being much preferable than the employment.

"The advice was taken. Colombe Val-de-Grâce was placed with an honest baker in the Faubourg Saint-Jacques in the capacity of bread-portress—a rather vulgar profession, no doubt, but the one she chose among many others that would have suited her protectors better. She said that she liked walking, going up and down stairs, from one house to another, getting up early and carrying a bread-basket on her shoulder. It was a marvel reminiscent of the prettiest frescoes in Pompeii to see her set forth from her employer's shop on a winter morning, with her basket wedged proudly on her left shoulder, displaying her pink nose, her pretty teeth, like those of a young lioness, her blue eyes and her blonde hair, through the violet November fog and the vapor exhaled by her excellent milk-loaves. They were genuinely superior to those of all the other bakers in the neighborhood; they were praised everywhere, and she was much in vogue.

"The baker in whose service Colombe was, a clever man, took advantage of the porter's fashionability to add fashionability to his products. That added to their value, so he had made a great deal of money and renown by the time that Colombe Val-de-Grâce informed him, with all imaginable circumlocutions, that she was going to marry a young painter-and-decorator of the Maçons-Sorbonne quarter, and that, in consequence, she would soon cease to be his bread-portress.

"The marriage became the talk of the Faubourg Saint-Jacques, from the Rue de l'Abbé-de-l'Épée to the Rue des Bourguignons, and all the way to the Gobelins. Everyone offered the most sincere and generous good wishes to the seductive and every-virtuous little bread-portress, now arrived very sweetly at her sixteenth year.

"Everyone offered her good wishes for happiness, as I said—except for César Caseneuve. The motive for that abstention is that César had experienced a great commencement to love for Colombe, whom he had known and appreciated for three years, since he had become an intern at the Val-de-Grâce.[14] He had not made any declaration, however, not daring to unite himself by marriage to a person of such obscure and dubious birth. He had waited, and had let the opportunity pass, and in the end, what always happens had happened, the chance he had not taken was lost. It is not impossible that Colombe would have been glad to be his wife; I was assured in the quarter that she had not been indifferent to the intern's tender assiduity—but all that remained vague and indecisive on both sides.

"Things having taken a different turn, as the frank vulgar saying puts it, Colombe Val-de-Grace made an-

---

[14] The author inserts a footnote here: "Monsieur Morel, the author of these memoirs, was therefore mistaken when he said the César Caseneuve's love for Mademoiselle Marthe Kanali was his first love." Actually, it was Sainson who said it, and then contradicted himself, so it would make more sense to credit the note to Morel. (Presumably it was too late simply to alter the earlier passage in the serial version of the story, which must already have gone to press.)

other choice. Her marriage-plans made rapid progress. Until the last moment, however, faithful to the establishment that had always been such a good mother to her, she wanted to bring the little loaves to her protectors.

"For the last time, therefore, she went into the Val-de-Grâce, whose pretty name she was about to abandon forever with a joyful sadness, with her basket laden as usual, to make her morning visit to Monsieur Kanali's guests.

"I've told you what a cordial welcome always greeted her there; imagine how she was received, with marks of amity, this time tinged with regret, when she told Dr. Kanali and all his friends that it was her last day for brining the bread. She was surrounded and embraced, and showered with the warmest farewells.

"Madame Kanali took from her jewel-box a garnet brooch she had bought in Carlsbad, the stones of which were mounted with superior skill, and gave it to Colombe Val-de-Grâce. Not wishing to be outdone in generosity by her mother, Mademoiselle Marthe took two golden bracelets from her wrists, surmounted by two beautiful pear-shaped topazes, and offered them to the delightful little bride.

"The poor child could no longer breathe; she trembled and quivered, weeping with happiness and timidity, joy and confusion. The excess of emotion got the better of her; she was obliged to sit down on the divan.

"A few minutes' rest did not calm her disturbance; she was seen to grow pale, turn white, and then to complain of a great oppression in her stomach, and to look around her with cavernous astonishment. She began coughing: a harsh, dolorous, incessant coughing.

"What was wrong? My God! The whites of her eyes became blue-tinted; a great chill overtook her; soon, her teeth were chattering. But what was it?

"'It's cholera,' said the celebrated Dr. Desroches to his colleagues, taking Colombe's hand in order to make sure that he was not mistaken. 'Yes it is,' he confirmed. 'She's doomed.'

"Colombe was immediately transported into one of the neighboring rooms; she already had, on her cheeks, her neck and her arms, which were as rigid and cold as ice, the well-known signs of decomposition. Four hours later, she was finished. The Indian demon had forced itself between her jaundiced arms and choked her. It was over. The Dove was dead.

"Turning toward César Caseneuve and pointing at the icy body of the poor little bread-portress, Dr. Kanali whispered in his ear: 'Finally, I have what I need!'

"Great God! What did such words—'I have what I need?'—signify in the presence of such a scene and such grief.

"Then the doctor added: 'It's six o'clock. Be in the same place this evening at eleven. I need you for a great operation.'"

Before recounting that great operation, we shall say something—or, rather, Dr. Sainson will once again tell us—about Madame Kanali, because Madame Kanali plays an important role in this story, to which it is now time to pay heed, in the general interest of the story, and which is strangely connected with what Dr. Kanali meant when he referred to "a great operation" in speaking to the astonished César Caseneuve.

Madame Kanali, Marthe's mother, was the daughter of the famous chemist Salomon Kanali, whose name she had kept when marrying a man who bore no resemblance at all to him. Salomon Kanali had been born in Dalmatia, and after having carried out successful studies of various kinds in the savant universities of Italy and Germany, he had obtained the chair of chemistry and natural history at the Archigymnasium of Presburg in Austria.

A man combining imagination and science, like the majority of Dalmatians, and having been appointed a professor in a land much given to exalted beliefs, he had devoted himself wholeheartedly to alchemy, that admirable distraction of great minds. He had even gone beyond the frontiers of alchemy, for he had not sought to make gold, but to do something much more extraordinary than the fabrication of that precious metal. Step by step, through the caverns of meditation and the calm of long nights of reading, he had pursued a much greater work, the most temeritous and formidable of all.

Convinced, like all the impious, although he was not impious himself, that the saints and prophets had only carried out resurrections with the aid of scientific methods unknown to the vulgar and carefully hidden from the crowd, he had tried to resuscitate the dead.

He even believed that the problem of resurrection had already been solved by a few scientists who were too wise to say anything, for fear of being burned as sorcerers. In his eyes, that miracle, since it was called a miracle, extraordinarily difficult as it might be, was not much more difficult to achieve than certain operations of chemistry that had similarly passed for monstrosities, sacrileges, and impossibilities before chemistry had resounding proved that wrong. He did not rank the problem of resurrection, as a difficulty to overcome, above the efforts of genius that Columbus had required to discover America or Newton to affirm gravitation—and he set out from there to immerse himself in the most ardent research, the most bizarre and boldest experiments and trials.

Was he mad, or merely deluded? Who can say? But Salomon Kanali thought he had succeeded in bringing back from oblivion, among others, a young man who had been dead for a moment. It was an unusual story, of which we shall find the trace and the echo in more than place in the life of his daughter, who not only shared with him that belief in the resurrection of humans by humans, but committed herself to beliefs more audacious still, if that is possible.

IV

Even if Salomon Kanali, the celebrated professor of the Archigymnasium of Presburg, never brought anyone back to life, it is certain that, while searching day and night for the means of brining about the phenomenon of resurrection, he obtained prodigious results—and, above all, prodigiously unexpected results. Thus, by submitting an individual who was no longer alive to a combination of chemical agents with whose properties he as experimenting for the first time, he encountered the secret of Ruysch, the famous Dutch anatomist.[15]

Ruysch's secret consisted of rendering to a subject completely protected from disorganization any age one desired, provided that the subject had reached it during life. Ruysch could render to the subject either the freshness of youth, the notable gravity of maturity, or the serenity of old age. What an advantage! How superior that method was to all the procedures known and practiced since the Egyptians!

He alone, therefore, Salomon Kanali, had recovered Ruysch's secret while trying to uncover God's.

---

[15] The Dutch botanist and anatomist Frederik Ruysch (1638-1731), immortalized in Jan van Neck's famous painting of "The Anatomy Lesson of Dr. Frederik Ruysh" (1683) used a *"liquor balsamicum,"* whose composition he refused to disclose, to preserve specimens; he was probably the first person to replace blood with an embalming fluid as a mean of preservation. He amassed a prodigious "cabinet of curiosities," which he sold to the Russian Tsar Peter the Great, along with his secret formula.

"It is known that Ruysch," says the *Dictionary of Medical Sciences*, "possessed a means of conserving in our tissues, after life, the softness and the majority of the properties that are their attributes. When the Dutch anatomist sold his cabinet to Tsar Peter I, he gave him a manuscript at the same time in which he made known the composition of the preservative liquid of which he made use, and declared expressly, in that manuscript, that the liquid was thing other than spirit of wine, brewer's spirit, to which was added, during distillation, a handful of white pepper. It appears, however, that Ruysch had not given the true composition of his liquid. Afterwards, it was thought that his means of conservation had been found. Geoffroy,[16] in 1731, was commissioned to carry out experiments, but the results did not live up to the hopes that had been conceived."

Hazard, that other great inventor, who is not a native of Holland but of everywhere, having delivered Ruysch's secret to Salomon Kanali, the latter made marvelously fecund use of it for his renown and his fortune, although he always regretted in the depths of his soul not being able to devote all his time and all his celebrity to the work of resurrection that he was pursuing so ardently. Those who have seen bodies embalmed by his enchanted hands proclaim loudly that nothing but the soul is missing from those beautiful creations of his genius. The Egyptians, much too highly praised, profaned the

---

[16] Claude-Joseph Geoffroy (1685-1752), often known as "Geoffroy the Younger" to distinguish him from his brother Étienne-François, who was also a chemist, although that sometimes led to confusion with his son Claude-Francois Geoffroy, who became known as "Claude Geoffroy the Younger"

most sacred parts of a human being, the heart and the brain, in order to conserve the less noble parts. The moderns, under the pretext of embalming, make a white man delivered to them into a veritable negro of the African coast, a being of pure jacaranda wood or true mahogany.

The glory of Salomon Kanali was no more sheltered from the bites of envy than that of other men. His enemies objected that his means of conservation, perhaps good in certain climatic conditions in ordinary circumstances, could not prevail against the venom of the Indian cholera, whose invasion was then threatening Hungary. He would never succeed, they said, in neutralizing the effects of the transcangenetic[17] scourge, the most rapid and most disruptive of all scourges, the most skillful at ravaging from top to bottom, in a matter of minutes, the sublime face that humans have received from their divine creator.

In every true scientist there is a hero; when it is not Pliny the Elder, devoured by Vesuvius, it is Pilastre de Rosier, falling from his balloon on the shore of the English Channel. Salomon Kanali accepted the challenge. He had only to wait for the epidemic, and he did not have to wait long. It ran with every wind that it encountered in its passage. The crisis of the decisive proof was getting closer by the hour.

Unfortunately, just as he was about to respond to the accepted challenge, Salomon Kanali suffered a deplorable setback. Having learned one day from a peasant

_____

[17] I have Anglicized the original text's *transcangénétique*, although I can find no trace of any such word in French or English; if it is a misprint, I cannot determine what the intended word might have been.

passing through the vicinity that a traveler had been murdered some distance from the city, on the edge of a forest known as Ulmenbaum, he immediately thought about his secret of recalling the dead to life. That idea, which never left him, distracted him from any other idea, and even from any fear of the senior clergy of Presburg, who had threatened him with the heaviest of thunder-bolts, the most frightful of anathemas and the darkest of their cells if he did not resolutely renounce that abomi-nable impiety.

When night fell, he headed by way of sinuous paths for the forest of Ulmenbaum, where he did indeed dis-cover, by the edge of a pond, a man killed several hours before by bandits. He believed that he had not been seen. He embarked upon his work—work judged to be diabol-ical, and further complicated by the duration of a long dark night.

Had he been followed, having always been watched? Had his informant set a trap for him? In either case, he was surprised by a nocturnal patrol of the local police, at the very moment when he was plunging a steel blade into the wound of the murdered man, doubtless in order to introduce some chemical substance thereinto. He was captured. He was accused of being the murderer.

There was a criminal trial. In vain he cited his offi-cial position, his irreproachable morals. As he dared not admit to the law, for fear of making his position worse, that he had gone to find the body of the man in the forest not to kill him but, on the contrary, to bring him back to life, he was considered to be the true guilty party. He would go to the scaffold, nothing less. He was regarded as already doomed.

A few young people from noble families of Buda and Pest, however, who were former pupils of the doctor, succeeded by means of maneuvers and gold to get him out of prison and obtain a pardon. He made honorable amends, swore that he would no occupy himself any further with either resurrection or alchemy, and, in order to give a certain guarantee with regard to the regular existence into which he promised henceforth to enter, he got married.

He married a young woman from Agram, who had also had a rather extraordinary event in her life, which we shall relate.

Before marrying Dr. Salomon Kanali, the young woman had been due to marry the Graf von Markfeld. The Graf von Markfeld had already been married twice, both times to charming daughters of Agram, a Hungarian town renowned for the fine aristocratic beauty of its women. After two years of marriage they had died, both of languor, it was said; others sought a more precise cause for those sudden deaths, but did not find any. Beautiful as those women had been, however, they were far from equaling him in bodily and facial perfection. Without the strange whiteness of his face—a matt whiteness without any analogy to known pallors—he would have had no reason to fear any comparison with antique marble statues. One very peculiar thing was that, although he was marrying for the third time, one would have thought that he had not aged a year, or a month, since his first marriage. He looked to be between thirty and thirty-five years old.

In addition to these details, from which his self-regard had the right to draw some pride, he exhibited two others of an even more personal character. A red spot, of such a vivid red that it was easily mistaken for a drop of blood, always pearled in the left corner of his lip; many people contended that it really was a droplet of blood. In that case, it must have been impossible to staunch, for it was always visible in the same place, to which the Graf von Markfeld continually put the tip of one of his fingers, as if he wanted to efface it.

He was, therefore, going to marry the woman who was destined one day to become the first Madame Kanali, wife of the celebrated chemist, when his bride-to-be observed, at first with curiosity, then with a certain anxiety, and finally fearfully, that her fiancé only ever offered her his left hand, whether at a dance or out walking. That intrigued and troubled her all the more because she had also noticed that the Graf von Markfeld was not left-handed. At table or at play, he made use of his right hand. However cleverly the young woman attempted to take hold of the Graf's right hand, she never succeeded in doing so. The hand incessantly escaped her. That was the second of the two singularities that remained to be mentioned.

However, the period of betrothal had passed, and the day chosen for the celebration of the marriage at the metropolitan church of Saint Martin approached. It arrived, with all its pomp. Saint Martin's was illuminated, the organs were playing their most beautiful psalms in the odorous fog of incense. The wedding procession had entered the sanctuary. The young spouses were already under the dais. How astonished everyone was when, at the very foot of the nuptial altar, the husband, or the man who was about to receive that title, the Graf von Markfeld, instead of offering his right hand to his young bride, again presented his left to her!

It was too much; the bride could not stand it any longer; she swiveled round abruptly, and grabbed that right hand, which was still concealed.

Horror! It was as hard and cold as ice.

"Beware," said a voice to her at the same time—that of a woman she could not see. "Beware, Mademoiselle; you are about to marry a brucolaque; you are about to marry a dead man; you are about to marry the vampire Bem Strombold."

The bride—who, from that moment on, was no longer the bride—uttered a scream of terror that cut through the church from end to end, and fainted beneath the golden dais extended over her head. She was taken to her father's house.

The metropolitan church of Saint Martin, considered to have been soiled by the presence of the vampire, remained closed for forty days, at the end of which it was purified by holy water and the appropriate prayers.

As for Bem Strombold, with the aid of one of those pretexts that one always has in the wake of a failed marriage, he was challenged to a duel by one of the young woman's brothers a killed by a sword-thrust—but they did not take the precaution of burying him with a stake through his stomach: an omission for which they paid dear. The brucolaque came back among the living several times, and caused great misfortunes in local families. We shall see the proof of that frightful assertion later, in what happened to the daughter of the woman who, by a providential stroke of luck, had avoided becoming the wife of the vampire Bem Strombold, and married Dr. Salomon Kanali instead.

While living alone with her father, who had been widowed at an early age, that daughter, who was Marthe's mother, formed a character strongly mingled with penetration and reverie, profundity and mysticism. Her father, although he had promised, and although he had sworn, had not renounced either alchemy or his research on the resurrection of humans by humans.

Well, the eternal preoccupation with another world within that young head, which followed in its flight all the deviations of her father—an ideal, unknown, apocalyptic world in which she lived far more than in the real world—had gradually drawn her to believe, quite naturally, in supernatural things: firstly, to believe, with her father in resurrection by human means; and secondly, to believe in vampirism, because of her mother's history of being loved by and having come to the point of being married to the famous vampire Bem Strombold, and also because of her own history, she having being born, like her mother, in Hungary, the fatherland of redivivi, brucolaques and vampires.

It was among her father's pupils that she met the young Hermann von Rosenthal. How and why did they fall in love? That is a question to which one can only reply with another question: why should they not have fallen in love? Both young and both charming, they were only waiting for an opportunity to come together, and the opportunity came of its own accord. They saw one another three times a week at Dr. Salomon Kanali's lessons, and Dr. Salomon Kanali, like all imaginable fathers, only perceived that a young man adored his daughter, and was adored in his turn, on the day when he came to make an official request for her hand in marriage.

Although Herr von Rosenthal was not of the highest nobility of the kingdom, the aristocracy of gold, he belonged to a family sufficiently well-titled and rich enough to alarm the doctor, who had imagined a more modest position for his daughter. He gave his consent nevertheless, even though he would have preferred some honest scholar for a son-in-law, brilliant in physics and mathematics and capable of aiding him in his research.

Rosenthal was not much of a scholar himself; he much preferred hunting chamois in the mountains to assiduous work in the depths of a library. Moreover, he bore all the signs of his resolute temperament; he was a sturdy fellow, hewn in the heart of oak of all true Hungarian hunters. That firmness, however, did not go as far as making him very bold in the presence of the woman he had chosen as his future companion. Even in the presence of her father, he had never dared to kiss her hand.

His comrades were astonished by that reserve—a reserve so excessive that a few of them sought bizarre and impossible explanations for it. The doctor's daughter, however, saw it as nothing but an honesty of soul, on which she counted, and which made her love him more. For others, it was indifference, coldness toward Dr. Salomon Kanali's daughter. His only true love, they said, was the hunt.

Even he seemed to be trying to prove them right. He often absented himself for a fortnight in order to follow, breathlessly, some young lord's hunt through lakes, marshes and bogs.

His blue eyes, of a savage limpidity, open in the oval of his colorless face, gave him an exceptional expression in the midst of the familiar types of the Slavic race. He therefore lacked the vigor of complexion with which tradition leads us, habitually, to redden the faces of hunters. He did not have that. Like the Black Hunstman of the German ballad,[18] his skin was as uniform and white as if he had only ever pursued deer by the wan light of the moon.

---

[18] The folk legend on which Carl Maria von Weber's opera *Der Freischütz* (1821) is based.

That great passion for hunting was to prove fatal.

His marriage to the only daughter of Dr. Salomon Kanali was about to take place when, during a hunt on the shores of the Danube at the castle of Graf von Stork, he was killed while emerging from a thicket by one of his friends, who doubtless mistook him for a roebuck breaking cover.

His death struck the woman he was to have married a few days later in the heart. She fell from despair into resignation, and from resignation into a long melancholy in which her health faded away. She was visibly perishing, in spite of the care she received and all the curative means invented by her father—as expert a physician as he was a chemist—in order to halt that rapid consumption.

There was something peculiar about that state of languor, in which she was soon seen to melt like a candle in the heat of a fire, taking on a joyful serenity as she became increasingly thinner. She was transfigured; her eyes lit up, more vivid and sparkling; her cheeks blazed momentarily against their profound pallor; and she often leaned over as if to listen to someone talking to her. By contrast with other invalids, she waited for the return of darkness with and anxious and agitated impatience.

One day, when the wasting process had brought her to an extreme of weakness, she told her father, with a reluctant confidence, as if long suppressed, that she had a great desire to make him a confession and wanted him to do something for her. Encouraged very affectionately to speak, she then told Dr. Salomon Kanali that since the still-present and still-dolorous loss of Hermann von Rosenthal, she saw the latter every night in a dream, and in the following manner:

The dark background of her room opened and was illuminated by a gray and vaporous light; then, at the extremity of a pathway prolonged into the far distance, she saw Hermann heading slowly toward her. He advanced silently to the side of the bed, and then, parting the curtains in the same silence, he leaned over her.

Although she was very glad to see him again, she felt a mortal, insurmountable terror on feeling his lips settle upon her. Sometimes they were applied to her arm, sometimes to her neck. They remained stuck to her flesh for a time she could not measure, she said, but which seemed to her to be very long. That mouth was icy, and all the time that it remained attached, she thought she could hear her blood falling, drop by drop, and leaving her.

"It's a dream, like all dreams," her father said. "To search it for a meaning would be folly." *All the more reason to expel it from her mind*, he added, privately, *if it gradually leads her to believe, like her mother, that she is the victim of the dogged and pitiless domination of a vampire—but such dreams are meaningless.*

Not entirely sharing her father's opinion that she was merely under the yoke of a dream, Marthe's future mother continued her confidence in a low voice, as she had begun it, although there was no one there to hear. She told Salomon Kanali what service it was she expected from his constant and benevolent affection. Since his enlightenment, he claimed, had led him to communicate a second existence to those who had lost it, it ought to be much easier for him to render it to one who had only partly lost it, like Hermann. The young man was only partly lost, one could say, because he returned every night and only disappeared at daybreak, at cock-crow.

Although he cherished his daughter, Dr. Salomon Kanali was painfully affected on learning the kind of service she expected of him. It was only by a miracle, it will be remembered, that he had escaped the rigors of the law for having attempted the resurrection of a murdered traveler. To expose himself again...nothing would save him if he were caught. However, paternal affection overcame the dread. He promised to make the most violent and reckless efforts of science to grant his daughter's wish. He began work immediately, and his daughter began to hope.

Before attempting anything against oblivion, it was necessary to assure himself of the state of conservation of his former pupil in the monument that had been erected for him by his comrades. The night for that preliminary inspection was chosen.

Having left the town very late, and alone, after several quarters of an hour walking across country, Dr. Salomon Kanali reached the desired spot. No spy had followed him. With the aid of an iron bar that he had brought, he loosened one of the marble slabs that formed the base of the monument and went down several steps. Having arrived at the last one, he lit a torch; the vault was illuminated.

To his great astonishment, the cavity was empty—utterly empty! There was no one there!

V

Its inhabitant had gone. There was no longer anything there but the branch of box-wood that he had held
between his interlaced fingers—for all eternity, it had
been thought.

It was certainly here, though, Dr. Salomon Kanali
said to himself, with a mental surprise equal to the most
formidable fear, *that Herr von Rosenthal was deposited*.
He had seen him deposited with his own eyes. To what
could such a phenomenon be attributed?

Pensive, his features distraught, he went home, and
in the morning he hastened to tell his daughter everything. She was momentarily struck by the same amazement, but, preferring to think that her father was mistak-
en to admitting that her Hermann was not resting a few
leagues away from her, and going further still, in sus-
pecting that her father, for fear of compromising himself
once again with the magistrates, had made use of the
pretext he had given for not undertaking his task, she
pretended to accept his story—or rather, in her view, his
lie—and went herself in the morning to the place where
her Hermann was sleeping peacefully beneath the trees.

There she searched for the stone that her father said
that he had loosened, sure that it would not be there. The
stone had been detached from the others that retained it!

Courageously, she went down the steps, into the
crypt. She looked...

Her Hermann was still there. His beautiful hands
were still crossed over his bosom, and between them was
the branch of blessed box-wood that she had placed there

three months ago, when she had been taken into that calm, cold vault.

After a fervent prayer, she went back up to the ground, went home, and said to her father, with the bitter discontentment of a heart brushed by a lie, that he had deceived her. Herr von Rosenthal had not budged. She had seen him; she had just seen him.

Convinced that he would have fulfilled his promise to his daughter, although it would have cost his scruples dearly, which he had confessed to her without hesitation, Monsieur Kanali swore on the Bible that he had not deceived her, and, to prove his veracity, offered to return with her to the same place the following night. He believed with all his heart that he could demonstrate, his daughter being with him, that he had not made an error in his expedition.

His daughter accepted. They went out of the city gate by night, went into the country, and arrived silently at the designated spot.

Before going down, Monsieur Kanali lit a torch—something that he had only done the first time when he had descended into the interior, but which he did in advance this time, for fear that his daughter might slip on the steps. They both went into the vault thereafter.

They did not stay for long. A few moments later, the father and daughter reappeared, terrified, trembling and white-faced, as if they themselves had been pale inhabitants of the subterranean dwelling from which they were escaping.

Why that terror? Because the tomb was empty.

Their double terror is self-explanatory, if one has followed the events that preceded it. A man appears every night to the doctor's daughter; he is not found during the night in his tomb. She finds him there by day. The following night, neither of them find him. There is, therefore, no longer any doubt: Hermann too is a vampire, a vampire like Bem Strombold. He is the same vampire, who is attacking the daughter as he attacked the other twenty years earlier, and who, instead of having the icy hand that he had twenty years ago, now has icy lips.

To complete the unfortunate annoyances, the light of the torch lit in the open air by Dr. Kanali attracted attention, betraying his presence, and that of his daughter, at a superstitious hour of the night and in a very suspicious location. They had been seen, recognized and denounced; they only just had time to escape. Rapid horses transported them over the Julian Alps. They took refuge in Italy.

For the doctor, accustomed to the studious and calm life of the lamp, such a displacement was a dire revolution in his life. Thus, after a few years of bitterness and incurable discouragement, he died in Zara, his birthplace. Science lost a star. It was to his daughter that he left his numerous manuscripts, including his great *Treatise on Resurrection*, which contained a supplementary account of the conversation of bodies by the rediscovered method of the celebrated Dutch anatomist Ruysch.

A year after the doctor's death, a victim of his genius and his paternal devotion, his daughter, in order not to succumb herself beneath the weight of so many various ordeals, summoned up a few distractions, in response to the solicitations of her friends. Among those that she created, there was one whose consequences were most unexpected.

A troupe of French actors, chased from town to town by their unlucky star, had come to give a few performances. There, as elsewhere, they collected nothing but poverty. Touched by the plight of those poor people, the ladies of the town opened a subscription on their behalf, and at the head of that good work, to manage it, they set the daughter of the late Dr. Salomon Kanali. For that reason, she made the acquaintance of the director of the wayward and disorganized troupe.

That director, an actor himself, was an intelligent young man, full of fire and very personable. He was called Belleville, although that might not have been his real name. Perhaps he had performed in Belleville, a locality on the outskirts of Paris, and owed his topographical name thereto. Belleville and Mademoiselle Kanali thus found themselves connected. They met frequently, and felt disposed to love one another.

One day, Belleville dared to propose himself as a potential husband; the offer was not judged too bold. The doctor's daughter, free to dispose of her hand and her fortune, accepted. She consented to become the wife of the actor, but on the express condition that, on becoming her husband, he would take the name of Kanali, a tribute that she thought she owed to the memory of her father, the illustrious Salomon Kanali. The marriage took place.

In the leisure of his new position, Kanali, the second of that name, began one day to read the manuscripts left by his father-in-law, and it was in consequence of that reading that the idea occurred to him of profiting on his own account from some of the great discoveries mentioned therein. That of embalming seemed to him to be the least problematic; he settled on that, studied it in depth, and got to the bottom of it. He remained convinced that his fortune was there—or, rather, the indefinite increase of his fortune, for he had entered into possession of a considerable income by marrying the daughter of the celebrated chemist.

Many years after his marriage to her—about eighteen years—the Indian epidemic having revealed itself for the third or fourth time in Europe, it then being 1849, he thought seriously about exploiting he admirable method of conservation of bodies developed by his father-in-law. However, he avoided with the greatest care putting it into practice either in Hungary, where he dreaded meeting the same fate as Salomon Kanali, or in Italy, where it was no less dangerous.

All liberty loves France. He therefore came to Paris in 1849, in the epoch of the reappearance of the Asiatic scourge in that capital, and he went, as has been reported at the beginning of this story, to take up residence in the Val-de-Grâce with his wife and daughter, the young Marthe Kanali.

An account has also been rendered of the lavish and distinguished manner, thanks to letters of recommendation from Austria, doubtless obtained by his wife's credit, in which he was welcomed among us. He was treated as a colleague, and he merited that favor, for during twenty years of residence in Dalmatia, Italy and Austria, he had applied himself to the study of medicine and the serious sciences connected therewith—but without ever losing entirely, in contact with that elevated endeavor, either the enjoyment or the blithe philosophical insouciance of his original profession as an actor. He loved that profession in the depths of his heart, although he was not gratified when people talked to him about it without some precaution, out of respect for the gravity of his new position.

Kanali, who was counting a great deal, as we have just explained, one the advantages that he anticipated receiving from posthumous embalmings and rejuvenations, had thus only entered the Val-de-Grâce with the hidden but unique objective of carrying out experiments on bodies damaged by the afflictions of the devastating scourge.

Installed in his apartment, he occupied himself relentlessly with his project. He needed, above all, an intelligent, special, discreet, zealous and devoted assistant who belonged to the establishment, who could procure him bodies and make them available for his experiments. César Caseneuve seemed to him to fit the bill marvelously. By degrees, therefore, he attracted the young man to his home, encouraged his assiduities with regard to his daughter, and when he was sure of holding him by means of the love that Marthe had inspired in him, he judged the moment favorable for making him his accomplice—and, of course, associating him with his glory and fortune.

After the indispensable voyage that we have just made with our reader through the past of our characters, let us now return to the point at which we deviated—which is to say, to the rendezvous arranged by Dr. Kanali with César Caseneuve beside the bed of Colombe Val-de-Grâce, struck down in a matter of hours by the epidemic. They were to meet, it will be remembered, at eleven o'clock.

They did indeed meet at the indicated hour, which was the most convenient time for the endeavor meditated for a long time by the doctor. People were coming and going in the wards; the physicians, interns, consultants and service staff were crossing one another's paths in all directions in order to get everything done, and they were scarcely sufficient for the formidable demands of that difficult moment, when the patients from outside came in quantity and in disorder to take the still-warm places of those who had died and would be taken away by the long wagons that have been mentioned.

In response to a few words whispered by the doctor in the still-bewildered ear of César Caseneuve, the latter swiftly rolled up the delicate and charming body of Colombe Val-de-Grâce in her bedclothes and put it over his shoulder. No one on the ward paid any attention to that movement, and, if they had noticed it, would never have guessed the objective with which it was executed.

Preceded by the doctor, César, who still had no precise idea of the project with which Kanali was associating him, silently went down the steps leading from the ward in which Colombe had been deposited to the garden, and with the same contained discretion, they continued their nocturnal expedition, with a muffled tread, on the mute sand of the paths through the dormant hornbeams.

After a certain distance, César, perceiving with astonishment the direction in which the doctor was heading, stopped and turned toward him.

"But doctor," he said, "one would think that we were going to my lodgings."

"Of course—that is where we're going. Walk."

"But why? Why are we going there?"

"You'll soon find out. Keep walking."

"But..."

"Just keep walking," repeated the doctor, in the tone of a man who has no time to waste on the meager pleasures of argument.

César Caseneuve continued walking behind the doctor, but he experienced an anxiety that did not quit him as he felt the light and gentle body of little Colombe swaying gently and trembling on his shoulder: Colombe

Val-de-Grâce, his first love; a love undoubtedly replaced, but not effaced; a rosy love that had appeared momentarily in the pale and monotonous sky of his early student days spent in the depths of the Saint-Jacques quarter—the quarter of poverty, science, resignation and love.

The sweat that streamed in an inexhaustible flood from his forehead, as if he were walking in bright sunlight—the night, it is true, was as hot as midday—added to the anxiety, the uncertainty and the unknown of such a situation in the midst of silence. Add to that, too, César's incurable fear of the yellow invasion and you will have some idea of the mental state of his tormented being. Half past eleven having chimed on the little clock in the lofty dome, he was gripped, as that drop of iron fell upon him, by such a sudden nervous tremor that he almost dropped his burden before they arrived at the building.

A few words about that isolated building, lost at the extremity of the garden, adjacent to the wall of the long Rue des Charbonniers: it had been ceded to Caseneuve; he had been relegated to it when his room was taken over to increase the space available for the invalids who had become too numerous. Now, let us explain the intention with which the doctor had thought it appropriate to put into action when he had exclaimed, beside the dying Colombe: "Finally, I have what I need."

What he needed her for was his experiment in embalming. To carry it out, he not only needed to procure a body, although that presented enough significant difficulties, but also, and above all, a distraction that would win him some notoriety in the quarter, and the city, in order that everyone, seeing the features of the individual seemingly recalled to life and beauty, would exclaim:

"It's her! It really is! It's marvelous! It's a prodigy! She's smiling at us! She's going to speak!" Renown, fame and fortune were there, infallibly there, for previous so-called embalming processes, as Kanali and many others had said, were nothing but a ridiculous and hideous masquerade, to the profit of mahogany and ebony. Only the ebonists were able to guarantee a resemblance.

Let us continue. Once a body marked in the neighborhood by that indispensable notoriety had been found, it was still necessary to ensure a place where the experiment could be carried out without being seen by anyone; that was a condition of the greatest importance. Senior physicians and administrators do not readily lend themselves to the temerities of innovators. But what place could be chosen for the successful completion of the operation of which Kanali had dreamed for so many years and was finally about to attempt? It was not easy to find a house with the facilities, the space and the isolation necessary for the operation. Kanali thought of César's pavilion.

We could now describe the whole of that important operation, but are not indicate exactly the various chemical elements that entered into the savant composition employed by the doctor, following his illustrious father-in-law.

It has been supposed that Ruysch, whose secret Kanali possessed, put into that composition, in strictly calculated proportions, myrrh, aloes, cardamom, rosemary, styrax, benzoin, cypress, mace, imperatoire, tacamahaca, cassia lignea, germander, spikenard, oregano and enula campana, but Salomon Kanali dissolved these mostly-oriental products in a liquid that was neither spirit-of-wine nor brewer's spirit, as the Dutch anatomist had indicated in his memoir to Peter the Great, in order to deceive posterity. It was another liquid, and the composition of that other liquid—the one that Ruysch had not consented to reveal—Fabricius Kanali, the son-in-law of the great Kanali, knew, protecting it under three impenetrable seals.

He was ready to make use of it that night: that night full of feverish and nameless anxieties for César Caseneuve.

Although we shall not divulge Kanali's secret here, we can at least reveal the result that he expected, with a certainty guaranteed by abundant probabilities already obtained.

Of all embalming processes, the most complete, in Kanali's view, was the one called, in specialist treatises, "the embalming of the mummy of the sands"—which is to say, the conservation procured by the sands of the desert, a conservation due to the dryness with which those privileged sands grip bodies. Now add to that dryness produced by the sun the gleam of rediscovered color and you will have conquered both the eternity of duration and the eternity of youth and beauty.

"In the countries of Africa situated beyond the Nile," says Père Kircher,[19] "is a desert of sand whose immense waves appear in a limitless horizon similar to those of the sea. Stirred by the wind, these sands produce such frightful tempests that they bury travelers, beasts of burden and merchandise beneath their enormous mass.

---

[19] Athanasius Kircher (c.1601-1680), best known for his studies in Egyptology and geology, was also an early microscopist, who hypothesized in consequence a version of the germ theory of disease, with specific reference to the plague, and suggested corollary methods of preventing infection, but he failed to convince his contemporaries.

The bodies thus buried are desiccated after long years by the ardor of the sun's rays and the virtue of the burning sand. They are desiccated to the point of becoming as light as if they were made of straw."

But what Père Kircher also says is that bodies thus calcinated become as black as Ethiopians—a disadvantage that cancels out all the benefits of the desiccation.

The new and admirable aspect of the sublime discovery of the great Salomon Kanali is, therefore, that one obtains by that means the incorruptibility produced by the sun and the desert sand, without deterioration of the tissues—on the contrary, while retaining its original paleness and coloration. Now comes the astonishing part of the discovery.

Understandably, not having the centuries to come and the sands of Africa at his disposal, it was necessary for the inventor to substitute chemical agents for them. They were substituted. It was necessary to pass the body through a rapid current of flames. That was not a slow combustion but a simple ballast of fire, rapid, radiant and overwhelming, which, by opening the pores, permitted the substance created by the great Kanali to fill and color the veins and the entire mucous network, the source of human coloration. That operation thus summarized and concentrated within itself, admirably, the effects of time and heat, the sunlight of several centuries.

Once they had arrived at the pavilion, where the doctor, having procured the key, had prepared everything necessary for the experiment, he and César went in. Kanali immediately locked the door and the windows and drew the curtains.

César then deposited Colombe on a large, perfectly-horizontal sheet of burnished metal. When she was laid out on the plate in question, the doctor picked up a brass vase full of the special composition from a corner and spread it over Colombe's face, breast, arms and legs, which were already coal-black by virtue of the well-known effect of disorganization that arrives instantaneously in the wake of the infernal malady by which she had been struck. After handing the brass vase to César, he occupied himself with anointing the young woman's body with the liquid, initially deposited in patches.

When that was done, he set fire to the edges of the liquid at the extremities of the feet and the top of the head, in order that, in meeting up, the two flames would envelop the entire body.

Immediately, the blaze occurred in the anticipated conditions, and immediately, Colombe's youth, her complexion, rosy flesh and frank ingenuous smile—all of her, in sum—appeared and blossomed in the dazzle of that magical light.

It was a complete success. The process had produced the consequences of which the doctor had dreamed for so long with such pride—for the entire quarter would testify the following day, on seeing Colombe resuscitated in youth and beauty, to Dr. Kanali's victory over oblivion.

César ruined everything. Delighted to the point of fear by the spectacle displayed before him, and doubtless also emotional at seeing the child almost alive once again whom he had carried to his lodgings in a condition so far from life, lost his head. He became disturbed, and with a nervous movement that it is not difficult to understand, he brought the liquid that he was holding in his trembling right hand—a liquid more flammable than gunpowder—too close to the lamp that he was carrying in his right hand, and the entire pavilion went up in flames.

Never had a more violent blaze burst out in such a restricted space. The pavilion, saturated with gas to the ceiling, cracked and split; the roof was blown into the air, while part of the walls collapsed with a detonation similar to that of a mine-explosion.

The deflagration was followed by a broad and continuous jet of flames, which rose straight up to the level of the cupola of the Val-de-Grâce, lighting up the smallest architectural details for all the people of the faubourg, easily woken up by that enormous noise and immense glare. It was all the easier because in that epoch, in 1849, people were prompt to pay attention to anything, and to be irritated by anything, seeing hostile intentions in the slightest incident. Suppositions were therefore ignited in the four corners of the vast quarter, and made rapid progress.

"That's coming from the Val-de-Grâce," was murmured on the streets and crossroads, from one back alley to the next. "What's happening there?"

"What's happening is that they're burning the sick," said someone who had already looked over the wall and into the blazing crater of the pavilion."

"That's it—they're burning the sick, to be more quickly rid of the embarrassment they're causing."

That malevolent, venomous, deadly rumor ran around, and grew as it propagated. It soon became a cry, general howl; "They're burning the sick! They're burning the sick!"

An angry group joined the malevolent group; it became a mob; it became a tempest; the garden wall in the Rue des Charbonniers was scaled and the boldest went in. Guided by the flames, they reached Caseneuve's pavilion.

What a spectacle! Their rage no longer knew any bounds; they had perceived in the midst of the diabolical fire the body of a young woman, half-burned—a young woman they recognized: the love, the grace, the joy, the delight and the idol of the quarter: Colombe Val-de-Grâce, devoured by the flames. They had not even known that she was ill! The least they wanted was to massacre Caseneuve and Dr. Kanali, to burn them on the pyre to which it was impossible for them to attach any significance at all, except that of the commission of an abominable crime.

Fortunately for the two individuals, so close to being thrown on to the fire, the staff of the establishment came to their rescue. The police followed. In sum, they were saved.

The mob was told that the fire had been started by accident in César Caseneuve's lodgings while he was busy studying the character of the malady that had afflicted the body of Colombe, who had died several hours before. The mob withdrew, grumbling, but there had been a great excitement. It goes without saying that a profound silence was recommended and observed concerning the event.

The next day, the intern César was sacked, and Dr. Kanali, for his part, was requested to find other accommodation.

And that that is how the doctor came to our establishment, where no unfavorable rumor preceded him or followed him, since all rumor had been prudently stifled.

From now on, I shall no longer be recounting what others have told me—it is Monsieur Morel who is speaking—but what I witnessed myself.

To begin with, I was witness to the somber melancholy that Mademoiselle Marthe Kanali brought in settling among us, a universal languor of which I shall reveal the cause straight away, although I only discovered it sometime after the family's installation.

Monsieur Kanali, who had only allowed César Caseneuve to establish himself within his familiarity, and to build up hopes of becoming his son-in-law, because he needed him, as an intelligent aide and devoted accomplice in his experiments, no longer wished to hear any mention of him in the deplorable wake of the success in the pavilion. As he held César Caseneuve solely responsible for everything disastrous that had happened to him on that memorable night—the fire, the invasion of the local people, his dismissal from the Val-de-Grâce; in sum, the complete ruination of his endeavor, on the brink of victory—he banned him from his home, conceived an aversion akin to hatred for him, and forbade his wife and daughter not only to continue to see him but even to pronounce his name. There is nothing like ambition to engender those black antipathies, those savage hatreds toward those who have upset the apple-cart in some way.

Marthe bowed her head in order to let the storm pass, but she promised herself not to forget her love, and such a promise is far-reaching. The ardent Italian woman drew upon her German firmness and her French mental resources to triumph over momentary ill-fortune.

As for her mother, Madame Kanali, the latter wondered whether she ought not to thank Heaven for having removed that young man from the threshold of their house forever—she assumed that it was forever. Never having vanquished the frisson that ran in icy threads through all her limbs at the sight of Caseneuve, who was evidently afflicted in her eyes with a unfortunate resemblance to some profoundly antipathetic individual, she had seen him depart with pleasure. With pleasure for herself, that is, albeit with some grief for her daughter, although the grief in question was still relative—for she had said several times to the divine confidant, in her prayers, that the day when Marthe married Caseneuve, if it were written in the stars that she would marry him, she would die at that very instant, of dolor.

We shall soon know what the reason was for Madame Kanali's insurmountable repulsion for César Caseneuve, whose remarkable intelligence, great honesty and well acquired science she did not deny—not to mention the other advantages that she did not refuse him either: an attractive face full of nobility, a distinguished stature and charming manners.

It remains to say now what César's situation was after the fatal misadventure of the pavilion, that shipwreck of all his hopes. It was not good. He was so explicitly banished by the doctor, the day after they had both been expelled from the Val-de-Grâce, that he did not have the courage, imperious as his love was, to present himself again at the Kanali family's new lodgings. It was one of those dismissals after which no hope remains, except for exalted lovers: supreme heroes such as the Des Grieux, the Werthers, the Saint-Preux,[20] and perhaps also for the César Caseneuves.

In any case, this explains perfectly the reason for the prudence with which Monsieur and Madame Kanali, with different motives, both asked me, with so much precision, during the first days of their residence, what time the gates of the sanitarium were closed, about the height of the walls, etc.

I have said that Mademoiselle Marthe Kanali's passion was combined with a great finesse; I do not know whether, in advancing that character trait, I have sufficiently characterized her new mental situation. After all, where is the young woman who does not have finesse at the moment when passion grips her? She acquires finesse because there is danger, and there is danger because there is an enemy.

An enemy rises up against every love; that enemy is either the family, or society, or the entire world. An impenetrable enigma! Marriage is made a necessity—the most obligatory of the necessities of life, for a woman— and yet there is no act in life to which more obstacles are raised for a woman. How many reasons there are for opposing it! Reasons sometimes based on the disproportion of ages, sometimes on the inequality of fortunes, sometimes on the difference of status. People are astonished to see so many old women on the sidewalk of celibacy; what astonishes me is to see so many other young wom-

---

[20] The Chevalier Des Grieux is the hero of Abbé Prévost's *Manon Lescaut* (1731); Werther is the hero of J. W. Goethe's *Die Lieden des jungen Werthers* (1774; tr. as *The Sorrows of Young Werther*); Saint-Preux is the hero of Jean-Jacques Rousseau's *La Nouvelle Héloise* (1761). It is worth noting that none of those classic love stories has a happy ending.

en marry, when I think that it only requires two mouths to say "I do" in front of the Maire, whereas there are thousands and thousands who have no other desire and no other function than always to be saying: "No, no, no."

Having reached this point in the road mapped out for them, the story of the Kanali family finds its characters in the following disposition:

Madame Kanali believed more than ever in vampires, which was easy to see in the questions that she had addressed to me since her arrival in the sanitarium. The reflection that she had made in front of her husband, intended for him—"Oh, it's not thieves we fear"—sufficiently emphasizes the continual preoccupation of her redoubtable belief in those creatures from beyond the grave.

That same credence explains to us the general panic that had invaded her at the sight of César Caseneuve and her terror when she discovered that he bore—like the vampire Bem Strombold, who had been on the point of marrying her mother, the wife of the great Salomon Kanali—a kind of little blood-red mark in the corner of his mouth. Except that Bem Strombold never offered his right hand, and César never refused it. No matter! Madame Kanali, because of that bloody sign, had shivered in all the delicate fibers of her heart on seeing César approach her daughter and fall in love with her; she thought that Marthe would be the victim of the third apparition of the same vampire in their twice-tested family, and that poor Marthe would die of that obsession for the very reason that her grandmother, the wife of the first Kanali, and herself, her mother, had escaped it.

Marthe would not have the same good fortune. A young victim was absolutely necessary to that great accursed creature; Marthe offered all the signs of the deadly predilection. A vampire is always preceded by languor, and Marthe's languor was evident to every eye; consumption accompanies him, and consumption was corroding Marthe pitilessly; he is surrounded by an aureole of pale colors, and pale colors covered Marthe's face. Therefore, Marthe would belong to him!

Now, add that Madame Kanali had only attached her attention with so much fixity to the windows of our long gallery of invalids because of vampires, that it is the recognized tradition in their stirring history never to appear in such great numbers as in times of major epidemics—and that we were, unfortunately, in one of those epochs.

Thus are explained the terror and anguish of Madame Kanali for her daughter, whom her eyes no longer quit. Marthe was followed and spied on by her with neither respite nor mercy. And that tyrannical surveillance of Marthe, born of excess maternal love, did not exclude that of Monsieur Kanali, whose anger against César Caseneuve had not weakened in the least. Far from it; it was one of those colossal scholarly hatreds, one of those hatreds compared to which the hatreds of the rest of humankind are almost amity.

All the incessant pressures exerted upon the love of César and Marthe, however, instead of cooling it, had only serve to exalt it to the point of delirium, to fever pitch. Having become, in one as in the other, the unique aliment of their thought, the inextinguishable flame of their brains, and their only reason for living, it rendered them incapable of anything else except loving one another.

The world was entirely contained within their love; there was nothing in the world except them and their love: it was a sublime egoism, a holy madness, that only those who have passed through that inferno of felicity once in their life have any possibility of understanding.

Here, naturally, arises the long sequence of difficulties, obstacles and dangers that Marthe and César would encounter before them whenever they sought to communicate their sensations.

César tried to write to Marthe; his letters were diverted and taken to the father and mother, whose surveillance and mistrust were augmented. He tried to climb over the garden walls; he was caught by the warders and risked being arrested as a thief. He renounced those means. Let us say right away that no means was successful for him, but that his multiple failures irritated instead of extinguishing the love of the two young people.

We have just seen that the love in question produced disappointments in Caseneuve; in Marthe it led from one discouragement to another, to a kind of dreamy idiocy, of one finds examples in young women tormented, as she was, by their most tender penchant. Her life became more distant by the hour from her connections with everything surrounding her, gradually isolating her within herself.

Mademoiselle Kanali walled herself up inside her love as if in a cloister, and from there, she no longer gazed upon the world, the sun and the living with anything but indifference. Her pallor increased further in the silent retreat of her love into the depths of her soul. Marthe was no longer anything but an earthly shade.

Before saying by what means, of which it is utterly impossible to form an idea coolly, Caseneuve final introduced himself into the sanitarium, it remains for me to describe he personal conduct of Dr. Kanali since he had been in our midst.

The doctor had not abandoned, and one would have been wrong to think otherwise, his project of embalming and rejuvenation, in spite of the serious check he had received at the Val-de-Grâce. He had come to our house in the Faubourg Saint-Denis with the sole objective of taking a triumphant revenge. My readers will not conserve any doubt in that regard when I have conducted them, in due course, to a certain establishment that I pointed out myself to Dr. Kanali, fatigued as I was in the end by always being asked the same question: "Monsieur Morel, can you tell me where the grave-diggers congregate?"—a question that he had asked me, as you will perhaps remember, during our first conversation.

Let us get back to the love of Marthe and César.

Marthe's melancholy soon became, by virtue of an effect often observed in young women afflicted with thwarted love, an exaggerated piety. Mademoiselle Kanali did not even stop at the exaggeration that takes the form of spending nights in prayer and taking communion on Saturday; she wanted to be a nun, and, in order to sanctify her novitiate, declared that she wanted to share with the sisters of St. Vincent de Paul the mission of caring for the sick.

Her frightened mother protested; her father revolted at the idea. What did such a determination signify? Was it destiny, the vocation of a young woman brought up for society, rich and celebrated by virtue of her grandfather and father?

Marthe was inflexible. She would let herself die, she said, if she were not allowed to devote herself entirely to the salvation of the sick. Arguments and pleas were futile. Nothing would make her renounce her resolution—a very imprudent resolution, I said to myself, as the indirect witness of these family disputes.

I would never have allowed her to prevail if I had been in her father's place, because it was doubtful that forbidding her to become a sister of charity would have caused her to die, while it was almost certain that she would fall victim to her devotion by going to breathe the subtle poisons of the epidemic at the bedsides of its victims. Already, out of ten sisters of St. Vincent de Paul who had come to care for out patients, seven had disappeared forever, and they were women accustomed to fatigue, hardened to long vigils, immune to any repugnance and whose morale was certainly sheltered from dread, for it was precisely the danger they were braving that they sought, and loved more than anything else.

It became futile to oppose Marthe's desire any longer, so firmly decided was she to devote herself, in a religious sentiment, to caring for the sick. She was abandoned to her recklessness. She went down into the wards and began her service. She made her debut at an exceedingly perilous moment.

Developed by the excessive heat of the month of June, the malady suddenly took on a more sinister character. We saw the black days of 1832 again. Already much weakened by the political situation, commerce disappeared completely. The shops scarcely opened; they were briefly opened to answer the demands of material life and closed again as soon as night fell.

The nights were hard to traverse. At distant intervals, red lanterns indicated the ambulance stations where one could go in search of first aid. Silent and deserted, the streets were furrowed in all directions by long files of stretchers, and toward midnight, when the inhabitants were imagined to be asleep—and they slept very little in that epoch—the carriages whose usage has already been mentioned outlined the exaggerated grimace of their shadows on walls shivering with fear: phantom carriages laden with phantoms. In order not to strike fear into the depths of houses that were always nervously on edge, the wheels were wrapped in thick cloth. It was a wasted precaution; fear always extends; it extends when there is nothing to be afraid of and it extends far more when there is something. There was a lot.

It was on one of those lamentable nights, impossible to forget, when our wards had no more room for anyone, that I saw a young man arrive, supported by two of his friends. His eyes were half-closed, his face anxious, his body arched by painful contractions, his breath halting and brief. His incoherent speech left no doubt as to the redoubtable name that had to be given to the disease by which he had just been struck down.

VII

Strangely enough, however—although I was perhaps the only one to notice it—he appeared, on entering
our wards, to be at least as frightened by the scene displayed to his right and his left as by his own situation. I
believe, in fact, that he forgot his own situation—which
is not ordinarily the action of any sick person—in order
to abandon himself immeasurably to the impression of
superhuman terror that froze him at the sights he perceived.

His lips suddenly became violet, almost black; his
eyes retreated beneath the somber arcade of his pale
forehead; his hair stood on end—a phenomenon in
which I had never really believed—like steely needles;
and he murmured between his teeth, which were chattering as if with extreme cold: "No, I don't want to stay
here! Oh, staying here is too horrible. All these people
are specters; they scare me; in a little while, I'll be a
specter like them. Take me away! Take me away!"

We succeeded in calming him down, though, or he
succeeded in mastering himself, and when he was a little
less agitated, his friends asked me for a separate room.

Coincidentally, alas—I do not say fortunately—the
patient occupying the cabinet placed in the middle of the
room, near the chapel, the only one that was vacant that
night, had bid farewell ten minutes before, even though
she had only come in that evening. People passed on so
quickly then! We put the newcomer in that room, and his
friends confided him to our care. They left immediately;
people did not like to stay among us long in those days,

so pernicious in character. The customary treatment was about to commence for their protégé.

God only knows what that treatment would have been! There were so many! Would they work on him with fire or with ice? The intern summoned to give him primary care declared that he would not last the night, that any effort to save him would be futile, and that the best thing to do, instead of seeking to martyrize him at will, was to subscribe to the latest and ultimate expression of his will, which was that a sister might come to sit beside his bed, charitably, to recite a few final prayers.

Mademoiselle Marthe happened to be there; she heard what the intern said, and immediately offered to be that pious reader.

The offer was accepted all the more readily because no other sister was in a position, at that moment, to dispute the precious task with her. They were occupied elsewhere, in medical services that claimed them without respite—for, in spite of their number, zeal and devotion, they were far from sufficient for their courageous and sublime mission.

Mademoiselle Marthe, therefore, went in to the new patient's room. The entrance to the cabinet—set, as we have said, in the middle of the huge gallery—was masked by the double fall of the large pleats of a long white curtain. Mademoiselle Marthe went in by herself, and remained alone with the patient.

She was enclosed in that refuge of silence and pious prayer for about three hours, and it was two hours after midnight—you will see that I have a reason for specifying the time with such exactitude—when a storm that had long been brooding beneath heavy, warm and stifling clouds broke over Paris, unleashing all the meteorological horrors into the atmosphere as it did so.

I shall never forget the disastrous effect of that storm on our poor invalids, and that is why the occasion is fixed in my mind. A poison—even prussic acid—could not have had more immediate or more frightful results on their organism. Each of them was snuffed out in turn, like a series of candles over which a horizontal wind has passed.

The rainwater was streaming in cataracts over the window-panes and livid flashes of lightning rain through the wards from one end to the other; the thunder never ceased to rumble and break forth in strident blasts. I had never seen anything like it in my life, but I was far from having seen everything.

At that moment, I saw Dr. Kanali and his wife arrive at the end of the ward at a precipitate pace, looking around anxiously. I deduced their intention; they were looking for their daughter. By means of a gesture I drew them to my station.

"What a night!" Madame Kanali said, as she drew near. "What a night!"

"Hard to bear, Madame—oh yes, very hard!"

"And my daughter?"

"There," I replied, pointing to the cabinet veiled by the white curtains. "Praying beside a patient."

"But that's intolerable!" said Monsieur Kanali, containing his rage, although, at that moment, he could have spoken as loudly as he wished; the storm had not diminished and its racket overwhelmed all other sounds. "It's intolerable! I don't want her to stay in this terrible place any longer. She could perish here in a matter of minutes. Let's snatch our child away from this poisoned gulf."

"But she's praying," I repeated, in a voice that I moderated because of a momentary pause that had just been produced in the patchier release of the tempest.

"Praying or not, I'm getting her out of here," retorted the doctor, also lowering his voice, as if he were seeking to reconcile his habits as a physician with his paternal wrath.

Then I saw him advance toward the cabinet with the white curtain; his wife went with him; I followed both of them.

The doctor lifted the curtain. What astonishment! What a surprise! What a circumstance!

Marthe was not praying; her hands were in those of the invalid, who seemed to me to be far less imperiled than I would have imagined, given the condition in which I had seen him when he arrived. They were not a moribund and a charitable angel helping him to pass peacefully from this life to a better one, but two lovers ecstatically delighted to find themselves together, fusing the surges of their soul in the same happiness.

The noise of the storm having prevented them from hearing our approach, they retained the same attitude before us. Sitting next to the bed, Marthe had placed her head on the pillow where that of César Caseneuve rested—for I shall not make you wait any longer to tell you that it was him, César Caseneuve, who was there with Marthe. And just imagine how they were praying together!

Many words of love must have been spoken in that sad space during the three hours that that tête-à-tête on the same pillow had lasted. Words of love! What power that love of the springtime of life must have had, in order for that young man to have braved a malady that no one in the world feared more than him! To have given him the miraculous strength to spend, in such a place, a night that might have been his last, as it was for so many others! No, I would never have attributed so much determination and valor to the sentiment in question. I had thought ambition alone capable of that heroic scorn for danger. I was mistaken.

The danger to which the two lovers had exposed themselves, which they had both prepared at leisure—for Marthe had only demanded to care for the sick in order to get closer to César Caseneuve—rendered them more interesting in my eyes that it would be possible for me to say. Courage, which changes everything, rendered their aberration very excusable: the sin of loving one another, of seeing one another, in spite of the will of their parents, in spite of the world entire. Who would not have been disarmed by so much heroism in passion, so much abnegation in the midst of so many dangers? Who would not have pardoned that love, if only because one might have thought it the last love remaining on earth, at that moment when the material world seemed to be plunged into physical distress, the moral world into the confusion of political opinions, and both were nearing their end? Who, we ask ourselves, would not have pardoned them?

Two people, however, did not pardon them—but one of them represented wounded pride, and the other fanaticism, which are equally pitiless. They were Dr. Kanali and his wife. The spectacle of their daughter, delivered to Caseneuve, awoke all Madame Kanali's superstitions and reignited her believe in redivivi, brucolaques, vampires and all those supernatural beings in which so many peoples of the Orient have believed, still believe and perhaps always will believe.

"Yes, it's him," murmured Madame Kanali, in a low voice, squeezing her husband's arm with a visible tremor. "It's him; recognize him, now; it's him, the imperishable, eternal persecutor of our family, the demon who has waged war successively against my mother and against me; against my mother under the fatal name of Bem Strombold, against me under that of Rosenthal. He is now pursuing our dear daughter in France, under the name of César Caseneuve. Yes, now it's our child's turn; and it's here, in the circumstances I which we find ourselves, in the place where we are, that he had to reappear—and has reappeared!"

What gave Madame Kanali's words a quasi-prophetic quality, and led to the denouement of the scene, were those of the two lovers. I shall report them as I heard them:

"Marthe, is this truly determined in your mind and your will?"

"Yes, my friend."

"You consent, then, to follow me, dear Marthe?"

"Yes, anywhere it pleases you to take me."

"Anywhere?"

"Anywhere."

"Think hard—you won't regret it one day?"

"No."

"Whatever happens, you'll never curse me?"

"Never."

"Well, then, let our destiny be accomplished; under cover of the tempest we'll quit this house; we'll go way from Paris toward the storm and the darkness, and we'll be together forever."

"Let's be together forever," Marthe repeated. "Death alone can separate us."

"Even death will not separate us," said Caseneuve, hugging the doctor's daughter in his arms with passionate effusion.

It was on hearing that vow, so solemnly expressed by Caseneuve, that Madame Kanali uttered a cry of maternal terror and revealed herself to her daughter and the man who spoke of remaining attached to her beyond the grave.

Deeply troubled, but fundamentally less convinced than his wife about the existence of vampires, the doctor took his daughter by the arm and dragged her back to his apartment, saying to her that he finally knew why she desired so much to be a sister of charity and nurse. Madame Kanali followed them.

I have no need to tell you that César Caseneuve did not present any symptom, however slight, of the disease that he had usurped as a pretext for introducing himself to Mademoiselle Marthe's presence—no symptom, except for an immeasurable desire to see where she was. It was that fear and the absence of any malady that gave the punishment that he was about to receive from Marthe's father an originality as burlesque as it was moving.

This is what the punishment in question was.

When Monsieur Kanali had taken his daughter back to her apartment—which only took a minute—he came back to where he had left Caseneuve stupefied by surprise, and where I was still suffering the effects of astonishment myself. Adopting the tone and authority of a doctor attached to the house, even though, if he was a doctor, he was not attached to the establishment, he told two interns who were accompanying him: "This young man is very ill. Examine him."

"Monsieur!" protested the astonished Caseneuve. "There's been a mistake. I came here to..."

"He's very ill, as you can see, Already, his disturbed mind no longer has any real consciousness of what he has done..."

"I tell you, Messieurs, that I'm not ill at all, and that I came here..."

"Terminal cholera!" continued the doctor, placing his hand on Caseneuve's bed. "Terminal cholera!"

"But Monsieur!" cried Caseneuve, again, very agitated by the threat that attributed a disease to him of which he was so terrified. "I repeat to you that I'm here for..."

"Incessant cramp!" the doctor continued, obstinately. "You see—his body is entirely contorted."

"But Monsieur, I'm not experiencing any cramp, and in truth..."

"Hippocratic face—see!"

"Me, I have a Hippocratic face?"

"Exceedingly Hippocratic—so called because Hippocrates was the first to describe its characteristics. Observe those characteristics on his face."

"What, this face!"

"On his face: the skin of the forehead taut..."

"My skin is taut?"

"Don't interrupt the definition of the father of medicine!"

"Even if he were the grandfather, you couldn't prove to me..."

Kanali resumed, authoritatively: "Skin of forehead taut, dry or covered in cold sweat; eyes sunken in their orbits; nose pointed."

"But my nose..."

"One more, don't interrupt the divine Hippocrates. Nose pointed, temples hollow, cheekbones protruding, ears cold and drawn back, lips discolored, livid and slack. Hippocrates has spoken."

"I too will speak!"

"Shut up!" Dr. Kanali continued, addressing the two interns. "Notice, too—a magnificent diagnostic—that he has opaque corneas."

"Me?"

"You have opaque corneas..."

"Yes, he has opaque corneas," the intern repeated, in order to agree with the master.

"I affirm to you, Messieurs..."

"He will soon be overtaken by lipothymia."

Exasperated, Caseneuve raised his arms to the heavens, murmuring in a sigh: "Lipothymia!"

"Lipothymia!" Kanali repeated. "Weakness, lipothymia; *deliquium animi*: lack of soul and courage; instantaneous loss of movement and sentiment, although respiration and circulation still continue—until, in syncope, the latter two functions are suspended. The invalid is lying there before our eyes, and is therefore struck with lipothymia, since sentiment is extinct within him, and he is still breathing."

"Of course I'm still breathing!"

"Yes, you're still breathing a little," said Kanali, "but soon, accidents such as respiration will..."

"What will happen?" demanded Caseneuve, becoming desperate and making efforts to leap out of bed.

"Syncopes, carphologias, spasms of the tendons," Kanali replied.

"But for the hundredth time..." Caseneuve said, howling with rage—or, rather, tried to say, for again he was interrupted and held down in his bed by the doctor.

"See how agitated he is! That's the spasms of the tendons. He's passed through the algid phase, the cyanic or blue period; he's approaching the most serious phase, the asphyxiant phase. It's a superb case!"

Fear finally succeeded anger in Caseneuve's soul. After having denied, then doubted, he now believed, in the face of the doctor's persistence, that he had contracted the Indian plague, by coming to breathe the air of one of its most active nuclei.

The doctor did not surrender his ascendancy.

"Look, Messieurs," he went on. "See how the glacial chill is gripping him; he's shivering; his limbs are stiffening. Observe!"

On hearing these last words, Caseneuve thought that he was about to perish—and he no longer had the slightest doubt when Marthe's father had terminated his anatomical description by saying: "He's doomed."

"Doomed?" demanded César, his eyes, mouth and entire body lurching forward. "Doomed!"

"However," the pitiless and ironic doctor went on, "We're going to attempt an energetic, desperate treatment on the subject."

"I don't want it!" César Caseneuve still had the strength to cry, beneath the weight of the denomination, so familiar to him, which eliminated a person from the number of the living: *subject!* He was no longer anything but a subject!

Without paying any heed to César's resistance, the doctor immediately began his prescription.

"First, frictions on the breast, all the way to the quick."

Moans from Caseneuve.

"Vesicatories on the epigastrum."

Lamentations from Caseneuve.

"Copious sanguine emission."

Louder lamentations from César.

"Vomitives."

Choking sounds from César.

"Quicklime around the body."

At the thought of that last treatment by quicklime, youth got the better of fear in Caseneuve. He bounded out of bed. He was determined to put an end to those threats, which he believed to be on the point of turning into deadly realities for him.

He was about to react against the evil by smashing the doctor's skull with the aid of the first object that came to hand, when someone was brought into the room, with a movement multiplied by footsteps and words, for whom the cabinet we were in was required. The cabinet was demanded in such a fashion that I believed that César Caseneuve would have been thrown out even if he had really been ill, in order to take unceremonious possession of his bed—but he was not there; he had taken advantage of the confusion caused by the newcomer's noisy entourage to get dressed in haste, so far as he could, and run away as fast as his legs could carry him.

There was only me, I'm sure, who heard the words that he darted behind him as he fled: "I wasn't able to steal her away while alive; I'll come and steal her away when I'm dead."

Then I saw him reach the far end of the ward and, by way of the stairs, which he went down in three bounds, take flight into the courtyard and the street—where, one may suppose without difficulty, he was very glad to exercise the liberty granted to his entire person.

What significance can now be attributed to that unexpected threat uttered by César Caseneuve—"I'll come and steal her away when I'm dead"—unless, like Madame Kanali, one believes in vampires?

VIII

The sick man who had come to take the place of César Caseneuve was brought in on a stretcher by a crowd of anxious, extremely agitated people, as distressed as if a member of the family had been struck by the disease. Their great number astonished me at first. How, at such an hour of the night, and on such a night, had so many people been gathered together? My second astonishment arose from the no less singular detail that all the people knew one another.

The commotion produced by their mass entrance into the ward having settled down somewhat, I attempted to obtain some enlightenment from one of them. I learned that the person—or, rather, the personage—who had just been transported into our midst, escorted by so much sympathy, was a celebrated club-member of the Salle Martel; he was the orator with the largest following, the most influential and the most popular.

You will not know the exact significance of the words *orator, club-member* and *Salle Martel* if you have forgotten that we were, in 1849, a Republic, or very nearly a Republic, in an epoch in which clubs were much in vogue, and when, by consequence, orators attracted universal attention, with their success, their clientele and their influence—an influence often greatly redoubted.

Among these clubs, much the most famous at the time—the only one still remembered today—was the club at the Salle Martel, placed less than a quarter of an hour's walk from our sanitarium. There, people agitated and discussed the most burning questions of politics and social philosophy; people agitated so strongly that there were sometimes fisticuffs beneath the speaker's podium—but an understanding was often reached, and at the end the session, fellow feeling was manifested in the street by the hymns of Pierre Dupont,[21] which were sung in chorus, to the great patriotic alarm of the inhabitants of the Faubourg Poissonnière and the Faubourg Saint-Denis.

Now, our personage had been touched by the wind of the epidemic during one of those oratory nights in question, in the very midst of his admirers in the Salle Martel; he had been very seriously afflicted. It was not a repetition of César Caseneuve's performance. Felled in the midst of his triumph, his friends had hastened to bring him to our establishment, where he arrived in a very serious condition. The effervescence of passions produced cases that were almost invariably incurable, and I was told, in fact, that it was during a debate in which the orator had abused his strength, pushing the heat of his words to the extent of enthusiasm, that he had felt wounded in his entrails. The blade steeped in the Indian poison had traversed him while he was launching an inflamed reply at his adversaries.

Save for the remarkable face of Caseneuve, I had not seen a specimen as correct and handsome as that of the orator of the Salle Martel. He was a man of about thirty-five or forty. His black hair, which was very long—as it was then the Republican fashion to wear it—descended like black velvet gauze over his superbly

---

[21] Pierre Dupont (1821-1870) was a song-writer who performed many of the fervent works he composed during the Second Republic at working men's concerts in the Salle de la Fraternité in the Faubourg Saint-Denis.

white neck: a striking contrast, easy to grasp because of the other fashion reigning in that epoch of wearing the short-collar broadly turned back over the shoulders. His beard, similarly pure black in color, terminated in a point, in the manner of the kings of Babylon, over his athletically-developed breast—and, in fact, are not orators also athletes?

One might have thought that one were looking at one of the young satraps of the colossal Biblical city, a city emerged from its ashes expressly in order to show us a greater beauty than Greece, a greater elegance than Athens, closer still to the ideal grandeur of demigods. There was nothing as simultaneously mild and majestic as his gaze, although it was already considerably weakened by the disease whose atrocious grip he was supporting so heroically. His portrait has remained in the memory of some of his contemporaries. He enjoyed the popularity, unfortunately very ephemeral, of the photography of circumstance.

Although the memory of his name has faded somewhat today, like the memory of his face, into the violet mist of a distance soon destined to be nothing more than vapor, colorless air, I shall not describe him in all his integrity. Everyone knows that one can wound someone even by praising them, when one touches on the still-dolorous past of our civil discords. I shall only hint at his identity; let us say that he was called Jean-Paul Désormeaux; that slight alteration of his name will not go so far, evidently, as silence regarding his noble origin, which he did not conceal—a frankness that had not harmed his popularity.

With his immense oratorical talent he combined, let us add, personal qualities of an exquisite humanity. Possessed of a fairly large fortune, he only retained what he needed to live in a small room in the Faubourg Saint-Martin. The rest went to the poor, for whose health he also cared, for he was a qualified physician, and he had practiced in Brazil—to which, I believe, he had followed the little phalansterian colony of Fourier.[22] That leads me to tell you that he harbored no illusions as soon as he was afflicted by the murderous breath of the epidemic, and he proved that to us with an admirable calmness as soon as he could pay attention to his situation without distressing the brave men who had accompanied him to our sanitarium.

When they had gone—and God knows how many times they looked back in order to see him again before leaving him—he said to Dr. Nivière, who was interrogating the rate of his pulse with his infallible experience and simultaneously examining the contraction of his pupils: "Nothing will save me, Doctor, but if you will permit, I can suffer less than one usually suffers in my condition. Put me in a bath, and ask that I be left in peace to write my last thoughts in favor of the people."

His wish was immediately satisfied. He was placed in a bath-tub and he wrote for two hours as if he were experiencing no pain. It was Roman fortitude. Underneath, agonies was racking him cruelly; by the third hour they were the stronger. Sometimes, the cramps were so violent, so intolerable, that the paper fell outside the bath-tub and the pencil into the water. Several times he

---

[22] The utopian philosopher Charles Fourier (1772-1837) proposed that the ideal egalitarian society ought to be organized on the basis of communal dwellings called *phalanstères* [phalansteries]; his works inspired numerous experimental communities, including one established in the Sai region of Brazil in 1841.

was restored to a sitting position, and with great efforts of will he tried to resume work, but toward first light his head slumped; weak and fainting, it rested on the edge of the tub, while his extended arms and the whole of his inert body were under the water. The orator of the Salle Martel, the thunderous Jupiter of the clubs, had passed on.

It was at that indecisive moment between light and darkness that I saw Dr. Kanali coming toward me.

He immediately drew me into the cabinet where the great clubman Désormeaux had just expired. Without having needed to take me to one side, for there was no one around us within earshot, he said: "Do you know, Monsieur Morel, that you have a heavy task on your hands in this house, especially in infernal times like those we're going through."

"Oh, very heavy," I replied. "But that's life; it isn't easy for anyone. Habit and resignation..."

"And you're suitably rewarded?"

"Not exactly in the manner of a Maréchal de France..."

"But all in all...?"

"A drab existence," I continued, smiling, having no idea where that dialogue, growing almost devoid of roots, was leading us. "Very drab—but the satisfaction of serving honest folk..."

"It's necessary, however, not to neglect an opportunity to be useful to oneself, and you aren't rich, I can see, judging by what you've told me, Monsieur Morel. Be careful!"

The warning of such a danger made me smile. "Oh, certainly not—I'm not rich, and probably never will be. But what can one do?"

"Perhaps you don't like money anyway? In which case..."

"On the contrary, I like it well enough—but it doesn't like me, and that's why we're never seen together." Once again, I wondered where the conversation as leading.

Monsieur Kanali began to speak to me in an even lower tone. "You could have ten thousand francs, if you wanted."

"What do you mean, if I wanted? Who doesn't want ten thousand francs? With ten thousand francs and the little nest-egg I inherited from my father, I could go to live like a little lord in Normandy, in a corner of the beautiful valley of the Auge, near Lisieux. Oh, how I'd like to have ten thousand francs!"

"That depends on you, Monsieur Morel."

"To have them?"

"To earn them."

"That's just it. It depends what one has to do to earn them."

"Easily—oh, very easily."

Diminishing the range of his voice, and drawing me next to the bed on which I had deposited Jean-Paul Désormeaux, he said: "You don't doubt," he went on, pointing to the famous clubman, "the universal impression of regret and grief that the unexpected death of such a man, so popular in Paris, will create?"

"The grief and regret caused by his loss, I agree, will be immense in Paris, but it's an irremediable misfortune."

"Oh, not entirely irremediable."

I looked at Monsieur Kanali with the same sentiment of close discretion that he had put into the final sentence.

"Not entirely irremediable," he repeated, meeting my interrogative gaze.

"I don't understand," I told him, finally, "the singular restriction that you seem to be bringing to the affirmation of the most evident and most irreparable fact in the world. That is a life utterly extinct, and you can't reanimate him."

"Perhaps, I tell you again, Monsieur Morel."

"There's no perhaps about it, and great doctor though you are..."

"I beg your pardon; if you mean that I can't resuscitate the man who is lying there before our eyes, as motionless as a stone, then you're right, although ambitious men have appeared on earth, temeritous rivals of God, who have claimed...but that's not what concerns us."

"Not in the least," I agreed. "You mentioned my earning ten thousand francs."

"Precisely—and I'm getting there," said Monsieur Kanali, his voice taking on something of the emphasis of the charlatans of the public square, to the point at which I thought I saw the apparatus of a vanishing-trick between his fingers and his suit turning into the red multipocketed apron of a trickster. "No, I don't have the ability to resurrect that man," he said, "but I can render him the physical superiority with which he was endowed before he was as he is now—which is to say, unrecognizable, thanks to the fatal hand of destruction. I have the ability to restore his rich complexion, his solid and ardent pallor, his eyes full of genius and rebellion, his mouth armed with irony, like those of all popular orators, from Demosthenes to him, via Mirabeau.

"And what renown would ensue, what a triumph that would be, for the man who brought about that transformation, who contrived that embalming, a great work with no resemblance, thank God, to the imperfect and infamous work of those pretended conservers with patents, whose art consists of rendering the subjects delivered into their maleficent hands ever uglier, more disfigured and more unrecognizable than they were before being entrusted to them.

"That man's glory would be marvelous, enviable among all the glories of the present and all time; people would clap their hands and cry miracle when they see him pass by; they will come from afar to see him. The State would not remain indifferent; it would be eager to reward the creator of that prodigy. He would be showered with distinctions, honors, medals.

"If positions and rewards have been heaped upon a clever man for having said that there is one star more in some distant crossroads of the sky, as if that star had not been there before him and would not always remain when he is dead, what would not be given to a man who had discovered something very different from a useless star, to a man who had given human beings a means of only making a partial exit from life when their hour comes to quit it?

"That man's glory would be as immeasurable as the service rendered—and that glory will perhaps be mine."

"Well, what's preventing it from being yours, Doctor? What's stopping you?"

"One thing, Monsieur Morel, just one."

"That's not very many."

"It's up to you to decide it," the doctor continued, putting his arm around me with the familiarity of one colleague to another. "I need this man to be left entirely at my disposal for forty-eight hours."

"This one?"

"This one."

"Forty-eight hours!" I protested. "When the authorities demand, imperiously, that he be disposed of within twelve hours, because of the excessive elevation of the temperature, and because...of many reasons. It's impossible!"

"The authorities, the authorities!" Monsieur Kanali murmured, impatiently, but with a great deal of suspicion in his disdain. "Of course, the authorities... however, if the man were hidden from the authorities, and another substituted for him... anyone at all... there are so many here at present..."

He cast a significant glance over the gallery, where all was silence—sufficient to permit the doctor to carry out the substitution that he planned without exciting the slightest protest. He concluded: "In that case, what would the authorities say? What would the authorities see?"

When he had finished, I said in my turn: "Who would dare to carry out that substitution?"

"You."

"Me!"

"I've told you the rather handsome price; I believe that I can count on your condescension."

"You mean my complicity."

"Complicity, condescension—what does it matter? Words are just words. Say yes, and in exchange for these banknotes"—he opened his wallet—"you'll deliver to me that man, whom, in a few days, when all his enthusiastic partisans think that he is gone forever, I shall cause to reappear in the light, strikingly handsome, real and superb in expression, almost alive. Do you accept the bargain?"

I confess that I hesitated momentarily. It seemed to me at first glance that I would not be committing any reprehensible act by accepting—but reflection, that conscience of the intelligence, immediately intervened, and I understood that putting one body in place of another was a grave contravention of the authorities' orders—orders which, respectable at any time, become sacred in times that are hazardous to public health. I told myself that it was bad, from the religious point of view, to summon on behalf of one individual the prayers destined for another. I thought, as well, about the moral censure that I would bring to the house when the substitution became known, as was bound to happen with a man like Monsieur Kanali, a hero of fanfares and acclamations.

I told myself all that, without forgetting that it was after a experiment similar to the one that he was proposing to me that the doctor had been expelled from the Val-de-Grâce. I therefore refused my tempter's proposition point-black, and rejected it in such a way to leave him no desire to renew it.

He was about to go away, for daylight was invading the wards, but he retraced his steps to say to me: "Since you have the deplorable weakness of not consenting to earn ten thousand francs, I beg you to do two things."

I listened.

"The first is that you keep the conversation we've just had secret."

"I can promise you secrecy. What's the other?"

"To tell me immediately what you didn't want to tell me the first time I asked you: the location, which must exist in Paris, of the place where the gravediggers habitually meet up."

"I didn't answer the question the first time you asked because I didn't think it was serious, but I see that I was mistaken," I said to the doctor, who was all ears. "The gentlemen in question meet every day at six o'clock in the Rue Myrrha in Montmartre, at the Crémerie Myrrha, where they eat together."

"Well," Dr. Kanali told me, laughing, "I shall dine at the Crémerie Myrrha this very day. You were wrong not to accept my offer, Monsieur Morel."

And he went away, humming a vaudeville tune: "It's so good to get rich when you're in love..."

IX

The Rue Myrrha is in Montmartre; it begins at the Rue Chaussée-Clignancourt and changes the name of Myrrha to that of Constantine in the very middle. To tell the truth, neither the Rue Myrrha nor the Rue Constantine gives rise to any idea of beauty; the two halves are as bad as one another; the beginning is as ugly as the end.

No other street in Paris is as incorrect, tortuous, bumpy, ill-constructed, badly paved, deformed and deplorable to the feet and gaze as the long Rue Myrrha. It is reminiscent of those absurd provincial streets that are named the Rue de Paris to honor Paris, but do that honor great disservice. Descending, or, more accurately, falling from the backbone of the Chaussée Clignancourt, the Rue Myrrha resembles a horse's saddle whose girth-strap has broken; it slips.

What a street! Oh, what a street! Here, the tall, thin houses rise up, stretching as far as they can, so to speak, as if to say: look at us, passers-by! Then, beside those houses run to seed, a steep gap suddenly opens up, only stopping at the flat roofs of another row of houses, with a single story. After these single-story houses, hanging on the flanks of the larger ones, other houses spring up, even taller, but much uglier. The latter are overburdened with balconies: balconies on the first, second, third and fourth floors. The Rue Myrrha is crazy about balconies. In the final analysis, all those big houses stiffly all the small houses, the former pumping the air and light from the latter.

It is the same throughout the street; one continually sees observatory towers on Eskimo huts and Eskimo huts on observatory towers. Sometimes, one encounters something even better though. There are groups of houses gathered into heaps and decorated with the name of "cities." A gate denounces their presence on the street; an avenue of rickety trees leads to them. One has before one a development of walls pierced with holes, like a bottle-rack. Those holes are windows. And as those windows have not shutters, they look as if they have been stripped after an attack, a looting or a gust of wind.

It's crazy and sinister. Summer there is horrible; one sees sweaty men with bare arms, children more than half-naked, and women with unkempt hair and dresses gaping, floating in rags and tatters, all going up and down, appearing and disappearing all day long through the spirals of these houses; urchins slide down the banisters of the stairways in order to get down more rapidly, and the wooly heads of workers stick out here and there through the snuff-box roofs, opening their mouths to breathe. Higher still, finally, there is nothing—the sky and the swallows.

At the foot of these houses, more unequal than—or, if you prefer, as unequal as—their human inhabitants, shops offers you, as in the center of Paris, everything that desire and need could wish, but with a particular character of accumulation, bad taste, abandonment and impropriety. The clothes-merchants seem to be selling clothes already worn, the cobblers shoes that have long lost their freshness, the hatters headgear that has already been introduced to water and has retained dust, the furnishers beds that have taken the road to the auction-house more than once, the grocers comestibles saved from a shipwreck, the milliners hats beneath which one imagines that one can see the vile heads that have worn them out, the clockmakers pendulum-clocks three days behind time and pocket-watches that emit the gleams of saucepans.

This is not an effect produced by bad taste and bad maintenance, but is reality itself and not appearance; it is the pitiful proximity and antipathetic cohabitation of all those shops: the coal merchant's dust blackens the ice-cream seller's wares; the plaster-merchant's whitens the butcher's cutlets; the cake-merchant is haplessly perfumed by the scented soap-water that the barber eternally squirts outside his door; the barber, in his turn, is overwhelmed and obscured by the resinous smoke of the bakery; the midwife's sign, unhooked, hangs down over the umbrella-merchant's sign, while the tinsmith's serves as a visor for the stationer, who, in his turn, extends is display into the midst of the apricots and salsify of his neighbor the fruiterer.

A charming street, the Rue Myrrha in Montmartre.

We have said that it changes its name in the middle; the middle in question is indicated by its intersection with the Rue Lévisse, which cuts the Rue Myrrha perpendicularly. It is shortly before the Rue Lévisse, still in the Rue Myrrha, that the creamery of that name flourishes, about which we are going to talk.

The Crémerie Myrrha offers its friends, and its enemies, a surface development that consists, to the right and left of its entrance door, of a system of shelves in sheets of coarse crystal, defended by a glass case. The shelves are poorly defended, the crystal being of a slightly bottle-green shade, but they are numerous and have an agreeable variety of products. That variety is astonishing and intimidating at first, for the term "creamery," strictly speaking, indicates an establishment where one can buy milk, eggs, butter and cheese.

Could anyone, even Herodotus, have described everything sold, found and encountered in that singular creamery?

For instance, through the dubious purity of the right-hand display-window, one perceives a metal-plate bowl, ornamented with a ladle in the same metal, a double utensil indicating sufficiently that punch is sometimes drunk in the establishment falsely dedicated to dairy produce. One is gripped by regret on seeing it that time has devoured the shallow layer of silver extended over the bowl's flanks; the copper has vanquished the silver. Half a dozen large cups in fake porcelain, around which run a double pale-blue stripe, are arranged next to the bowl. None of them is intact; this one is scuffed, that one chipped, a third cracked from top to bottom like the tower of Coucy-le-Château. Let us not dwell on the injuries of the others. So one can take coffee as well as punch at the Crémerie Myrrha?

One can even get milk there, for here is a varnished earthenware jug full of milk. The milk in question is half-covered with flies, which would cover it entirely if their caresses were not shared with another chipped jug in which prunes are floating. These charming insects go from the milk to the prunes without anything troubling their pleasures. It's marvelous to behold the traces of their sojourn in the Crémerie Myrrha. Everything is embroidered by their feet and ingenious mouth-parts: the mirrors, the window-panes, the woodwork, the chairs, the wallpaper, the curtains and the ceilings have suffered to such a degree from their incrustation that one can say without exaggeration that the windows are already crystal and flies, the paneling wood and flies, the ceilings plaster and flies, on their way to being nothing but flies.

The second floor of the creamery shows to passers-by another enormous bowl full to the brim, and sometimes brimming over, with chocolate à la crème; the cream has disappeared, the chocolate can be deduced. The place of honor between that yellow-tinted lake and a sort of faience pyramid from which seasoned pipes emerge, stuck in by their shafts, is occupied by a bright red piece of veal enveloped in excessively-developed loins—loins that could become, in time of war, artillery ammunition. On Sunday, an oval is designed with carrot slices round the master morsel, but the piece of veal is often replaced itself by a rabbit placed on the tray in a picturesque pose; one might think that it were about to run away.

That rabbit forms a ridge; over that ridge an ingenious hand usually scatters, instead of carrot slices, slices of onion, culinary hieroglyphics signifying that the rabbit will be "*aux petit oignons*"—which is to say, delicious—and to prove that there is no error of natural history on the part of the cook, a live cat, of a russet hue particular to cats in suburban restaurants, is asleep on the shelf next to the rabbit.

Beyond the veal and the rabbit one sees bottles of beeswax, an ungilded tea-caddy, a bottle of cherries and a plaster bust of Béranger, all dotted and disfigured by little fly-specks.

At the top—right at the top, on the uppermost shelf—one can make out commemorative porcelain mugs, two vases with artificial roses, and a basket, similarly in porcelain, but pierced with diamond-shaped holes. Sometimes, one can see tufts of packing-material sticking out through these diamonds. Why? Because one puts eggs that one wishes to conserve therein.

The wall against which these shelves are backed was once painted with coarse frescoes representing subjects drawn from cynegetic pleasures relevant to the table. Half way up there was a boar-hunt; above it, a deer-hunt. That eloquent painting has disappeared; it had too much irony built into it for the regulars ever to request its restoration. What possible connection was there between their meals and roebucks or wild boar?

What, then, is eaten at the creamery on the Rue Myrrha?

The shelves placed to the left of the main doorway emphasize that one can also drink there.

On the first, unequal in size but densely-packed, stand bottles of cognac, old rum and cheap brandy, of which people seem to be extremely fond in the Rue Myrrha. Liqueurs flourish here too; the ladies are not forgotten. On illustrious labels one can read *Walnut Elixir; Jasmine Flower; Tears of Adonis, Spirit of Béranger, Lip Dew, Cream of Cassis, Angel Water* and *Milk of Love*. No, the ladies are not forgotten, for beside a slab of Gruyère, in summer, one can see half-price tickets for the Bal du Château-Rouge scattered in a soup-bowl, in winter, tickets for balls at the Opéra, and in all seasons, reduced-price tickets for concerts and other amusements.

The shelf-unit that overhangs that one belongs more particularly to fruits and the *toilette* of the fair sex. I have seen a corset on that shelf, with all its whalebone bristling, displayed between a basket of nuts and a basket of lady-apples; the apples seemed to have become effeminate by gazing at the upper part of that ornament, which bore an inscription pricked with a pin, in which one could read: *Bargain.*[23]

In the second part of the same set of shelves, there is a stuffed partridge, as if to prove that game is not entirely unknown in the Crémerie Myrrha. That small masterpiece of taxidermy rubs elbows with a hunk of lard stood on end, a symbol much truer than that of the partridge, larded soup being far more readily available all year long in the establishment than partridge with cabbage. The end of the shelf is devoted to the exhibition of a superb calf's head destined to be adored *à la poulette, à la vinaigrette* or in its shell. It awaits its fate in a melancholy fashion, with a sprig of parsley in its nostrils.

As for the third shelf-unit, it is entirely taken up by printed squares stuck to the glass itself. On these rarely-renewed squares one can read *Beef Broth, Fried Eggs, Breaded Cutlets, Beef with Cabbage, Soup of the Day, Tripe, Dumplings, Prunes* and *Raspail Tonic Liqueur.*[24]

But half past five is about to chime on the telegraphic clock of the Église de Montmartre.

Dr. Kanali stopped outside the scarcely-monumental entrance to the Crémerie Myrrha. He had arrived. Before going in, he sought to make sure that this really was the establishment that I had indicated to him

---

[23] I have translated *Occasion* as "bargain," as that preserves something of the intended double meaning; the word could also be translated as "opportunity."

[24] François-Vincent Raspail, a leading figure in the 1848 Revolution and a candidate for the Presidency of the Second Republic, was a chemist and physician; in 1845 he published *Histoire naturelle de la santé et de la maladie*, which contained a recipe for a famous antiseptic "elixir." He was another anticipator of the germ theory of disease who failed to win over his contemporaries.

that morning, without having had the time to describe its features with an engraver's precision, to the point that he would recognize it without hesitation. He had imagined it much less grand. Thus, on going in, he was quite surprised by the sight of the interminable rows of tables that one encounters, along with the equally-extensive rows of whitewashed joists supporting the ceiling. He was disturbed by it; he thought he was confronted by the refectory of an entire population—and there was some truth in that.

He went forward, and then saw that the depth was terminated by a high glass partition, behind which he saw other benches and tables. Finally, he saw beyond those two gigantic rooms, in the far distance, a large blazing fire, a Hellish kitchen, a Gargantuan fireplace, in which torrents of flame were steaming upwards, in which crackling and spitting armfuls of dry wood were incessantly being fed to the flames, and in which six pairs of skewers were rotating—a cheerful, noisy spectacle, as lively as could be, which would certainly have merited being seen were it not for an excessively strong odor of food and boldly buttery cooking not gripped you in the throat and eyes.

At the sight of that sumptuous space, Dr. Kanali permitted himself more than one reflection, and, in going to stand in the middle of the creamery, into which the diners were already flowing, he thought that he would never have supposed that men of the particular species of which he was in search were so numerous in Paris. His astonishment, already great, was doubled by an even greater astonishment when he saw quantities of women coming in at least equal to those of men.

The majority of these women were unaccompanied. They took their places around tables unceremoniously.

Many of them immediately started chatting to the men in terms of the broadest familiarity. Who were they? In his corner, Kanali racked his brains for an answer, and especially for a means of explaining satisfactorily how gravediggers came to have such easy and expansive manners, and to mingle in this way with the society of women—who, in general, whatever their status, are not very disposed to welcome and treat kindly people of the unattractive profession to which he supposed the entire assembly to belong. He was destined to go from one surprise to another, as you shall see.

Who did he recognize in many of these diners, arriving at the Crémerie Myrrha in groups with every passing minute and taking possession of the tables. Former comrades of the theater! Yes, actors! Actors with whom he had once played comedy. Like him, of course, they were twenty years older, but they had aged well; he discovered them in his memory—which made him fear, for the same reason, being recognized by them. He huddled close to the pillar on to which his table backed, and enveloped himself in the fumes of his soup. We shall see that the precaution was no great help to him. But what a strange thing! Actors there, where he had come in search of gravediggers.

Had he mistaken the place? No...he really was in the Crémerie Myrrha. Did both categories gather there? Was that plausible? Laughter and tears together, at the same time, over the same tablecloth? No—it was impossible to admit. Besides which, where were the tears? He could certainly see the laughter, but he saw nothing that betrayed dolor, even official, even obligatory, even habitual. All these people, without being models of elegance, were very gaily dressed. They wore straw hats, creole waistcoats, white trousers...

There must, therefore, be an error in his presence, he reverted to thinking—and he thought that perhaps I had intended to made fun of him...

While he was ruminating these reflections, however, someone came to sit down at his table, and that someone looked at him intently. He tried in vain not to notice that he was the object of persistent attention; hat gaze made him impatient, and he became so impatient that he saw that he would either be obliged to leave the table or to ask the ill-bred individual why he was staring at him in that way.

"It seems to me, Monsieur..." Monsieur Kanali said to him.

"It seems to me," said the impertinent fellow, interrupting him, "that I'm Saint-Aimable and you're Belleville."

"I'm not Belleville."

"What! You aren't Belleville? You're definitely Belleville. I recognize you; we've appeared on stage together. First, begging your pardon, at the Luxembourg, at twenty francs a month; then at the Folies-Dramatiques, under Père Mourriez, who similarly paid us very little, but treated us very badly; then at the Gaîeté; then..."

"I haven't appeared on stage anywhere, Monsieur, I tell you!" exclaimed the doctor, ashamed and happy at the same time about the encounter, wounded in his pride but charmed in his memory, ready to strangle Monsieur Saint-Aimable, whom he wanted simultaneously to hug with all his strength.

"You've never been on stage anywhere, you say?"

"No, Monsieur, and the unwonted familiarity with which you're addressing me..."[25]

Kanali made as if to get to his feet; Saint-Aimable held him back by the arm.

"The proof," he said to the doctor, "is that you're acting right now—a little better, admittedly, than you used to do..."

"Monsieur! Put an end to this!"

"It isn't the end yet—we're only in the prologue, my dear Belleville."

"Monsieur! This gross importunity..."

"Will you accept a glass of Madeira in honor of your return to our midst?"

"To your midst? To whose midst?"

"To whose midst, he asks, O immortal gods! Our midst: actors, hams, bohemians, anything you like, who come every day to take our meals here, when we have the consideration and bounty of payment. For we're not well-off, Belleville, since the recent revolution, which was not—oh no!—made in our favor. But tell me, will you accept the dry Madeira that I'm offering you?"

"No, Monsieur," said Kanali, who was nevertheless yearning to clink glasses with the old comrade of his youth.

"Oh, that's too bad, Belleville, that's too bad. You could have told us about your Italian campaign, which wasn't as fortunate as General Bonaparte's. Michelin, the juvenile lead of that traveling company of which you were a part, is the only one who returned alive to Paris."

"Michelin isn't dead! He's here!"

"You know him, then? Ah, you know him!"

---

[25] The actor is addressing Kanali as "tu" rather than "vous," as an old friend would.

The doctor had given himself away. He stammered: "No...there are so may Michelins... I knew a Michelin once...a surgeon...that's why..."

"See how you've unmasked yourself! Waiter, Madeira!"

Kanali, utterly defeated and realizing that he was compromised, got up resolutely this time and half-turned in order to go. He felt himself forcefully retained by two arms and held against a voluminous chest. He gazed into the enormous mouth of a comedy financier, which said to him, face to face, while laughing and stifling him with his embrace: "Michelin! To whom you fed lines so long ago! Little Michelin—now big Michelin."

Emotion got the better of pride. Softening, the doctor embraced Michelin in his turn—and then all three of them embraced.

"But don't give me away," the doctor said to them. "I'm no longer an actor."

"What are you then, wretch?"

"I'm rich."

"You're rich!"

"I'm famous."

"Famous!"

"I'm a physician."

"A physician!"

"I'm even German."

"And German!"

"German."

"Is that all? Then tell us, milord, by what miracle...?"[26]

---

[26] It is truly remarkable the Monsieur Morel can quote this conversation, not to mention the play featured in the next two chapters, word for word, when he was not present. One might

X

"Not just now. You first, I beg you—tell me where I am, for I confess to you that everything I've seen here in the last hour has confused me to the point that I'm no longer conscious of myself."

"But you're in the famous Crémerie Myrrha."

"All well and good—but I expected to find in that creamery..."

"What? What were you expecting?"

"No...once again, you talk...you wouldn't believe me if you knew why I came here...and how far I am from finding what I sought. I beg you, Saint-Aimable, tell me all about this place...in order that I know..."

"A superb place!" said Saint-Aimable, while the doctor ordered the best wines in the house—which could not be said to be the finest vintages. "Let's begin, if you please, with the mistress of the establishment.

"The person that you see sitting at the counter is Mademoiselle Zélie Patriarche, who has run it for ten years. She has, so to speak, conquered it, for before being the sovereign of the Crémerie Myrrha she was, a long time ago, a modest client, its subject. One day, as her charms were declining and her savings had reached an elevated level, she bought the creamery. That's how she mounted that mahogany throne, which is sometimes a podium and sometimes a confessional. It's from the

almost think that he were making it up. At any rate, it seems highly likely that the introduction to this chapter, as well as much of the next two, was originally a separate work that had nothing to do with Morel at all.

149

height of the counter, when it's also a throne, that she commands, giving her orders to her employers—kitchen-staff, waiters and waitresses; it's there that she receives complaints, and then it's a podium, from the guests who pay and want to be treated in accordance with their money; finally, it's there that she listens to the avowals of those who don't pay much and the sighs of those who can no longer pay; then the counter changes into a confessional.

"Zélie Patriarche loved and she was beautiful, my dear Belleville. One can still see the superb ruins that her back reflects in the tall mirror behind her. She still has magnificent blonde hair and richly arched shoulders. In society, she could still make two or three conquests of much younger men if she experienced a belated pride in making use of her beautiful debris, but she prefers to conserve them for the sake of the dignity of her house. It is generally unknown, moreover, how much more complete and sincere renunciations of society are among women like her than women who lead an honest and conventional life. They retire much more rapidly and resolutely from the stage to go back into the wings. Their philosophy is profound; the excessive rigidity of their mores becomes evident when the time comes for them to convert to good. Then it's more than a change of mores that takes place in these great sinners; it's almost a change of sex; they become men by virtue of the elevated maturity of their intelligence."

"But I wasn't familiar with that world."

"Know it thoroughly then, my dear Belleville." Saint-Amiable continued: "Without having attained that final perfection, Mademoiselle Zélie Patriarche had already been able to acquire the good sense to put herself in a position to sustain the battle against the evil days of old age. She has built this fortress, from which she can see them approach without fear. She paid twelve thousand francs cash for this creamery, which has increased in value to thirty thousand since she bought it, and she has lived and paid off many old debts on top of that.

"Few people, it's true, would have been in a position, as she was, to increase the value of the establishment. She knew so many people and so many professions before retiring here! Those were the people she attracted; they are her true clientele. That clientele came to add itself to the one she had bought in buying the establishment, and those two populations of regulars offer an exceedingly varied physiognomy. You have before you type-specimens taken from the two sexes that sit down at these tables every day: look and listen.

"Over there are dried-up petty clerks earning between twelve and fifteen hundred francs a year; over there are widows whose husbands left no more trace behind them that Captain Franklin; over there are chronic debtors pursued through Paris from street to street, house to house and roof to roof, who have finally taken refuge in the impenetrable fissures of Montmartre and Batignolles; over there are petty landladies of the Rue des Martyrs, the Rue Rochechouart and a hundred other streets of the same family, who never dine at home because they dread kitchen odors and are not cooks; over there are shady, crooked and fraudulent businessmen who buy merchandise in the morning on credit and sell them for cash an hour later at a fifty-per-cent loss; their names are well-known in the Place du Palais de Justice; over there are aged female players of the stock-market, who offered their charms as guarantees when they had charms.

"Over there, near the window, are painters misunderstood for forty years, who have not even succeeded in becoming sign-painters, because being a sign-painter in Paris required a certain talent and special aptitude; over by the other window in the corner are promising writers; there beside them are writers who are no good; to their right are actors who are starting out and actresses who are finished; over there, between two poets, young actresses who still don't put on rouge in order to go on, and, further away, old actresses who put on more than ever because they no longer go on; there are juvenile leads with the chimerical dream of an engagement with the Palais-Royal or the Variétés; great coquettes whom the directors of the Porte-Saint-Martin or the Vaudeville always promise to come and hear their debuts at the Tour-d'Auvergne but have never been heard and never will be; young girls who claim to be pupils of the Conservatoire and who really are, unfortunately for the Conservatoire; and finally, over there, the directors who are always in the process of putting together companies for next season, a false pretext by dint of which they dine on credit throughout the time that precedes the famous season in question, which has never been indicated on any calendar.

"And then, further away—much further—there are hundreds of other characters, demi-characters, walk-on parts, human profiles, all of which I would tell you about, my dear Belleville, if we were not in such a hurry, my comrade Michelin and I, to know whether, among all the categories of people, man, women and professions that I have just caused to pass before your eyes, there is the one you came here to find."

"No, it's not there," replied the doctor, slightly stunned by the list reeled off by his old comrade without drawing breath.

"What! Not there!" cried Saint-Aimable and Michelin in chorus. "Who the devil are you looking for, then?"

"It's unnecessary to say, for the moment..." Kanali replied.

"No, it's not unnecessary. Come on, talk..."

"Once again, my good friend..."

"Once again, talk, if we're your friends."

"Well..."

"Well?"

"I came here in search of a gravedigger..."

"They're here."

"What! They're here?"

"Yes. There are as many gravediggers here as actors."

"Then I haven't been deceived?"

"Not at all, since you have two of them in front of you."

"Two what?"

"Two gravediggers, of course."

"Two gravediggers? I can only see two..."

"Well, Michelin and I are two gravediggers."

"Get away! You're two actors."

"That doesn't alter the fact. Thus, in the theater, I'm the second lead Saint-Aimable, and in the city, the gravedigger Piquelard."

"Can I believe my ears?"

"And I," said Michelin, "am the utility player Michelin in the city, and the gravedigger Fleur-des-Champs in the city."

"Good God! You don't say? To begin with, I'm heartily glad of it, in the interests of the motive that brings me here, but I can't help being surprised by its strangeness."

"There's nothing very strange in it, and when you know...anyway, you'll know right away why Michelin and I, and many others who are here, are actors and gravediggers."

"Ah! I'm listening with a double interest, my good friends."

But it was completely impossible, at that moment, to listen. The Crémerie Myrrha was in motion and abuzz, seething over its entire surface.

"What is it?" demanded the doctor. "What's happening."

"It's the custom of the creamery," Saint-Aimable replied, "that between dessert and the moment when coffee is served, the habitués enjoy a local diversion, a kind of improvisation. The dessert is finished and we're awaiting the coffee, so it's the moment when the scene in question is staged. We're therefore forced, if we want to hear one another, my dear Belleville, to delay for a few minutes the explanation you desire to have from Michelin and myself regarding our double profession of actor and gravedigger, and for you to tell us with why—for we're excessively eager to know—you came here in search of gravediggers."

"Messieurs et Mesdames," said a rich and sonorous voice—the voice of a stage-manager, which must surely be that of an unemployed stage-manager—"we have the honor, myself and my comrade Tavel de Saint-Georges, of enabling you to hear today, if you care to do so, *The Echoes of the Damned City*. Let everyone, in consequence, retake their seats in order that silence can be established."

"What does he mean by *The Echoes of the Damned City*?" Dr. Kanali demanded, immediately.

"That's right," replied comrade Saint-Aimable to comrade Belleville. "Having been absent from Paris for more than twenty years, it's quite impossible for you to divine the significance of the words *The Echoes of the Damned City*."

"Educate me, then."

"I'll do so briefly, for the play's about to begin. Draw a line from the Faubourg Poissonnière to the Madeleine; from the two extremities of that line draw two others that converge here, where we are, in Montmartre, and you will have outlined an area vast enough to contain a city at least as big as Toulouse. That city, whose contours you've just traced, has a distinct population: a population classified since its origin under the heading of fallen women."

"Oh yes—I've heard mention of...*lorettes*."[27]

"Shh! Fool...you're in their territory here, you're surrounded by them...don't get yourself into trouble...let's speak in whispers. There is, therefore, in Paris, as I've just explained—in the very heart of Paris, at the center of the boulevards, theaters and railways, an immense city uniquely populated, from north to south and east to west by the women in question. They have an entire city to themselves. Anyone who wishes can see it. You could see it; you could see these ladies' little cardboard town houses, the apartments constructed for their

---

[27] An argot term approximately equivalent to the Anglo-Saxon "slut" in meaning, but with an inevitable French euphony that dignifies it somewhat.

use; you could also see their markets, their fountains, their theaters, their promenades—and you would know the physiognomy of the *Damned City*."

"I've beginning to divine it from your description."

"A few more details of mores and you'll comprehend, like all of us, the setting of the *Echoes*, which is about to be performed before you.

"People get up very late in the damned city, because they also go to bed very late. When the Paris on the other side of the Boulevard Montmartre, the Boulevard des Panoramas and the Boulevard des Italiens already has its shops open, its cafés awake, its circulation established, everything is still closed, barricaded and asleep in the idle quarter—the Rues Bréda, des Martyrs, Rochechouart and, generally, all the daughter and granddaughter streets of those districts. No café is open in that zone, no fiacre is clattering along the road, no shop has yet exposed its widow-displays. Only the milk-sellers, the eternal milk-sellers who have been in the same places since Julian the Apostate, since the foundation of Paris, are stationed in their corners at the thresholds of doorways.

"The moment comes, however, when all the door on the streets I've just named open slightly, and then one sees appear, here in profile, there only represented by a hand sliding between the two battens of a door, there in a short skirt, there in furtive slippers, there in sparse tresses, there in a bonnet still rumpled by the tempests of the nights, there in a headscarf, there is a simple checkered peignoir and bare legs, the same women that were seen the previous night, only a few hours ago, coming home in delivery carts, in fiacres, in cabriolets, in phaetons, in américaines, getting down therefrom in elegant costumes, with big bouquets collected in the corridors of the Opéra and the greenhouses of the Galeries Jouffroy.

"They're the same women; one sees them in the evening in the Bois de Boulogne, at the Bal d'Asnières, the Château des Fleurs—all the spectacles of Paris; and one sees them in the morning coming in person, for want of a domestic, to buy their milk modestly at their door. Many among those ladies, so rapidly metamorphosed, venture as far as the end of the street to go in search, at the baker's and the grocer's, of the complement of the first meal of the day. And that bizarre merry-go-round, scarcely credible if one has not witnessed it, is repeated every day with the same contrast of sumptuousness and poverty.

"Now, my dear Belleville, suppose, on a clear and silent night, that you were floating high in the sky over the *Damned City* with us, all of us who lend ourselves to that fiction; suppose too that, like a new Asmodeus, you remain suspended in that manner until morning—and you will have the key to the *Echoes*, and a depiction much more exact and much more colorful of that double existence of supreme glamour and profound misery that I have just described to you."

A final call for silence was hurled over the assembly, and the two actors charged with playing the scene of the *Echoes* began.

Attention! Attention!

Nocturnal Echoes of the Rue Pigalle.

"Charming evening, Alphonse!"
"Delightful, Florentine!"
"Not so delightful for me—I lost ten louis at baccarat."

157

"Florentine, I'll give you double hat sum if you tell me with whom you lost it."

Nocturnal Echoes of the Rue Saint-Georges.

"Could I eat crayfish *à la bordelaise!* I've got a craving for them. Suppose we go get something else to eat, Gontran?"

"Do you think so, at two o'clock in the morning?"

"Why not? Crayfish are timeless."

Nocturnal Echoes of the Rue Turgot.

"The face of that Russian haunts me. He's ugly, but completely lacking in elegance."

"Pass me a cigar, Marquis."

"Paquita, you've already smoked five."

Nocturnal Echoes of the Rue La Bruyère.

"I want to go back to the cascade!"

"Me too; shall we go back to the cascade?"

"But my dears, the horses are exhausted."

"To the cascade! To the cascade!"

"Coachman, return to the cascade."

Nocturnal Echoes of the Rue d'Aumale.

"God! I could gladly swallow a maraschino ice-cream!"

"And me half a dozen sardines!"

"What if we went to supper?"

"Bonvallet's is closed now, Mesdames; what do you have in mind?"

"He'll open up for us. To Bonvallet's!"
"To Bonvallet's!"

Nocturnal Echoes of the Rue de La Tour-d'Auvergne.

"Mabille has definitely become too upmarket."
"What do you expect, Zoé?—everything in this world comes to an end."
"What happened on the Bourse today?"
"Please let me go to sleep."

Nocturnal Echoes of the Rue de Douai.

"Here we are at last, thank God!"
"Who's taken my shoe?"
"It was the stockbroker who lifted the foot this morning."
"No jokes—give me my shoe and stocking."
"Good! It's not just her shoe, it's her stocking now."

Nocturnal Echoes of the Rue de Navarin.

"James, you'll restock my window-box tomorrow?"
"Yes, my dear, I thought of that."
"And you'll send me fifty bottles of Ermitage-Bergier?"
"I sent you fifty bottles the day before yesterday.
"That's all right then—and six of Chartreuse?"
"Green or white?"
"Six green and six white."
"But that makes twelve of Chartreuse?"
"I won't say no."

Nocturnal Echoes of the Avenue Frochot.

"How do you like my mantilla, Delphine?"
"Admirable. How much?"
"Not dear."
"But from the shop?"
"From the shop, three thousand francs."

Nocturnal Echoes of the Rue Fontaine.

"Gaston, you'll get me a box at the Vaudeville?"
"You'll have it at midday, my darling."
"Not number thirty-three, you hear?"
"Why not? There's a perfectly good view from there."
"Yes, but one isn't seen."
"That's true."

Nocturnal Echoes of the Rue de la Tour-des-Dames.

"Who has a chambermaid to give me?"
"What have you done with yours?"
"She quit last night."
"Bah!"
"Word of honor! To go to work right away for a Brazilian widow."

Nocturnal Echoes of the Rue Blanche.

"Gentlemen, you're going to come up and take tea with me."
"It's very late, Mathilde."

"Pure *caravane*, as yellow as amber."[28]
"There! Coachman, stop!"

Nocturnal Echoes of the Place Bréda.

"Jules?"
"What?"
"You're not going, are you?"
"Why not?"
"You want to go to the Club."
"So what?"
"You're going to gamble."
"No, to read the *Moniteur*."
"Leave me my money, or you're not going."

Mesdames and Messieurs, the echoes of the night being exhausted, we shall pass on to the echoes of the morning.

---

[28] "Caravan tea," and its equivalents in various European languages, was once a general term referring to a range of aromatic Chinese and Russian teas, but this reference is more likely to be to a specific kind of Moroccan tea, sometimes known as "gunpowder."

XI

Matinal Echoes of the Rue Pigalle.

"Quickly, three sous' worth of milk."

"There you are. Do you need eggs, Madame?"

"How much are they?"

"Two sous each."

"Give me six—I'll pay you tomorrow."

"Then I'll sell them to you tomorrow."

Matinal Echoes of the Rue Saint-Georges.

"Where've you been, Rosine?"

"To the butcher's. I've brought this leg of mutton."

"And you paid?"

"Ten francs."

"Ten francs! It's made of solid gold, then?"

"It's on solid credit."

"I understand. It's like me—I paid forty sous for these cutlets."

"You got them on credit too?"

"Not entirely. My butcher sells me one on credit, the other for cash."

"And he steals twenty sous from you on each of them—he's much smarter than mine."

Matinal Echoes of the Rue Turgot.

"How much will you give me for this bracelet, Monsieur Munich? It cost three hundred francs."

"I'd be mad to give you fifty francs for it."[29]

"But that's armed robbery."

"Not a liard more."

"Oh, thanks a lot. You'll give me fifty francs?"

"Not so fast! Before giving you that, I have to accompany you home, and ask your porter whether you really live in the house you take me to. The police require it. There are thieves around here!"

"That's out of the question! You want me to let my porter know that I'm selling my jewels? That's atrocious."

"Complain to the police."

"Come on, isn't there a way?"

"There is a way, yes, one way."

"Ah! What is it?"

"One alone. Instead of giving you fifty francs for your bracelet, to cover the risk I'm running in buying from you without knowing you, I'll only give you forty francs. That's good of me, eh?"

"You're taking another ten francs off me?"

"Yes, yet—only ten francs for not going to make enquiries of your porter."

"Give me the forty francs and let's have done with it."

"There, in beautiful brand new five franc pieces."

"It's a hundred sous short! Brigand!"

"That's right. You're very pretty, you know."

"What are you saying? Oh, it'd have to be a lot shorter than that!"

---

[29] The pawnbroker's speech is rendered in a tortuous eye-dialect intended to represent the accent of a German Jew speaking French. I have not attempted to reproduce it.

Matinal Echoes of the Rue de La Bruyere.

"Restaurateur?"

"What can I do for you, Madame?"

"At six o'clock today, I need a superstitious diner: trout, fillet mignon *à la maître-d'hôtel*, *ris de veau* with truffles, chicken *à la financière*, artichokes *à la barigoule*, potato fritters, charlotte russe, a brie and two plums. For wines: Romanée, Conti, Médoc, Château-la-rose, Bouzy. The rest goes without saying: coffee, liqueurs..."

"Very good, but what doesn't go without saying is the money. The dinner in question will cost eighty francs, at least. You already owe me two hundred and twenty, and you've owed the since last carnival; if we add another eighty francs..."

"That will make three hundred francs."

"I don't know about that!"

"Do you know why I'm giving this dinner?"

"To have a good time, I presume."

"In order to pay you, you ingrate!"

"What?"

"At the moment, I have a young Moldo-Wallachian prince hitched up. He's already galloping quite well, but he sometimes bolts when he feels the bit. One more dinner and I'll have him broken in. Will you or won't you help me to tame the Moldo-Wallachian?"

"What time's the feast?"

"Six o'clock for quarter past."

"You'll be served on the dot by my waiters."

"One more thing, Restaurateur."

"What, Madame?"

"I need your silverware; mine's a bit short."

"The Ruolz?"[30]

"No, your silverware—the genuine article."

"So be it—but it'll be me, then, who has the honor of serving you."

"What a good opinion you have of me."

"Of you, no…but of Moldo-Wallachian princes..."

Matinal Echoes of the Rue d'Aumale.

"A four-livre loaf, Baker."

"There—that's sixteen sous."

"I'll pay you later."

"Certainly not!"

"Just four hours' credit."

"None. Pay, or do without the bread."

"Take this eighty-franc batiste handkerchief; I'll come and get it back at four o'clock and give you your sixteen sous. I'm taking the bread."

The improvised scenes of the *Echoes* ended there.

It was during the supreme moment consecrated to the delectation of the coffee that Saint-Aimable said to his former colleague Belleville: "It's time to tell you why Michelin, myself and fifty other castaways here combine the functions of actor and gravedigger. The '48 Republic has killed the theaters; they've been dead for more than a year, and will be for a long time yet. The Opéra takes two hundred francs in receipts, the Théâtre-Français between fifty and sixty. Where can we go? What can we do? To whom can we turn?

---

[30] Ruolz is an alloy of copper, nickel and silver, named after a French comte of that name, extensively used in ersatz silver-ware.

"There's a shortage of arms to meet the demands of the epidemic; we've offered ours; the funeral directors have accepted them gladly. *Saved! Saved!* as one says on stage in the boulevards. We were put to work immediately; we make fifty francs per day—I mean per night, given that we only work at night. Otherwise, we dispose of our time in the following manner: from six to eleven in the evening we perform on stage; from eleven until eleven in the morning we do what I said; as soon as eleven o'clock chimes we take off our prince- or shepherd-costumes, cast aside our wigs, wipe off our rouge and run gaily to the funeral director, who dresses us in black coats and all the conventional accessories.

"Now you know, my dear Belleville, the motive that has led us to become carrion-beetles, like the majority of the brave artistes that you see assembled here. Now it's your turn to tell us what motive, no less strange, brings you here in search of gravediggers."

Kanali told his two rediscovered colleagues about the scientific goal that he had been pursuing for years, through the difficulties raised up everywhere against him by ignorance and fanaticism, and confided to them that the goal might be obtained in the following manner: "You're not unaware, either of you, of the death of Jean-Paul Désormeaux, the adored, venerated clubman mourned by all the fanatics of the Salle Martel?"

"How could we be unaware of it? It's us—Michelin and myself—who will inevitably be charged with burying him tomorrow."

"You! That's my fortune, then!"

"Why is it your fortune?"

"And my imperishable glory!"

"Your glory? Always your glory...your fortune. What connection...what significance...?"

"Yes, it's my fortune and my glory, and a thousand-franc note for each of you."

"A thousand-franc note! Oh, Belleville don't give us false joy—we'll die of it."

"You know as well as I do, both of you," Dr. Kanali replied, who was about to make Michelin and Saint-Aimable the same offer that I had rejected, "the universal and fanatical regret aroused in Paris by the Republican party's irreparable loss. In Paul Désormeaux it lost a god. Well, I can give him back."

"You, Belleville?"

"Me, the celebrated Doctor Fabricius Kanali. Yes, I can give him back, if you'll consent to lent me your assistance."

"We're with you—talk."

Kanali talked.

After having explained to his two former comrades what the reader already knows—which is to say, the preservative superiority of his method of embalming by comparison with all known and knowable methods—the doctor said to them more intimately: "Listen to me; since it's you who will lower the body of the illustrious clubman into the grave, will you consent to raise him up again three days later, in order to deliver him to the great and sublime operation about which I've just told you, and delighted you."

Kanali's two friends consulted one another with their gazes, and were both of the same opinion, which Saint-Aimable took responsibility for communicating to the doctor immediately.

"What you're proposing isn't without danger."

"I know, but that's why..."

"That's why friendship makes its demand beneath the graceful features of a thousand-franc note," Saint-Aimable added.

"In sum, you accept?"

"We accept."

"Ah!"

"But..."

"There's a but?"

"There's only one."

"Let's have it, quickly!"

"The place where the great clubman, the Republican of the Salle Martel, is being laid to rest tomorrow," Saint-Aimable went on, "was only consecrated to the designation assigned to it a short time ago; it's still frequented by crowds. It won't be possible, at any hour of the day or night, to carry out the removal with which you want to associate ourselves without the risk of being discovered, and being discovered would ruin everything—the operation, you and us."

"That objection has some weight," said the doctor, "but how long do you think it will be before the terrain you mention is free, returned to its original solitude?"

"At the rate things are going, I estimate that it will be about twenty days."

"Yes, twenty days," Michelin agreed, swallowing the last drop of his cognac.

"Well, let's not hurry; let's postpone the execution of the project for twenty days," said Kanali. "On that condition, are you with me?"

"Oh, entirely."

The doctor opened his wallet and handed each of his old comrades a hundred-franc note, by way of an advance, as a guarantee of good faith.

"So I can count on you both?"

"For life and until death," replied Saint-Aimable. "It's agreed, to be done twenty days hence." He rose to his feet. "I beg your pardon, but we need to bid you farewell; we're performing this evening at the Palais-Royal at the benefit of an artiste's widow, and we're in the first piece."

"Go, my friends. How lucky you are to be on the stage!"

"Yes, but at eleven o'clock we quit the stage for the other music; it's not as cheerful."

"I know, but you also know that Boileau, the legislator of Parnassus, said: 'Happy is the poet who can pass with light veneer/from grave to smooth, from pleasant to severe.'"

"What if we were to have, on Boileau's advice, another glass of smooth?"

"To the theater, Fleur-de-Champs!"

Saint-Aimable and Michelin left the room, followed by their old comrade. The session had ended anyway; the diners of the Crémerie Myrrha, men and women alike, where flowing out into the streets and alleyways of Montmartre, some to play comedy, some to sing, some to dance, but all to exercise, by gaslight or in shadow, some meager industry that would bring in what was needed for the next day's dinner.

I could tell, by the way Dr. Kanali treated me, that he was no longer counting on my collaboration to bring his project to a successful conclusion. He did not mention the clubman or the Salle Martel to me again, nor the clandestine substitution of one body for another, nor embalming, nor any of what he had said so much about on the memorable night of the great storm. He devoted all his attention to his daughter Marthe, whose mental condition required all his concern. The discouragement and chagrin of having been thwarted in her beautiful temerity of love had severely disrupted her health.

What had she hoped to result from that action, daring among the most daring? Does passion see anything else but the moment, though? Is not the moment everything to it? Her happiness had been destroyed—and it had been quite sufficient—by snatching away the veil of her tenderly hypocritical devotion to all the sick, when she was only preoccupied with one, and one who was not sick as yet. That hypocrisy had not succeeded, and how many deceptions were enclosed within that one!

For the time being, Marthe declined, without being able to stop herself, toward the dreamy melancholy into which her mother had once descended when Herr von Rosenthal was struck dead on the Hungarian plain while hunting. That also darkened the grief of Madame Kanali, frightened by the many points of resemblance between her daughter's love and her own. What more redoubtable confirmation could that resemblance require than the little red spot that César Caseneuve had in the corner of his mouth, like Bem Strombold the Vampire?

Besides which, for Madame Kanali, Bem Strombold and César Caseneuve were but one and the same apparition, permanent within her family, within her race, perhaps destined to march side-by-side with her race and her family until the end of time. What a frightful predestination!

However, Madame Kanali said to herself, *since my mother and I were both saved from the persecutions of the evil genius that reproduces itself incessantly in our house, why should Marthe, thanks to my perennial daily and hourly surveillance of her threatened life, not escape it?*

Madame Kanali forgot that there is one moment among all moments by means of which the love of a young woman escapes, whatever surveillance is mounted around her; that moment is not marked on any clock-face; it is not called a minute, or a second, or a fraction of a second; it is nameless; but it chimes, it vibrates in the brains of the amorous like the most sonorous bell. Marthe was on the lookout for that moment, and when one is stubbornly in the desire for just one thing, one obtains it—that is the great power of inventors and lovers!

How did Marthe obtain it? You will doubtless recall the bizarre bird of which Madame Kanali was fond: the bird of ill-omen that you have seen, one evening, perched on the back of an armchair; the sinister owl with the round, plaintive yellow eyes. Marthe appeared smitten in her turn by a great passion for the owl, and the owl, for its part, a bird as gentle and faithful as sadness, followed Marthe anywhere that Marthe desired. Sometimes it posed on her wrist like a falcon, sometimes on her shoulder like a parrot; and in the evening, when the young woman went to sit down, at dusk, on one of the most isolated benches in the depths of the garden, she then set the owl free—which took advantage of it to take flight, with the heaviness characteristic of birds of that sort.

Once, however, I noticed that it flew up rather high into one of the linden-trees that formed a curtain at the back of the garden, and that it assumed a attitude of attentive meditation on one of the branches nearest to the wall.

The accentuated physiognomy of those birds is familiar; not only do they seem to be thinking, but also reflecting, pondering, meditation with profundity. They are the philosophers and metaphysicians of the ornithological race. It is impossible not to notice their preoccupation. They have eyes in the form of headlights, which beckon like the radiance of lighthouses. Those of Marthe's owl stopped me that evening with a singular tenacity of expression. They forced me to look at it. It tilted its head to one side, also one does when listening with strict attention, and its gaze also seemed to be listening, so oblique was its direction.

For what was the owl listening. What was it trying to grasp in the tranquil immobility of the air? Strongly intrigued, in order to see better without being seen, I took up a position some distance from the bench on which the doctor's daughter was sitting, her eyes turned toward her bird, which seemed to be covering her with its wings, while Marthe seemed to be trying to fascinate the bid with her gaze. Add the fixity of mine, poised between Marthe and the funereal bird, and you have a tableau of the most magnetic coloration, something in the dark manner of a drawing by Albrecht Dürer, the Michelangelo of witchcraft.

At the moment when this was happening, the guttural cry of an owl sounded in the air some thirty or forty meters from the spot from which I was observing, and the owl I was watching above Marthe's head immediately replied to that cry. Evidently, I thought at first, it's some owlish love-affair that I'm witnessing. Why shouldn't owls love one another?

I was confirmed in the opinion that I was witness to a tender affair of the heart between two birds of mourning when, following the raucous cry that I had just heard, I saw Marthe's owl rise ponderously from branch to branch and hurl itself from the last one to pass over the wall of the garden, which it left behind. It disappeared. I was about to go away when, remembering my Buffon, I recalled that the month of June, which we were then in, is not the mating season for owls. My petty erudition as a naturalist held me in place. It was not, in fact, a matter of love.

Having heard a few *crou crous* and a few *pou pous* through the branches, I saw the owl return from its expedition. It did not pause in its original position; it descended from the topmost to the lowest branch, only stopping at the bench where Marthe was sitting. She welcomed it and set it on her knees. Thanks to the lipid clarity of the night, I could distinguish the young woman's hands; they were occupied; I had seen them make anxious searching movements at the bird's neck. She detached therefrom something white, doubtless a piece of paper, some note.

It was a note, which she unfolded and read—assuredly some message of love, for Mademoiselle Marthe, while reading the note brought from the other side of the trees, kissed the great tufted head of the night-bird, evidently trained by the patience of the two lovers to perform that trick.

If it was a love-letter, though, who else but César Caseneuve could have written it? Had love, therefore not perished in the night when the two young people had been caught by a father wounded in his diabolical pride as a scholar and an inventor, and by a mother crazed by superstitious terrors? Was it really César Caseneuve who was on the other side of the wall? How I admire love in those insane individuals given to other things than our prejudices, who overturn everything in order to reach their goal—and get there!

Thus, it was in a hospital, and in a hospital cruelly tested at the hour at which I am writing these lines, that love joined two hearts, exiled from one another, pining for one another; and it was an owl, the redoubtable osprey of the ancients, that was bearing the messages of love exchanged by those two your hearts in turmoil, around its neck!

Having become party to the secret of that aerial correspondence between the two young people, I asked myself whether I ought to betray them to Marthe's parents. My internal response was that morality did not demand that severe intervention from me, for the simple reason that the day after I had revealed it, they would have devised, I was sure—who could have doubted it?—another means of exchanging their thoughts. To whose advantage, then, and for whose benefit, would I be playing the ever-equivocal role of informer? Besides which, I did not have the leisure to worry for long about the question of whether, in the circumstances, I had a moral obligation to remain silent or to speak; a most unexpected event came to cut everything to the quick.

I shall describe that event.

XII

Shortly after the scene in the garden, one morning when I was fetching ice from the cellar situated under the window of the Kanali family's apartment, I heard the murmur of heated words, punctuated by intervals of moaning. I listened; the words were being spoken by Monsieur Kanali; the moans were being exhaled by Mademoiselle Marthe. Over both floated confused exhortations, confused for me, but which I nevertheless recognized as emerging from her mother's mouth. The sum of the words and plaints indicated that some unfortunate incident had recently occurred.

Having carried my blocks of ice to the little pharmacy where they would be distributed according to the exigencies of service, I ran to the Kanalis' to discover the cause of the plaints and lamentations that I had heard under the window. I did so with my customary discretion; I found a plausible pretext for introducing myself into their apartment at a time when I was not in the habit of going there.

The pretext was, in fact, unnecessary. Scarcely had I gone into the drawing-room than Monsieur Kanali, who was very animated and red in the face, pacing back and forth, said to me: "Don't be surprised, Monsieur Morel, by the state of agitation in which you find us. This newspaper"—he handed me *La République*, a paper much in favor then with the Montagnard[31] party—"has

___

[31] In the Convention established after the 1789 Revolution the "parti de la Montagne" was a group occupying the highest-places benches in the Chamber, which always voted for the

informed us this morning of the death of a person…of a young man we knew in the early days of our arrival in Paris…a young physician attached to the service of the Val-de-Grâce. We liked him…we liked him a great deal. But what can you expect in the accursed days that we're enduring? It's necessary to expect anything. Today one, tomorrow another…"

With the same hesitancy of ideas and expression, not knowing whether he ought to be mortified or to talk about the accident with indifference, the doctor continued: "Certainly, he was a fellow who didn't lack knowledge… quality… a veritable aptitude for medicine. It's regrettable… very unfortunate. One doesn't know, word of honor, whether one will be alive tomorrow…this evening… in an hour's time. Eh? My God, after all… it's destiny... At the end of the day, one has to resign oneself… yes, resign oneself…"

"And what was the young man's name?" I asked the doctor.

He replied to me while setting his watch to the hour that he could hear chiming at Saint-Laurent: "César Caseneuve."

On hearing that name pronounced by her father, Mademoiselle Marthe experienced an involuntary and violent nervous movement in her hand, which was clutched in Madame Kanai's. She withdrew it; her mother tried to retain it; my attention was summoned in that direction. Mademoiselle Marthe had hidden her face in a white handkerchief thrown over her head, which was tilted backwards on one of the cushions of the sofa.

---

most violent measures. Just as the Jacobin "clubs" made a comeback after the 1848 Revolution, so did the Montagnards.

On seeing her thus veiled, I was reminded in an entirely personal manner of the intention of the painter Timanthes, who, in my opinion, was not so much seeking to mask a dolor that he recognized, so it was said, that he was unable to reproduce with his paintbrush, but to render human suffering in a new way, taken to its culminating degree of exaltation.[32]

That white handkerchief did not mask anything: neither Marthe's eyes, very apparent under the fabric and swollen with tears; nor the ridge of her nose, outlined like that of a corpse beneath its shroud; nor her cheeks, to which that pale veil was stuck and over which it stretched; nor her lips, whose edges lifted it up by virtue of their moist and staccato palpitation. Uncovered, hr face could not have expressed as distinctly the ill-contained ravages of her soul.

Madame Kanali completely lost sight, in sharing her daughter's immense affliction unrestrainedly, of what César Caseneuve's sudden end had rid her. She forgot that she was freed from the perpetual dread that he had imposed on her, as a vampire—although it is true that vampires die repeatedly, since they come back to earth repeatedly.

I have forgotten to report the content of the newspaper, in which the doctor invited me to read the lines relating to Caseneuve's death. I read them, and this is the text of that necrological paragraph:

The ranks of young physicians, already so cruelly decimated, have experienced another sensible loss in the

---

[32] Timanthes of Cythnus, who flourished in the fourth century B.C., was famous for a painting of the sacrifice of Iphigenia, in which Agamemon is shown veiling his face, supposedly because the artist despaired of his ability to depict his grief.

person of an intern full of talent named César Caseneuve. He died, we may boldly say, a martyr of science, for it is recognized that young Caseneuve, wishing to prove the non-contagious character of the reigning malady, dared to introduce himself into a Paris hospital and lie down in the still-warm bed of a victim of the Asiatic scourge. He had made use of a ruse to enter and have himself admitted to the hospital; he had been able to imitate to a surprising degree of verity the particular symptoms of the disease. The physicians and employees were duped for several hours by that heroic act, but after he had been there for a certain time, accepting with a stoic firmness the energetic treatment meted out in such circumstances, one doctor more clear-sighted than his colleagues perceived that César Caseneuve was not afflicted by the infection whose tortures he was feigning, and he was immediately discharged. The interesting intern thought that he had remained exposed to the peril long enough, however, and spent sufficient time on the battlefield, no longer to have any doubt about his medical theory—which is to say, to sustain unshakably henceforth that the scourge was not contagious. A fatal error!—literally fatal! On arriving home the young doctor was struck in a pitiless manner by the same disease that he claimed to have vanquished. He had breathed in the deadly germ[33] in our wards. He expired in the night.

---

[33] It was not until 1864, some years after the publication of this novel, and long after 1849, that Lois Pasteur made the speech in a debate at the Académie des Sciences that is nowadays viewed, in retrospect, as the crucial landmark in the establishment of the germ theory of disease attributing infectious diseases to tiny organisms rather than "miasmas" or some other vague source, but it had been proposed several times previ-

César Caseneuve, the new Empedocles, who precipitated himself into the abyss of the Indian disease in order to make its acquaintance, and who, like Empedocles, was devoured by it, had not yet reached is thirtieth year.[34]

I handed the newspaper back to Dr. Kanali, and immediately withdrew in order not to disturb a grief to which I could only bring embarrassment by my presence. I should not omit to report, however, a highly characteristic remark that I heard emerging from the doctor's mouth as I drew away.

"Come, come, my child," he said to his daughter, gripped by a new nervous crisis. "Don't distress yourself so. *I'll embalm him.*"

A fine consolation, you see, for a young woman who had just lost the man she loved madly! What magnificent egoism! What scientific egoism!

That family scene had moved me considerably—me, to whom Mademoiselle Marthe was nothing—but, distressed as I was, I could not help a few reflections occurring to me relative to the young man's death. The newspaper had told the truth in writing that César Caseneuve had dared to brave a formidable danger when he came to us—for it was here, in the sanitarium, as the newspaper had not said, that he had put his life at risk for the sake of his experiment...oh, not for his experiment, but his love, if you please. It had also told the truth when it added that Caseneuve manifested no symptoms

---

ously and the author was presumably aware of it, as he mentions two of its earlier proponents in his text.

[34] The pre-Socratic philosopher Empedocles was said to have vanished, leaving only a sandal on the rim of the volcano Etna, thus implying—rightly or wrongly—that he had jumped into the fiery crater for some unknown reason.

of the disease that he had braved when he was sent home—but what appeared to me to be less evident in the paper's story was what came after the incontestable assertion of those two facts. It added, however, that the reckless young man had expired the following night at home. That seemed to me to be impossible, since eight or ten days after that night he had come to correspond with Mademoiselle Marthe at the end of the garden via the intermediary of the owl. Unless he was not the one who had been exchanging love-letters with the doctor's daughter over the garden wall...but who, then...?

These reflections, I alone was in a position to make, for Marthe's parents were completely ignorant about the nocturnal rendezvous of the young woman and Caseneuve—if, that is, I repeat, it really was him who kept those amorous rendezvous. On the other hand, though, if it was not him, why that desolation; why were Marthe's tears so hot and abundant at the news of his death? She could not have been subject to two passions at the same time, conducting two intrigues...that was an absurd supposition.

These preoccupations troubled me for two days; after those two days they left me—I had others to bear! Augmented by the political overexcitement to an alarming degree, the sick imposed an impossible task on the staff. We did not have enough arms to service wards that were never less than full. I shall pass over days and nights whose scenes, if they were recalled to my memory, would render me mad or idiotic. Thirty years of experience had not yet hardened me to the point of considering coolly what my eyes have seen.

And with that, an exquisite temperature! There was never a more radiant summer than that of forty-nine; nights worthy of Sicily or Naples. It was scarcely for a few hours of those beautiful Oriental nights that I allowed myself the rare leisure of a little stroll in the gardens.

It was during one of those nocturnal relaxations, which I only permitted myself between midnight and two a.m., that I had the opportunity, which I had desired for a long time, of a deep conversation with Madame Kanali regarding her belief in the existence of vampires.

If anyone is astonished to find Madame Kanali awake so late and wandering around at those advanced hours of the night, they have forgotten the excessive heat of the summer of 1849—a summer during which staying in a apartment had become a scourge; they have forgotten the impossibility of sleeping under the fearsome burden of those asphyxiating nights; they have forgotten the vigilant character of Madame Kanali, born for the night, born for insomnia as for meditation, like all the great thinkers of ancient and modern times. She was a woman similar to those Rembrandt painted, her chin sunk into the pensive hollow of her hand, her elbow leaning on the window-sill, her gaze endlessly searching the limitless mystery of the stars and the immensity of space.

On the night in question, Madame Kanali, lying back in an armchair, enveloped in a peignoir with green and gold stripes, entirely adapted to Dalmatian tastes, was dreaming between the little basin and copse of the Jambe-de-Bois. One day, I will tell the story of the man with the wooden leg who gave his name to the basin.

The circumstance was favorable. I approached Madame Kanali and said to her, with the familiarity that her natural generosity authorized: "I'll wager, Madame, that at this moment, you're thinking about vampires."

"In which you doubtless don't believe?"

"I'd like to see one—just one—in order to believe in them."

"Oh, don't make such a wish! Never see one! But you Frenchmen don't believe in anything; you're the sons of Don Juan, who only believed that two and two are four. Will you even go as far as that? I'm afraid that you might have surpassed Don Juan! A strange contradiction! You admit without reluctance phenomena much more surprising and much more extraordinary than vampires, but that of vampires leaves you incredulous. In your country, incredulity is in the blood. One mystery more frightens you, as if everything around us—around you—were not a mystery, from birth until death. The sun that returns every morning, the stars that appear every night..."

"Oh, I beg your pardon, Madame, that's science; it's astronomy. The sun and the stars return quite simply by virtue of the movement of the earth."

"Quite simply! Since it's as simple as you say, go on. Tell me, Monsieur Morel, who gave this movement to the earth, which it certainly did not adopt of its own accord? If you have faith, you will reply: it was God; if you don't; you don't have any reply to make to me—but the earth turns nevertheless; I defy you to deny it. Well, it's exactly the same with the existence of vampires; if you believe, you'll reply that they exit because God..."

I interrupted Madame Kanali at that point in her statement, not wishing to embark upon a debate with a woman ready to confuse her faith in vampires with her faith in religion. "So you, Madame," I said to her, in a tone that did not stray far from the line of a mere doubt, "firmly believe that there are men dead for many years, who escape from the tomb and come to apply themselves by night to the living, in order to aspire their blood drop by drop, and of whom the living can only be rid by piercing their hearts after cutting off their heads?"

"Yes, Monsieur, I firmly believe it."

"Are these men—these vampires—really dead?"

"Yes. God permits them to resume their original form in order torment certain persons condemned to their persecution, with an intention whose motive he keeps to himself."

"So you admit, Madame, that, although dead, they return as they were during their lives?"

"Oh, certainly I admit it, since, when they are killed, their blood runs as bright and crimson as when they were wounded in life."

"And there are many examples of such resurrections?"

"Many, especially in Hungary, Moravia, Poland and Greece, where they are called brucolaques. Do you suppose that intelligent and learned people like those of the countries I cite would profess belief in vampires if there were no truth underlying that belief?"

This time I refrained from making the slightest objection to Madame Kanali's argument. She continued thus: "If you had read a book entitled *Magia posthuma* by Carl-Ferdinand von Schertz, published in Olmütz in 1706,[35] you would know that four days after a woman had died, an extraordinary noise was heard at the extremity of the district in which she lived. It was eleven o'clock and the ground as covered with snow. At that

---

[35] This book is frequently mentioned in dissertations on vampirism, but all the references seem to be based on a citation in Dom Augustin Calmet's famous treatise; the details of the Paul case also seem to be taken directly from Calmet, as they contain numerous details not reproduced in *Infernaliana*.

unaccustomed noise, the inhabitants emerged from their doors, and they saw a white specter, which sometimes attacked a man and sometimes and animal, grasping their throats to choke them.

"Then there was a Bohemian shepherd who emerged every night from his tomb to cal to people under their windows, and who predicted the day and hour of their death. When his heart was transpierced with stakes, he uttered loud screams, but he was still living; it was necessary to burn him.

"And there was Arnold Paul—listen to this story— who, after having been killed by the weight of a hay-cart under which he was crushed, came back a month later and caused the death, pumping the blood by slow suction from beneath the left breast, of four people who happened to be on the road with him when he was killed. People in Madreiga—that was the Hungarian name of the town where Arnold Paul was born—trembled, but they remembered that it had often been said that Cassova-Kachau, a sizeable town, as you know, on the frontier of Serbia had been tormented by a Turkish vampire. Had that one's vampirism, then, passed like a venom into the blood of Arnold Paul? They determined to verify the matter.

"Arnold was exhumed, and it was found that his body was indeed intact. His fingernails, his hair and his beard had grown, his eyes were open—evident signs that he was a vampire, and a vampire of the most redoubtable species, for, shortly hereafter, four people weakened by him and annihilated by a consumption that carried them away became vampires. Those four new vampires aspired the blood of seventeen young women, who, after having also died of an incurable languor, emerged after a few months from the ancient cloister in which they had been buried and committed frightful ravages in their turn in the unfortunate village of Madreiga, which it as necessary to commit to the flames in order to finish once and for all with the legion of vampires.

"All these facts were examined carefully and attested publicly and in due form by the surgeon-majors of the regiments garrisoned at Cassova-Kachau and the principal inhabitants of the area. That legal document was then sent to the Imperial Council of War in Vienna, which appointed a commission to examine the fats again. After a scrupulous check, the commission determined them to be quite true, quite real, and confirmed them formally with the attestation and signature of its members, who were Battuer, first lieutenant of the regiment of Alexander of Wurtemburg, Clickstenger, surgeon-major of the regiment of Furstemburg, and Guoichitz, captain at Stallatz."

"Those are doubtless authorities," I said to Madame Kanali, "but I would prefer another to all those, respectable as they are."

"What other authority do you need? I've cited villages, towns, earnest witnesses, public officials, names belonging to great Hungarian families whose descendants still exist..."

"I'd ask for yours, Madame—your authority."

My reply was not merely a simple courtesy; it forced Madame Kanali, indirectly, to tell me what I had already heard from Dr. Sainson of the Val-de-Grâce. I was anxious to obtain that repetition, firstly in order to have absolute confirmation of facts that seemed to me to be very difficult to believe, and secondly to persuade Madame Kanali to tell me whether she really put César Caseneuve in the rank of vampires—and whether, if she did, she feared that he would come back, since he had not been pierced with a stake after his death, as is the custom with redivivi, oupires, vampires and brucolaques, in order to prevent them from ever returning among the living.

I only obtained half of what I wanted, in consequence of an event that interrupted our conversation, which I shall relate in a moment.

Madame Kanali began by confiding to me, point by point, everything that I had already learned from Dr. Sainson's mouth, firstly, concerning the vampire dogged in his pursuit of her mother, the daughter of the great Salomon Kanali, the one named Bem Strombold, who only made use of his left hand, and secondly, concerning the vampire Rosenthal, the successor of the preceding one, if he was not the same, who had a little bloody spot in the corner of his mouth. When she was on the point of replying to me on the question in which I was most interested, however: whether she feared seeing Caseneuve return to attach himself to the existence of her daughter Marthe, César not having been subjected after his decease either to perforation of the heart by a long stake or cremation—which is to say, destruction by fire—she suddenly stopped speaking.

I looked for the cause of that untimely silence. Madame Kanali was staring straight ahead; she was trying to make out an object in the white and powdery mist that the moon, on the point of setting, was amassing in the depths of the pathways. With a gesture of her hand and a furtive glance she commanded me not to disturb her attention.

"But it's not a single object that is coming toward us," I said, in a low voice. "It's a group—there are two people."

"I think so too," said Madame Kanali—and she added: "Look, Monsieur Morel; doesn't it seem to you that...?"

XIII

She stopped speaking. I finished: "Yes, one would think it were a young woman and a young man...an officer. I can see epaulettes shining."

Although the sanitarium was frequented at night by many more people than in ordinary times, I was nevertheless very surprised to see that couple strolling at an hour when no one came into the garden, especially strangers.

Madame Kanali resumed: "If my daughter had not gone to bed two hours ago, and if we knew an officer, I would say, in truth..."

"Indeed, Madame, there is a resemblance between the slim figure, and the gait...the sway of Mademoiselle Marthe and the appearance of the young lady who is on the soldier's arm."

"They're coming this way; we'll see at closer range whether the resemblance is as great as it appears to us at our present distance—although, in the increasing darkness in which the moon's setting is leaving us, it will be hard to distinguish..."

It was not only the disposition of the moon that threatened to take away any means of observing ore clearly the analogy by which Madame Kanali and I had been struck. Instead of taking that path at the end of which we were seated, the two nocturnal strollers turned right, entering a parallel path, and from then on it was only possible to catch glimpses of them through the tightly packed tee-trunks and the curtain of branches that separated that path from ours.

It was the end of June; the foliage is very thick at that time of year. There were moments when we could see very little of our young people: a patch of white dress, the glided line of the peak of a kepi.

By the time they had reached a point parallel to our position, we could no longer see them at all. On the other hand, we were briefly able to hear Marthe's voice—for it was her—saying to the young officer, who was doubtless very attentive to her slightest words: "What you're proposing to me for our next meeting is, you say, very bold and perilous, and you fear that I won't accept—but when one loves as we love one another, I don't believe one has the right to hesitate over what you're proposing without giving you reason to think that my love for you is weaker than yours for me."

That was the only sentence that we caught, the two lovers not ceasing to walk straight ahead, and, in consequence, to draw away from the position that Madame Kanali and I occupied. That unique sentence was, however, clear enough to leave us in no doubt as to the nature of the sentiment that Mademoiselle Marthe experienced for the young officer who was accompanying her, whose uniform I recognized as that of a captain in the Garde Mobile—a body of volunteers formed in 1848, you will recall, to maintain the order that was furiously imperiled.

Although I was momentarily astonished to see that uniform again in 1849, the Garde Mobile having been dissolved some months earlier, I immediately reflected that the officers had been given the right to wear it until the moment of their incorporation into the line.

What happened at that moment before my eyes confirmed the opinion that I had initially rejected with all my strength: that Mademoiselle Marthe had already replaced the unfortunate Caseneuve in her heart. How could there be any doubt of that henceforth? Marthe was there, hanging on the arm of a new lover, and at a nocturnal hour that one normally refuses as a meeting time at anyone's request. I expected some movement of just maternal anger on the part of Madame Kanali; I expected her sudden and threatening appearance before her daughter, and a scene of the most furious violence, to the extent that I was preparing arguments in my head to calm her down; but she spared me those pleas for clemency and moderation.

"I'm the happiest of mothers," Madame Kanali whispered to me, having difficulty containing the excess of her joy.

I looked at her with an astonishment that must have seemed imbecilic.

"Yes, the happiest of mothers: my daughter is saved!"

I sank even further into my amazement.

"She's in love!" she went on. "She's in love! She has forgotten, praise God, hat fatal César Caseneuve, who has henceforth lost his deadly ascendancy over her. Nothing but a new love was capable of extinguishing within her the love that consumed her night and day for the man whose presence, whose phantom, will no longer return to desiccate her youth and her intelligence, to deprive her of sleep and happiness, and slowly consume her life. She has been returned to me forever, when I thought her lost forever. The vampire Caseneuve has been driven back to the deepest of his caverns, to which he was returned for the first time when my mother escaped his icy clutch by marrying my father, and again when I rid myself of him in my turn by marrying the doctor. Now she is free too, returned to the pure air, to the healthy light, to liberty—in sum, to life. The spell is broken."

It was not only the unlimited joy of having recovered her daughter that was shining in Madame Kanali's flame-filled gaze as she expressed her gratitude to God in the most enthusiastic tones; it was also the fanatical intoxication of a woman of conviction who has triumphed over obsession with the evil spirit. Her whole face was radiant; she was floating in the mystic light of a redemption. It was as if I were dazzled by it, and I felt in spite of myself the force that was lifting her up and carrying her away. It overwhelmed me.

I had never understood so well until that moment how the intoxication of faith causes intoxications similar to its own, and how easy it is to make others believe when one beliefs so energetically oneself. Humankind is merely an electrical circuit extended by divine power from one end of the world to the other.

I will not venture to say that Madame Kanali forced me to share her exalted opinion about the existence of extrahuman creations; I confess, however, that she reduced me to no longer knowing what to say to her about the strange conduct of her daughter. Moreover, all of that—individuals and surroundings—vanished like a veritable apparition.

While Madame Kanali was talking to me about her happiness and I was listening to her, the two young strollers were eclipsed in the violet shade of the pathways; the moon had descended below the horizon; the harden, darkened by the obscurity, no longer offered the uncertain sight of any graspable form; and I could hear the unspeakable cart bearing away the day's funereal harvest passing by, grating beneath the arch of the sanitarium and rolling away with dolorous jolts over the roadways of the Faubourg Saint-Denis.

I went to get a few hours' rest.

Let us pass on immediately to the following day.

I was still utterly stunned by the previous night's adventure, and I was wondering how Mademoiselle Marthe's meeting with the young officer might be explicable when Dr. Kanali took me aside mid-morning and drew me along with him into a deserted pathway in the garden. I feared that he might be about to talk to me about embalming again, but it was nothing of the sort.

"Monsieur Morel," he said to me, "my wife told me at breakfast what you both saw, last night, here in the garden, and I assure you that I intend, at any price, to get to the bottom of that singular event. She mentioned a young officer…a young woman…but I won't believe anything, or admit anything, until I've heard from you."

"My God! I'm ready to tell you everything I know, Monsieur le Docteur, but I warn you…"

The doctor did not let me finish. "First, is there any officer being treated in the establishment?"

"None. Last year, in the same epoch, after the events of June, we received several, but since then…"

"So you can affirm that there is none in the sanitarium?" he continued, in a tone of anxiety and ill-humor.

"None, I assure you."

"Could one introduce himself clandestinely?"

"You know better than anyone," I told the doctor, "that no one can get in here without permission. By trickery, it's impossible. In the early days of your installation in the house you examined the height of the walls with me—a sufficiently reassuring height—and you observed all the other material impossibilities of getting in. Although, in the disastrous epoch that we're undergoing, the orders are sometimes relaxed slightly during the day—how can we argue with all the visitors who flock here to see their sick friends and relatives, about the authenticity of their entitlement to pass through the gate?—by night, I defy any anyone to get in without being seen and identified. It's as impossible as any impossibility in the world."

"But then, how do you explain the presence of the young officer you saw? You did see him, didn't you?"

"Oh, certainly."

"As you see me?"

Oh no, of course not! Not at such close range, or in broad daylight, as I see you."

"My wife had not caused you to enter into the chimera of her hallucinations? She has in imagination sufficiently extraordinary to do that."

"Madame Kanali might evaluate a fact mentally in a manner different from a man as positive as me, but I cannot grant her the faculty to make me see someone when there is no one there."

Without appearing to be entirely convinced by my reasoning, the doctor, still very agitated in spite of the efforts he as making not to let it show, to the point of forgetting, in his anxiety, that he had not thus mentioned the name of his daughter, for propriety's sake, said: "I love my daughter Marthe very much; I agree with her mother that she could only have made the choice of a man worthy of her—but still, it is my duty to find out who this young man is."

That paternal pretention would doubtless have appeared eminently reasonable to anyone in the world—except that the doctor brought to the manifestation of his incontestable authority a hidden agenda that was suddenly revealed in its full breadth at that moment of our conversation, without, however, showing itself as yet in its entirety. What, then, did that dull anger mask? What object of hatred was at the bottom of that seething anxiety?

"However," he went on, "we're not in an enchanted palace here. No one descends into it in a balloon. No one insinuates himself through the cement of the walls. And since it's a house like any other, a means surely exists of discovering who the man is whom you saw—the man who must have been here before and will come again."

"Certainly that means exists, and you've just indicated it yourself/"

"Let's have it, right away."

"It's a matter of hiding yourself in the place where Madame Kanali and I were at midnight yesterday, and waiting. If the young officer appears, you can reveal yourself to him immediately, and that way you'll know..."

"I've thought of that, so natural and so facile for me not to have thought of it immediately—but I'm afraid, and more than afraid, that in doing that..."

"Of what are you afraid?"

"Of getting carried away when I come face to face with a man who has not acted honestly, in loving my daughter thus without first introducing himself to us; I'm afraid, in that explanation from which moderation will necessarily be excluded, of offending, wounding or killing my daughter's affection for the young man—and it's to that affection that I don't hesitate to attribute, with her mother, her unexpected return to life.

"There's more: that passion once broken by my action, by the anticipated action of a legitimate violence, I'm afraid of similarly annihilating—and this is my greatest fear—the only reason that my wife has for not dreading that her daughter is still thinking about that accursed César Caseneuve; a dead which even his death has not tranquilized. Oh, far from it! Thus, since his death—you're doubtless aware of Madame Kanali's bizarre opinions...outré beliefs...superstitions...call them what you will, insanities, if you wish—all of that has returned to her mind, darker and stronger than ever.

"Well, this new love of her daughter has been a rainbow suddenly raised above the storm...it's over... entirely concluded, since yesterday...a few hours were sufficient. She's calm again, reassured, confident, happy. To reopen within her the immeasurable source of terrors and fears would be a crime on my part, an abominable cruelty...

"However, I shall pass with a firm tread over all the scruples, all these dreads, if necessary! There is beneath it, you see, Monsieur Morel...what is there? I can't guess, but surely...that sudden change in my daughter's heart...I must have an explanation! What I'm going to attempt is dangerous...but I'll master myself...I shall see this young man. Your advice will be followed, Monsieur Morel. I'll be there, in the place where you saw him last night."

"At the same time," I added.

"At the same time," the doctor repeated.

"There it is," I concluded, pointing into the depths of the garden."

"Very good! Until tonight!"

"Until tonight!"

The doctor left me. When I was alone, I became anxious, for different reasons than Dr. Kanali, about the presence in the sanitarium, in the middle of the night, of that young officer, who, as the doctor had said himself, had indeed not fallen from the clouds into a garden path in order to adore his daughter. But what route had he taken? I had no inkling. Although it occurred to me that he had corrupted the fidelity of one of our domestics, the possibility seemed too implausible to be admitted, even for a moment. Nevertheless, to soothe my conscience, I questioned the employees responsible for manning the gate. None of them gave rise, in his responses, to the slightest suspicion. It was therefore necessary for me to renounce for the time being any further attempt to explain the phenomenon on the fantastic introduction of the handsome nocturnal officer.

My resignation on that point did not, however go as far as permitting me to remain indifferent to circumstances that might give me some clue. I was so far from that resolution that I stuck firmly to my intention to lie in ambush for the young officer with Dr. Kanali and his wife, the following night, in the depths of the garden.

At the agreed hour, midnight, I therefore went to the place fixed that morning by the doctor and myself I order that we would find ourselves in the path of the lovers if their unlucky star led them to a repeat performance of the previous night's rendezvous.

It was not only curiosity, nor simply my desire to render myself agreeable to the doctor, that decided me to get mixed up in that adventure, with which, strictly speaking, I had nothing to do. My position in the house—a position already long-held in 1849—obliged me to keep close track of events therein, in order not to allow any bad publicity emerge into the light of day.

Monsieur Kanali and his wife had reached the rendezvous ahead of me; they were occupying the location I had indicated to them. The doctor's face had the same expression of umbrageous anxiety that I had seen imprinted upon it in the morning, while his wife was even more radiant with joy, if that were possible, than the preceding night. As soon as she perceived me, she hastened to assure me that she could now answer for the health and life of her daughter, to whom she intended to say, after the surprise that she and the doctor were about to give her in a few minutes, that she had been wrong not to confide her new affection to her parents. They were rich enough not to refuse her the right to chose a husband of modest means, if, in fact, it were the mediocrity of the fortune of the man she loved that was the cause of the absolute silence she had maintained.

"Isn't that your opinion?" she said to the doctor.

"Undoubtedly, undoubtedly—unless Marthe has other reasons for concealing this love from us."

"What other reason could there be, my love, to fear the slightest opposition on our part to a young man about whom she surely has no reason to blush?"

"I don't know, but..."

"Then why create one at will?"

"There might nevertheless be a reason..."

"That I deny."

"In that case, I'll say to you in my turn: why is Marthe so suspicious of us?"

"Firstly, because of the perfectly adequate reason that I've already told you, and secondly because, you see, my love, young women experience a kind of need for secrecy, for discretion...dissimulation, I might say...in order to give love a bitter and stimulating aroma of dread and dolor. And finally, remember too that Marthe, who was so madly in love with César Caseneuve such a short time ago is, so to speak, ashamed to expose another passion, born yesterday, immediately to the full light of day—an admissible passion, I repeat, which she will confide to you, I'm convinced, once that modesty has vanished. Do you understand a little better now?"

"Yes, yes," the doctor replied. "Nevertheless, I'm curious, and increasingly impatient, to see the man who has extinguished in a breath the love that was consuming her, and immediately ignited another in her heart."

As on the preceding night, the June moonlight was illuminating the immense cupola of the heavens with its dreamy light. The great silence of midnight floated over the great city. The hospital gate, which had just opened, as had been its habit for two months, to let the sinister cart pass through, had furtively closed behind it. Nothing, at that moment, troubled the universal calm extended over the old faubourg, through which the suburban market-gardeners were not yet passing, over the sanitarium and the garden where we were waiting for something to happen.

The event was not long delayed in occurring; the two shadows that had appeared the previous day were vaguely outlined at the extremity of the double pathway that has already been mentioned, and it was then a question of seeing which one they would take.

The idea occurred to me that, having taken the other path the previous night, this time, the two phantoms would take the path where we were waiting for them. On that inspiration, I suggested to Monsieur and Madame Kanali that we ought to move to the other.

They followed my advice, and all three of us immediately went into the neighboring path, where we did our best to make ourselves invisible.

My presentiment was justified. We soon saw the two shadows go into the path we had quit, advance slowly, with their arms linked, and then sit down on the bench we had abandoned, placed there expressly for lovers, and excessively propitious for sweet conversations by starlight.

Hazard determined that the young officer of the Garde Mobile had his back toward us, while Mademoiselle Marthe was placed in such a manner as to show us her full face—which permitted me to observe that, as her mother had said so delightedly, her new passion had indeed wrought fortunate changes in her entire person. I had never seen her so youthful or so lovely; nothing was as charming to contemplate as her complexion in the pale and delicate light of that radiant summer night.

XIV

As their confidences were being made in hushed tones—everything demanded that: their situation, and the silence of the night, which invites discretion—it was fairly easy for us to be able to hear them, but for the same reason, it would have been very difficult to recognize, by the sound of his voice, who the young man sitting next to Marthe was, if by chance he had already been known to us, for words have the same anonymous character when emitted without emphasis as when they are very faint; one is, so to speak, speaking in pencil.

"So, then," the young officer said to Marthe, "you firmly believe that your father will never consent to grant me your hand?"

"I'm convinced of it by virtue of his character, his ambition—in sum, by virtue of everything that he is."

"You see! You see!" whispered Madame Kanali to her husband. "I was right. Marthe is sure that you would never consent to give her hand to a mere officer, whose épée is probably his entire wealth and entire future."

"Listen," he doctor relied, dismissing his wife's reflection with a gesture of his agitated hand in the shadows. "Please, listen..."

"In that case," the officer said, "let's hope that my plan succeeds, my dear Marthe."

"And what is this plan, my love, which you mentioned to me last night and which I've been thinking about all day?"

"A plan as old as the world, but which is still the best one offered to poor hearts thwarted on earth. My plan is to abduct you."

At these words the doctor made a movement as if to pass from one path to the other. He was prevented from doing so by his wife.

"All this," she told him, "ought to appear to us as what it is, and that's mere childishness—pure childishness, given that we have, ourselves, the intention of marrying them, have we not? Look—the young officer seems to have a graceful and noble figure..."

"You're not replying, Marthe," the young officer went on. "You assured me last night, however, that you would consent to anything, not wanting to let me believe that you did not love me as much as I love you."

"Of course I said that, my love...but where will you take me when you carry me off?"

"A few steps away from here, to the house of one of my relatives, where we shall write to your father that we're already far away—very far away—and that we're going to leave for Russia is he persist in refusing us his consent."

"You hear that," Madame Kanali continued whispering to the doctor. "You hear that—it's still a romance. Oh no, dear child, no one will carry you off; you won't leave here without us, for you'll leave married, and married to the man you love, to the young officer to whom we owe it that you're alive and have been returned to us."

"And how will you abduct me?" Marthe went on. "It's not easy to get out of this place; by day my mother never leaves me alone and by night the gate is locked. We'd be seen, and then..."

"We won't be seen, my dear Marthe; we'll simply go out the way I came in. Has anyone seen me come in? No! For five nights running, however, I've got in."

Five nights running! I said to myself. *But how? How?* I resumed listening immediately, though.

"How did you get in?" the doctor's daughter persisted. "How do you get in, the gate always being locked?"

We were all asking ourselves the same question at the same time, waiting with extraordinary attention for the young officer's reply.

"Don't ask me that," he replied.

"Do you climb over the wall? It's very high."

"Oh no! How, in that case, would I get you over it, in order to get out of here?"

"Do you disguise yourself, and does some employee of the house whom you have bribed let you in by a secret door?"

"I haven't bribed anyone."

"It's the Devil, then," said Marthe, laughing. "It's the Devil who gives you the means to get in."

"If only it were the Devil!"

"So what is it, then?" said Marthe, astonished.

"So what is it?" murmured the mother, simultaneously, with a quiver in her voice, addressing her question to the more-than-attentive ears of the doctor, who had at that moment the face, the neck, the gaze and the tense attitude of a lion pausing, a wild beast that has just scented the suspicion of a prey in the air.

"Don't interrogate me any further, Marthe," the young officer replied—and I noticed that after that recommendation addressed to the doctor's daughter, he wiped his brow incessantly; one might have that his nerves, contained with difficulty by an effort of will, were being racked by an internal terror. Sweat was inundating him.

"No, I need to know how you get in here at night," Marthe insisted.

"If I told you, you wouldn't want to go with me."

"That's impossible!"

"I repeat to you that, in spite of your love for me, you wouldn't want to go with me if I told you what means I'm going to employ to abduct you, and which I've used until now to get in."

Again the young officer passed his handkerchief over his forehead.

Convulsively, the doctor gripped the two large branches forming the screen that concealed him, and Madame Kanali, whom I was observing, went suddenly pale, as if all her blood had been drawn away to her feet.

Marthe continued, taking the young officer's hand affectionately.

"It's very dangerous then, your means of getting me out of here?"

"It's...terrible."

"Terrible?"

"Yes."

"Tell me immediately, then."

"There'll still be time to tell you, at the moment of execution."

"And what if I don't want to go with you then?"

"You will, I know," said the adventurous young man, putting his arms around Marthe's lovely head.

"If that's so, why make me wait?"

The young man drew even closer to Marthe, whom her mother never quit with her gaze, looking at her with an indefinable emotion.

"Why? Because the fright I'd cause you now by revealing my means of escape wouldn't diminish the fright you'll feel when the moment comes. I'd rather only give it to you once."

"But my God, what is it, then?"

"Stop, Marthe—don't ask me about it anymore."

"César, I beg you, in the name of our love, tell me..."

"César!" cried the doctor, forcefully parting the branches that he was holding in order to launch himself from one path to the other. "César!"

And he launched himself.

Caseneuve, on hearing his name pronounced behind him, turned round abruptly. Madame Kanali saw his face then.

"The dead man has returned!" she screamed. "Oh, this time it can no longer be denied: It's Bem Strombold! It's Müller von Rosenthal! It's César! It's the Vampire attached to our family, to the blood of our house, vowed to his murderous lips. Death to him! A stake in the heart! A stake in the heart!"

Madame Kanali seemed terrible to me, veritably frightful at that moment, pale beneath her gray hair, crazy with maternal dread, crazy with magical terror, crazy on behalf of her entire family, as somber and unhinged as the redoubtable figures of German witchcraft, who danced barefoot by moonlight in the Harz mountains, when she cried for a second time: "A stake in the heart! A stake in the heart!" and looked wildly around as if to discover an actual stake to plunge into Caseneuve's heart. The latter, not having waited for the stake, had set off along the path at a run, at a phantasmal pace.

Someone else, however, was gathering speed in that hectic flight: it was the doctor, whom I also followed at a run, but at a much less rapid gallop. His intention was obvious to me; when he saw that César was heading for the arch of the main entrance, evidently to get out through the gate, which he supposed to be open, he got ahead of him by taking a short cut, and ran to place himself between the two halves of the gate—which was closed.

Now, as I was a few paces behind César, it was impossible for him to get away from us. Suddenly, however, I could no longer see him and judged that he had gone under the vault, where Monsieur Kanali was waiting for him. So I lessened my pace as I ran breathlessly toward the doctor, who was even more breathless than me.

"Well?" he said, on seeing me. "Did you get him? Where is he? Give him to me!"

"No—it's you who caught him."

"What, me? But he was there, in front of you…"

"Yes, but he was coming toward you."

"Undoubtedly…"

"Well, then," I said, "what's become of him?"

"What? You're not bringing him to me?" said the bewildered doctor, intoxicated by exasperation, replying to my question with the same question.

"No, I'm not bringing you to him, since it's you who…"

"Ah!" he said. "He's got away from us!" The doctor was choking with anger.

The fact was that César had got away from both of us.

"Has he gone underground, then?" said the doctor, flabbergasted by that strange and inexplicable disappearance. "Is there another floor underneath the house?"

Our doubt and colossal astonishment would have lasted several minutes more in front of that iron grille, through the bars of which César could not have passed, and where the doctor had mounted on stopping him, if someone had not suddenly moved us out of the way in order to open it—and to open it for something less poetic and, more particularly, less alive than our amorous fugitive: the *tapissière*, drawn by two strong horses.

This evening, the *tapissière* was creaking under the weight of its heavy load.

"In that case," said the doctor, two-thirds in despair but still sustained by a rage that took hold of him in a final third of hope, "he's gone back to the garden...let's search for him in the garden. Let's track him down...he mustn't get out...he shan't get out!"

After the scene that you have just read, I truly did not know what to think the next day when, by means of reflection, I sought to explain it to myself. I said to myself: *So here's César, who was dead but has come back in perfect health, more amorous than before, and more resolute than ever, since he's talking about abducting the doctor's daughter.*

Less bowed down beneath the heavy realities of his world, in truth, I might perhaps have yielded myself to the stirring superstition of vampires—which, all things considered, at least explains the extraordinary by the extraordinary, which didn't seem so false a form of reasoning now. As I wasn't entirely ready, however, and, rightly or wrongly, could scarcely believe what everyone in the world had previously believed, I did not feel that I had the strength, in spite of the marvelous aspect of the event and Madame Kanali's fanaticism, to accept the lady's convictions, any more than I had admitted them two nights earlier, when she had obligingly recounted to me at such length the facts relating to the vampires unleashed against her and her mother, which I shall willingly call vampires of the first and second kinds.

They were not my beliefs, and I promised myself to get to the bottom of the intrigue, in which, unromantic as I am by nature, I was progressively drawn to take an interest, and which I was eager to see through to its denouement.

You can imagine how glad I was, animated by such sentiments of research and curiosity, to accept the invitation that Dr. Kanali extended to me a few days later—an invitation that, in any other circumstances, I would have declined, as much out of modesty as propriety. He asked me to sit in on a kind of family council that would examine, from the viewpoint of resolutions to be made in everyone's interests, the facts concerning the night marked by the reappearance of César Caseneuve, fundamentally quite extraordinary whether he was a vampire or not. I stammered a few insignificant reasons to excuse myself for not being able to accept the invitation, but in the end, I did accept it and I went.

The three individuals comprising the family were gathered: the doctor, his wife and their daughter.

The owl was asleep on the mantelpiece.

I have no memory of any face more expressive in its desolation than Madame Kanali's. Cruelly put to the proof, it appeared, by virtue of the emotions of the still-recent night on which she had seen César again, that she retained in her terror-petrified features the surprise produced by that apparition. Distress hollowed out an infinite depth in her eyes, and her mouth seemed torn by the cries of anathema she had uttered. When I went in, she was leaning back on the sofa, tightly wrapped in a big black shawl that hung down to her knees.

Only mental excitement can bring about these somber ecstasies, which the greatest material dolors do not attain, because they break the body and in this case, the impact had gone beyond physical harm to strike squarely at the sensibility, the reason—in sum, everything that God alone has the secret of healing. The return of that young man, after the official certification of his death, had reminded her too dolorously of the return of the other two phantoms, which it had been so difficult to drive back into the caves of oblivion, not to trouble Marthe's mother, exasperating her to the extent of rendering her such as I saw her before my eyes.

Her own eyes only quit their meditative immobility to search her surroundings with the wild anxiety of monomania, as if she were expecting to see César Caseneuve emerge at any moment from the thickness of the walls. That dread was so powerful within her that she was holding her daughter's hands in the position of someone who is holding up a person fallen over the edge of a precipice or into a fire, striving energetically to pull her up in order to save her.

"What!" she began by saying to her daughter, plunging her gaze like twin épées into Marthe's astonished eyes. "You haven't guessed that you have been the victim of a deadly lie, when you have seen César Caseneuve appear before you again?"

The word *deadly* was not the least surprising to Marthe among those that had just opened fire upon her. Why deadly? Besides why, she was also wondering what lie there was in the presence of César—an extraordinarily unexpected presence, to be sure, but very real.

"Let's leave aside the question of apparitions, which we can discuss later if you still insist," said the doctor, "and ask Marthe how she explains the return of

César Caseneuve to this world, when it had been publicly alleged that he had quit it on a particular hour of a
particular day..."

"Isn't that what I'm asking?" Madame Kanali retorted, without letting go of her daughter's hands.

"Of course, but you set the question on the vaporous terrain of magic, while I'm putting it in the much
more solid ground of reality."

"Reality!" said Madame Kanali, ironically. "Reality! But that's what I've seen—it's what all of us have
seen that is the reality: an apparition escaped from the
world of darkness."

Although habituated since infancy to her mother's
mysterious ways, Marthe, to whom Madame Kanali had
never talked about her superstitious doctrines for fear of
frightening her and awakening presentiments within her
that she supposed to be only too disposed to gather and
develop, did not understand her agitation or her lan-
guage. She found it very difficult to understand the
bizarrerie of her mother's conduct toward her. One day,
she had given her to understand that she knew that she
had a new love in her heart, and had appeared very happy about it; the next, she had heaped her with reproaches
because she had discovered that she had faithfully returned to the returned Caseneuve. Why?

Marthe, however, had never noticed an absolute repulsion against the young man on her mother's part.
Marthe's reasoning was accurate on all points except
one, which is that her mother had always had considerable apprehensions in seeing César courting her daughter,
but had only confided the secret of her alarm to her husband.

"All right," the doctor continued, "your reality is
the right one—but I've already told you that we'll exam-

ine that side of the question later. I'll ask Marthe once again to answer me: Marthe, how do you explain the return of César Caseneuve naturally?"

"I'll explain it," Marthe replied, increasing disturbed by the ceremonious questions and her mother's increasingly haggard expression, "as Monsieur Caseneuve explained it to me himself. His physicians had left him so ill the last time they saw him that they thought him domed, to the extent that when they left his house they said to the concierge: 'Your young tenant is a dead man,' and the concierge immediately ran to make his declaration at the Mairie. Monsieur Caseneuve was not dead, and was so far from it that he got up the next day, went out the following day, and came here to the rendezvous that he had arranged with me."

"All that is, indeed, possible," said the doctor, when his daughter had given her explanation. I admit it without difficulty, but I intend..."

"Possible! Possible!" groaned Madame Kanali. "You admit it, you say, without difficulty. But it's insane! Just think..."

"Undoubtedly, it's quite possible," the doctor repeated, sensing the approach of a storm that he wanted to avoid at all costs. "I'll make Monsieur Morel the judge of it."

"My opinion is yours," I replied. "In times like this, declarations at the Mairie are not rigorously checked; names are inscribed on the list of the deceased more or less as one pleases. It's easy. It's a ready-made pretext for disappearing at will and reappearing when one deems it appropriate."

"Very good!" replied Madame Kanali energetically. "But consider, then, that the accursed creatures of whom you want to prevent me from speaking, always choose the best pretexts for reappearing on earth: they make use of the most natural in order to deceive the living more fully—and it's precisely because the pretext employed by César Caseneuve is natural that it's all the more necessary to be suspicious of it.

Madame Kanai raised her voice. "Besides which," she continued, "who has interrogated the physicians who said to the concierge: *Your young tenant is a dead man*? No one! Which of you has questioned the concierge who confirmed the judgment? No one! And furthermore, why was he, César, the man of the night, who has so easily advanced all these impostures, unable to say how he had introduced himself into this establishment? It's because pretexts were lacking on that point. The walls? He told you himself, when questioned: insurmountable. The employees? He said it himself: incorruptible. How then, did he get in? He made no reply; he had no reply to make. That's because, in order to get into the sanitarium, it's necessary to say what one is, and that is what he cannot say. Well, I'll say it: he's a vampire, a vampire, a vampire!"

XV

As we have just said, Marthe had always been kept distant by her mother from any precise confidence regarding the dangers run by the descendants of her family by virtue of contact with tenebrous beings in which, as we have just seen once again, Madame Kanali had a blind faith, incarnated in her by way of personal experience and natural prejudice. One can imagine, therefore, how her mother's final exclamation struck her with alarm and distress. Her blood froze in her veins, her nerves quivered, as if a detonation had suddenly occurred beneath her feet and hurled her into the air.

Horror! The man she loved, César, had suddenly passed, on the sacred authority of her mother, from the possible world, the everyday world of humankind, into that of magic, that of subterranean beings, vile and outcast creatures. She had mingled her young, innocent, delicate love with that of a being lower than a demon—for demons, at least, are in possession of the violent life of damnation; they enter into creation on a warrant from God; they are the persecutory genii commissioned by him for the punishment of human beings—but vampires do not enter into any order, any class or any calculation of creation. They belong neither to life nor death, neither oblivion nor Hell; they are the dead-alive, the dead that affect life; or, rather, they are the frightful grimace of one and the other. The dead reject them with the terror of the night, and the living fear them no less.

As Marthe only knew about them what she had read in books, she had never debated with herself from the viewpoint of their real possibility, had never found herself in a state of mind to deny them with the firmness of reason. On the contrary, her reason, taken by surprise, gripped, enveloped and carried away by the rapid whirlwind of fire emerged from her mother's fanaticized mouth, was lost, plunged into a crazed intoxication, into an immeasurable terror, and it surrendered her to her mother—a strange but not unique phenomenon—frisson for frisson, swoon for swoon, pallor for pallor.

Taking advantage of the bridgehead established, so to speak, by her frenetic verve, Madame Kanali passed over it to go directly to questions that, in any other circumstances, I would have found extraordinary coming from her mouth. It is true, as Molière has proved sufficiently in his *École des femmes*, that fear sometimes approaches naivety.

"When that monster spoke to you, Daughter, did you not feel invaded by an earthy vapor, which stifled you?"

"I don't know," Marthe stammered, confusedly. "I don't know...I felt so many things...it's possible...but no, no...no earthy vapor."

"That's because you wouldn't have noticed it," Madame Kanali went on, without letting go of her daughter's hands, which she squeezed even more energetically instead. "And when he took you by the hands, didn't you feel that his were horribly icy?"

"His hands...?"

"Yes."

"Wait while I try to remember...no, Mother, no...I even believe I remember having told him several times that they were hot."

"It's not general, in fact," Madame Kanali continued. "There are vampires who dissimulate that chill in several ways. Let's pass on. Tell me, Marthe...but I

213

don't know myself how to tell you…it's necessary, though…I'm obliged to ask you…"

Madame Kanali was very hesitant to explain herself with regard to one final point, which she judged most essential, but also very delicate, as is evident. There was a conflict within her between her respect for her daughter and the need to convince her nevertheless with the most incisive precision that she ought not to doubt for a single second that she had shared her love with a vampire.

"Marthe," she resumed, making an extreme effort, as if resolutely decided, no matter what the cost, to put the question to her daughter. In a faint voice, she continued: "Marthe, when the accursed one's lips touched you…."

Dr. Kanai interrupted. "Enough!" he said. "Enough! For the third time, I don't want you to stimulate the imagination of our child to the point of delirium, when it's quite simply a matter of telling her that the love she has experienced for this young man is a love that can have no result, no goal, no future for her, because I, her father, will never consent to her marrying a man that I have already refused—never! Since that, Madame Kanali, is where you want to get to, I've got there immediately, saving a great deal of time and unnecessary terrors."

"Unnecessary terrors!" cried Madame Kanali. "Unnecessary terrors! But if I hadn't led Marthe to the edge of the gulf, in order to unveil all its black profundity to her, she would never have had the salutary vertigo that she is experiencing; she would never have recoiled; she would never have know why her hand has been refused to a young man that she loved and whom she will now hate, execrate and curse as much as she loved him."

"I could never hate him," said Marthe.

"What! You don't detest him?" demanded Madame Kanali, astonished to see the approval of what she had just said and affirmed to the doctor vanish in that singular manner.

"Oh, on the contrary."

"Then," Madame Kanali continued in the same tone of naïve stupefaction, "you won't promise us not to lend yourself any longer to the attempts he will dare to risk in order to renew his relationship with you?"

"I can't promise that," Marthe replied, in spite of the fear that was still blanching her lips.

"But such a love will be the death of you!"

"Then it will be the death of me," replied Marthe, trembling.

"A slow death."

"Then I'll be happy for longer."

"But he'll take you with him!"

"Then I'll be happy forever."

"Well then, I'll kill him myself, I swear! I swear!"

"Then I'll be happy sooner, for I'll die with him," said the inflexible young woman, still in spite of the terror from which she had not emerged.

"Oh!" cried Madame Kanali. "Oh! That's how all these unfortunate young women fall under the influence of these abominable reptiles, who begin by fascinating them, in order to damn them thereafter and finally steal them away from the affection of their parents, from the eye of God, from the salvation of their soul."

After the final word of that last sortie against the vampires, Madame Kanali, sibyl and mother, somber and in tears, excited and in despair, wrapped her shoulders and head in the upper folds of her Indian shawl, and allowed herself to yield meekly to fatality—without, however, forgetting the oath she had just sworn: the fanatical oath to kill César Caseneuve, and to kill him as one defeats those of his species when one wants to make them die for good and all.

"You've employed all the means in your power," said Dr. Kanali, putting his hand on his wife to calm her down, "and nothing's come of it. Here's mine."

The doctor turned to me. "Monsieur Morel," he said, "you will draw up an account of our expenses in the house, which we shall be leaving in a few days' time in order to go to America. We'll see whether vampires can cross the Ocean."

Twenty days having gone by since Dr. Kanali's bizarre encounter with the actors Saint-Aimable and Michelin at the Crémerie Myrrha, the moment had therefore come when the two part-time gravediggers had undertaken to deliver Jean-Paul Désormeaux, the popular orator of the Club Martel, to him.

The doctor awaited the hour of this delivery with the most anxious impatience, in order to proceed with the embalming of that magnificent subject. He was all the more eager to take possession of it, and to enjoy the success of the operation—a certain, immense, infallible success—because he had decided, with an infallible determination, to leave France immediately after his triumph. As he had told me, he intended to go to America with his daughter Marthe, whom he intended, at any price, to extract from her fatal love for César Caseneuve—a love that had become, by virtue of a combination of natural or supernatural circumstances, the trouble and delirium of the family. Marthe, as we have seen, was under his spell; Madame Kanali had discovered in that a divine malediction, in a horrible form, and the doctor himself had ended up regarding it as an outrageous challenge to his authority as a scientist and a father.

There are such duels to the death in many families, between the desires of children and the demands of parents. Such conflicts are marked by a final day, a final catastrophe in which the bonds of affection, respect and blood, long stretched, break under the shock of a passion unjustly conceived or unjustly suppressed. Well, that final day, that final catastrophe, had sounded for the Kanali family.

Five days after the almost-magical appearance and disappearance of Caseneuve, Monsieur Kanali came toward me via the pathway of the Convalescents; he appeared, from one moment to the next, upset and radiant. I had just taken the *Journal des Débats* to the director and was about to take *La Presse* to the chaplain. I had paused at the circus around the large basin, where I was busy scraping away the moss and grass that had blocked the grating.

On Dr. Kanali's contracted features, usually much calmer, sudden joys burst forth and flared up at intervals. Evidently, sentiments of equal strength, but different in nature, were diving his heart; sometimes one submerged the other, sometimes they collided—and then, as in eclipses, light and darkness cut across his face, lending it a bizarre appearance. The pathway of the Convalescents being sufficiently long, I had the leisure to observe that picturesque conflagration on his physiognomy.

I went to meet him, for I had to talk to him about his own interests—and surely one of the two powerful preoccupations that he had as he came toward me, without having yet perceived me in the place near the basin that I had just quit. He was talking loudly and gesticulating a great deal, smiling to himself, threatening, increasing his pace, suddenly slowing down, and then becoming excited again; again he rubbed his hands with satisfaction, only to recommence his threats against an absent enemy further on.

"Well," I said to him, at a distance, "nothing new, Doctor. I haven't learned anything."

I pulled him out of his waking nightmare.

"Oh, it's you, Monsieur Morel. Nothing new about the young man, that is?"

"Nothing."

"However, since the night when we chased him so hotly and let him get away from us so easily—which is to say, five days ago—he's been back four times."[36]

"Yes, he's come here four times—and in spite of my vigilance, prepared for any ruse he might employ, it's impossible, Doctor, still impossible, to find out how he gets in and how he gets out."

"Four times," the doctor repeated, with an ager full of irritation. "Four times! He hasn't seen my daughter again, to be sure, for we don't let her go down to the garden by night or leave her alone in her room. Her mother has moved her into hers. Nevertheless, he's come, and come four times; I have the proof of it. The first time, he attached a bouquet under her widow, from which I took a note in which these words were written: *Hope, dear Marthe; in four days we shall be reunited.*

---

[36] The chronology of events has become slightly confused, and will remain so. If, as César said on the occasion of his last reported dialogue the Marthe, he had already got into the sanitarium five times, Dr. Kanali's current calculation would make a total of nine, with a tenth still to come; as the reader will see, however, that figure does not correspond with the arithmetic offered hereafter.

Do you understand than audacity? In four days they'll be reunited! The next day, another note, this time attached to the neck of the owl, which, unable to get into Marthe's room, since Marthe is no longer resident in that room—a circumstance unknown outside—ended up by returning to Madame Kanali's room. Madame Kanali saw, took hold of and has obviously read that second note and the words it contained. Those words were: *Continue to hope, dear Marthe; only three more days.*"

The doctor interrupted himself to say: "He persists, as you see, he persists, the wretch! What plan has he made? I'll go on: the next day, which was yesterday, a third note, slid under the door of the room when her mother was assumed to be asleep, and these words: *Always hope, always, dear Marthe, two more days to hope.* Well, what do you think, Monsieur Morel, of that impertinent security, that certainty, which renews its affirmation every day? Ah! Finally, this morning, a fourth and final note, which I found just now, pinned under the chair in which my daughter sits in the sanitarium chapel—here it is; I still have it in my hand, having just discovered it under the chair."

And the doctor read the fourth note, of which I will tell you the approximate contents: *Hope more than ever, dear Marthe; tonight we shall be reunited; the chloroform that I enclose in the ring hidden in this letter will put your mother to sleep for a few minutes, during which you can get out of her room without running the risk of waking her. Until this evening, then, where we usually meet, at the usual time. You have told me that in order to follow me you will not recoil before any means of getting out of the house; the moment has come to fulfill your dear promise, but I won't hide it from you that the method is terrible. Will you have the courage?*

"With the result that if I hadn't found this note," the doctor continued, "this evening, when my wife had been put to sleep by the chloroform, my daughter would have escaped, would have come here to the garden to join Caseneuve, and they would have left together." The doctor stamped his foot on the ground and struck a tree with his fist. "But it's enough to make one believe, like my wife, in black magic and white magic, in brucolaques and vampires, when one sees this indefatigable pursuit of my daughter, this persecutor of our repose insinuating himself into this house without anyone ever being able to figure out by what superhuman means, what unknown path, what fantastic breach in the wall, what door or what ruse—for you've discovered nothing in the last five days?"

"Nothing, I repeat—and yet, I affirm to you on my honor that I've put a guard on all the places by which it might be possible for someone to get in: the garden, the courtyard, the cellars, the grain-lofts..."

"And yet, he's not a spirit, a flame or a flash of lightning, is he, Monsieur Morel?"

"No, but he's ungraspable."

"Oh, not to be able to lay a hand on him! How glad I would be, how much pleasure I would obtain from catching him here and making him pay, drop by drop, for all the anger and all the rage that he has been igniting within me for far too long!"

"Dare I ask, Dr. Kanali, why, overcoming a certain reluctance, which I admit, but which I have difficulty admitting to be eternal in a man of great sense like yourself, you won't give your daughter to this young man, whose intelligence and honorability you have praised to me, who is due to be the heir one day, if I'm not mistaken, of a rich uncle—a young man who is a doctor like yourself?"

Monsieur Kanali did not let me finish.

"Why don't I want him for a son-in-law, you ask me? Why? I don't want him precisely because he is a physician, or, rather, because, having the title and the science of a physician, he does not have the qualities, because he does not have the most important of all: courage. A physician is a soldier; on many occasions that soldier is bound to rise as far as heroism. Danger is a part of our noble profession.

"On the battlefield, the physician runs through a hail of bullets, traverses webs of cannonballs, guides himself by the light of bombs, in order to bandage the wounded and pick up the dying. In our cities, he plunges continually into the atmosphere of the most murderous fevers; he breathes them in; he inoculates himself with them by contact. From the poisoned arms of the patient he is treating, a mortal drop often springs forth, which might kill him by landing on his hand or in the corner of his eye. And in our hospitals, Monsieur Morel, as no one knows better than you, is not the peril immediate, constant in all forms and all places?

"You see, in times of epidemics such as the one that God is inflicting upon us at this evil moment, it is almost certain loss of life for the physician within a given interval. Whoever recoils or hesitates before those conditions imposed on our profession is not worthy to exercise it, to wear the title."

The doctor continued, drawn to make allusion—I saw it coming—to his attempted embalming at the Val-de-Grâce, when, I knew, Caseneuve has lost his head. "Well, that young men about whom you are talking, whom you are astonished that I don't want for a son-in-law, does not have the courage that the profession of medicine demands; he is a poor soldier; he is afraid of the bullets of disease and the cannonballs of death. I would not want him in our ranks; I do not want him for my daughter. Let him tremble elsewhere. Don't speak of him to me again as a possible son-in-law—don't mention him to me at all! Rather than see my daughter Marthe in his arms, I would rather see her leave here this evening in one of those sinister carriages that I never see myself without an invincible shudder, wholehearted physician though I am."

Dr. Kanali stopped, astonished to see me take several steps backwards and go pale at the last words he had pronounced. "What's the matter?" he asked. "Are you feeling ill?"

"Nothing, nothing," I told him. "What I'm experiencing is all in the mind. Look, while I pull myself together—which won't take long—read this newspaper on that bench. I'll talk to you afterwards...I need to think for a few minutes."

XVI

Although the doctor did not understand my sudden weakness, he suspected that it had something to do with the disparate threads of the conversation that we had been having with regard to his daughter. He examined me, and then sat down on the bench near the basin to read the newspaper I had just handed to him, while I delivered myself to my reflections.

"Oh, great God, what am I reading?" cried Monsieur Kanali. "No, never has disappointment fallen so cruelly upon anyone!"

"What is it?"

"It done for me! Abomination!"

"But what is it?" I asked the doctor for a second time. "You seem overwhelmed by the weight of some terrible news. What have you learned from the paper?"

"I'm in despair, more than one can say—despair!"

"If I knew why..."

The doctor was choking. He paused momentarily to breathe. With difficulty, he went on: "You know that man from the Salle Martel, the political orator who was brought here one evening, dying, about a month ago...on the night of the storm?"

"Jean-Paul Désormeaux, I believe..."

"Yes, Jean-Paul Désormeaux. I had made plans to give him a second immortality by embalming him according to a procedure that would have returned him to the eyes of his partisans as handsome as ever. I'll pass over the details regarding the various trials of that sort that I've already attempted successfully, and which promised me an immense success."

Details which I know, I thought.

"This evening—this very evening," the doctor continued, "I was to bring about the miraculous transformation; everything was ready: location, isolation, chemical agents."

"Well? Has the newspaper warned you of some unexpected difficulty?"

"If it were only a difficulty!" cried the doctor, angrily crumpling the newspaper in his hands. "It's an impossibility: a radical, insurmountable impossibility. What a scoundrel!"

"Who's a scoundrel?"

"Him!"

"Who's him? Indignation is obscuring your ideas, and your words..."

"Him, I tell you!"

"Jean-Paul Désormeaux?"

"Listen to this article in the paper."

After having smoothed the creases out of the newspaper with his still-agitated hands, the doctor read in a voice trembling with passion the following article, to which I listened with all my overexcited attention:

"To the profound astonishment of the Republican party, it has just been discovered that one of the most popular orators of the club of the Salle Martel, the famous Jean-Paul Désormeaux, the virtuous, incorruptible Jean-Paul Désormeaux, was in daily communication with the police, to which he had always belonged. Convicted at the age of twenty for forgery, he had spent five years in Melun, where his first-rate education, his facile eloquence and rare aptitude for all mental exercises had distinguished him from the other inmates. When his punishment was concluded the police selected him out as a subject of whom they could make the best use. First, he was given a new name—an exchange by which he had nothing to lose—and under his new name he was able, without giving offense to the justly-suspicious Republican party, to make useful daily reports on the members and intentions of that party to the Paris police.

"Thus, it is claimed that he rendered great services to the administration of the Rue de Jérusalem in recent times. He was responsible for the arrest of several section-leaders, who are sailing for Nouka-Hiva at this very moment.[37] The Salle Martel was the field in which he labored with great success, to the profit of those whose gratitude was shown in the generous form of two thousand francs a month. It was there that he built an intimate rapport with the red party, which never suspected that a wolf had slipped into the fold, if it is permissible to make use of that rural comparison with regard to the gentlemen of the red party. Imagine their furious indignation during the two days in which the news has been circulating.

"There is talk of nothing less than exhuming Jean-Paul Désormeaux and plunging him into the sewer of the Faubourg Poissonnière. Although we disapprove of that excessive gesture of vengeance, we fully understand the horror that a traitor must inspire, whichever party he is selling. The silence of scorn is the only punishment that it is necessary to inflict upon him, especially when death has already removed him from the range of his enemies' blows.

---

[37] France took possession of Nouka-Hiva, nowadays known as Nuku Hiva, in the Marquesas Islands in 1842, after the U.S.A. and England, which had earlier fought over its possession, failed to make their claims stick. Its use as a venue of transportation was brief, and the French abandoned it in 1859.

"At any rate, Jean-Paul Désormeaux has passed in an instant from the luminous Capitol of popularity to the Tarpeian Rock of insult. We remain Roman in relation to this violent contrast in our manner of conducting ourselves with those who deceive us during great political upheavals, the touchstone of individuals as well as the masses."

Dr. Kanali's voice had altered when he resumed, and it was in a tone of despondency that he spoke. "And now, how can I be expected to embalm a traitor? Oh, the fine plan of rendering animation, expression and the coloration of life to a spy, an informer! The project is sunk, the affair gone up in flames!"

As Dr. Kanali concluded, I admired the quality of his oration while stifling a strong desire to laugh. "You see, Monsieur Morel, it's necessary never to let forty-eight hours go by between the death of a man and his resurrection. Three days later, it's already too late; the great man has become a bandit, recognized as a spy or a wastrel, exposed as a traitor or a thief, confirmed as a forger or a scoundrel. But what am I going to do now?"

The doctor answered himself, while trying to tear apart the bench on which he was sitting with his bare hands: "There's nothing more to be done. That's twice I've been thwarted in the same attempt. There's a fatality in it; I won't recommence my struggle against it. This country is against me. For me, then, it's another country, another fatality! I'm leaving France! And I'm leaving immediately. My decision is made. It's noon—I'll catch the three o-clock train to Dieppe. I'll go to London, which is where my family and I will be tomorrow. The day after, I'll embark at Southampton for New York."

Driven by excitement, the doctor stood up. He was about to go away, to carry out his project immediately.

I stopped him. "Doctor," I said, "give me until tomorrow."

"Until tomorrow? What for?"

"Just until tomorrow."

"But again, what for, when my destiny is forcing me to go?"

"I have a presentiment," I replied, "that a decisive fact will present itself here tomorrow which will change it."

"To my advantage?"

"I wouldn't ask you otherwise."

"No, it's impossible that anything that might happen here tomorrow will improve a situation even further aggravated by the acute family chagrin with which you're familiar. The only possible consolation that I might have had in the confusion into which I've been plunged by what has happened, my only consolation, my daughter, is afflicting me like all the rest—more than the rest, in afflicting her mother too. It's a family shipwreck. No, believe me, don't ask for a futile delay. Let me go."

"You won't experience that shipwreck—at least, I hope so—if you consent to what I ask."

"What plan have you got in mind? You have in your voice, in your gaze, in the hand that's shaking mine so cordially, preoccupations, sentiments…things of which you offered no glimpse when I arrived here a little while ago."

"Something you said, Doctor," I replied, "was a flash of enlightenment for me, a ray of fire in the darkness, Trust me, give me until tomorrow."

"All right—I'll give you until tomorrow."

"That's not all—I can't do it all alone."

"Speak! What more do you expect from me?"

"Go back to the chapel, from which you brought the note written by César Caseneuve to your daughter, and replace it under the chair. It's probable that your daughter will find it, read it and, by means of some sign of intelligence for which we need to be on the lookout, will reply to it in the course of the day. Her response is a foregone conclusion; she'll accept. Tonight, therefore, she'll be at the rendezvous given to her by the writer of the note. We'll be there too: you, Madame Kanali, and me. The denouement of this intrigue, obscure but not impenetrable, will burst forth immediately.

"It will be a denouement for everyone: for you, for your wife, for Mademoiselle Marthe and for the man whose influence over the fascinated heart and dominated will of your daughter have become a persecution that Madame Kanali shares and which is increasing, every hour of every day, the personal terrors of her beliefs. Be ready, therefore, tonight. The 'usual time' of which César Caseneuve speaks is about half past midnight I'll come to find you a quarter of an hour earlier. During the day, you'll alert Madame Kanali, and the three of us will go down to the garden in silence. The rest is up to the course of events."

After these final arrangements, the doctor went to do as we had agreed: replace the note he had taken and bring his wife into the secret of the ambush set for the two young people.

I had much on which to reflect after his departure.

I had taken a great responsibility on myself by making a promise to bring enlightenment and peace into that family tormented by so many various passions, but it interested me to the highest degree, and I had a sincere conviction that this affair, like all those in which people lose their heads, required more common sense and reflection than effort to avert misfortune. Those who are drowning do not require a continent beneath their feet; much less will suffice; it is often on a piece of wreckage that one survives a shipwreck.

That item of debris, for me, was César Caseneuve; he was destined, in my thinking, to bring the olive-branch into the house. But where was César Caseneuve? Would he come, as he had promised? Might not the ruse that he employed to get into the house, which I believed I had finally discovered, and which was the cornerstone of all my hopes, fail on the very day when it was important to the success of my calculations that it achieve the great result for which it had been imagined?

Let us admit that the ruse would not fail, vanquished by ill-luck, and that César would get into the house, as he had promised. Was that all? What other means did I have thereafter of making him acceptable as a son-in-law to a father and mother set against him, exciting one another to a peak of irritation? The events that will follow, from which we are separated by a matter of hours, will tell whether my method was sound, and whether the prophetic opening created in my brain by the involuntary remark that Dr. Kanali had made was or was not a hallucination.

Circumstances presented themselves in the best conditions imaginable, as I had foreseen, and as I would have arranged them myself had I been the invisible order of the world.

We allowed Marthe to administer the chloroform to her mother—who, forewarned of the occurrence, took care not to breathe in while the phial was placed under her nostrils. Then we allowed the young woman to go down into the garden in complete confidence—two characteristic facts that permit us to have no doubt that she had found and read the letter pinned to the wickerwork of her chair.

We went down to the garden in our turn, and, the moon no longer illuminating the last nights of the month, were able to reach, without being seen or our presence suspected, the bushy location where the two lovers' last conversation had take place, and from which they were planning to depart forever.

After due reflection, I decided to tell Monsieur Kanali and his wife the reason why I had brought them; it was not appropriate for me to maintain the mystery any longer.

"Your daughter is there," I said to them. "In a few moments, César Caseneuve, whom she is expecting, will be with her, and this time, if I'm not mistaken about the means that he has contrived to get in, it will be easy for us to catch him, no matter how clever he is in eclipsing himself or how nimble he is in fleeing.

"The means that I attribute to him, which I don't want to keep secret any longer, is this: in order to slip into the sanitarium, César must be taking the place of the cart-driver who brings the *tapissière* here every night. There is no other supposition to make, and I have made it. Yes, underneath the smock of that nocturnal carter, whose function he purchases for a few hours—I don't know at what price—he wears the costume of the Garde Mobile in which I have seen him. Once he's inside, he folds up the smock, throws it over his arm in the guise of a cloak, and, after his meeting, with your daughter, he puts it on again and takes his place at the head of his horses. Search for the officer; he has disappeared.

"That's the skillful game he has played every time he has got in here by fraud, and it's with the aid of that rapid change of clothes that he's escaped us. He won't escape us this evening, but let's be prudent. Let's allow him to accomplish half his transformation, then allow him to come this far, where we are, costumed as an officer in the Garde Mobile—and when he's on the point of withdrawing with your daughter, of getting out of the house by the means that I suspect, catch him…and everything will be settled."

When I had finished speaking the doctor looked at me with the phenomenal astonishment that I had experienced myself when the thought of the means employed by Caseneuve to slip furtively into our midst had occurred to me. He was all the more astonished because he knew better than anyone what immeasurable fears the young man had in that regard. What love! What passion! What a folly of passion and love César must therefore experience for his daughter Marthe, since, in spite of that infinitely boundless fear, he made himself into a personification of fear: the fearful man became a conductor of shades and a collector of phantoms in order to get close to her!

"The struggle with such a fear," the doctor murmured, "is almost courage!"

Madame Kanali did not say anything; she was awaiting events for the last word on that legend of the Middles Ages. For her, Caseneuve remained what she had always said he was: a vampire.

The half hour after midnight chimed on Saint-Laurent, and on that warning of the imminence of the crisis, the doctor and I imitated the granitic immobility of the eccentric woman, with her dark and distant superstitions.

A few seconds after the last vibrations, we heard the gate of the sanitarium open, and over that noise passed another: that of the wheels of the tapissière rolling under the arch.

After a few minutes, footsteps caused the sand of the pathway where Marthe was waiting to rustle.

"However impatient you are," I whispered to the doctor and his wife, "restrain yourselves. Listen, and don't move. Let it suffice for now to be sure that he can't escape you, if it's him that we can hear coming."

It was him.

He was wearing the costume of the preceding nights, that of an officer.

After thanking Marthe for coming to a rendezvous that would by unlike any other, he said to her: "My dear Marthe, we have ten minutes to spend together; listen to me solemnly, for what I have to say to you is solemn."

"I'm listening," Marthe replied, slightly surprised by the authority in César's words; he had been more amorous than grave in his speech thus far.

"I've already warned you," he went on, "that you'll only be able to get out of here by accepting the means that I use myself to come in."

"Haven't I already said, for my part, that I would consent to anything in order to go with you. Why go over it again?"

"Yes, you've told me, and that's good."

"It's neither good nor bad, my love; it's because I love you," said Marthe, whose voice, less confident than during preceding meetings without being less tender, testified to an emotion surely due to the influence recently exercised upon her by her mother. The traces of Madame Kanali's conversation were still fuming—the conversation in which, you will remember, she had forced her daughter almost to allow herself to be convinced that César belonged to the frightful family of beings rejected

232

both from the bosom of creation and that of oblivion. Drawing all her energy from the finest sentiments of the heart, although Marthe continued to love Caseneuve in spite of what her mother had said, she nevertheless could not entirely pass over what her mother had said. At her age, there are no two ways of receiving the impressions of the external world. She believed César because she loved him; she believed her mother because she loved her—but that hesitation in her voice had much to do with the similarly hesitant utterance that escaped César, which he had perhaps been holding back on previous occasions, or which, even better, he had thought of not pronouncing at all.

"Well," Caseneuve resumed, after Marthe's protest, imprinted with devotion, that she was ready to accompany him, "I still doubt it."

"What do you doubt?" she asked.

"That you have the strength to fulfill your promise."

"But I've told you that I will have the strength to follow you anywhere it pleases you to take me."

"Anywhere?"

"Anywhere."

"Even into the tomb?"

On any other occasion, that outré expression of hackneyed vocabulary—but always new to lovers—would only have been an image for Marthe, beyond which she would have gone in search of César's true meaning. On this occasion, however, remembering her mother's attack upon him, she was, in spite of the natural solidity of her constitution, gripped in the heart by a sudden, nervous, involuntary fear; she saw in César what that fear made her see: a different being, a different creature. His pallor seemed to her to be dull, verging on the immobility of marble; his eyes, stuck by a supernatural fixity; his hands, which held hers, as cold as those that her mother attributed to vampires.

"Oh, it's not into the tomb, exactly, that I want to take you," Caseneuve went on, smiling, "but it resembles it strongly."

To that response from César, which had just confirmed his nature and his intentions in Madame Kanali's eyes, the latter made a movement as if to precipitate herself into the other pathway. I held her back and, at the same time, stifled a cry on her lips with a hand that prevented its explosion.

Caseneuve continued: "If you knew, Marthe, if you even suspected the means by which I have come..."

"It's time—tell me," Marthe replied, in a curt and choked voice.

At that moment, in the air the enveloped us all, actors in and witnessed to that scene, there was a particular fluid of excitement that gripped and twisted our nerves to breaking-point. We were like sappers waiting avidly for the ignition and explosion of a mine stuffed to the brim.

"Yes, it's time, my dear Marthe," Caseneuve continued, "to tell you by what means I've come, and, in consequence, by what means we'll go."

We listened.

Then Caseneuve told her the strange things you are about to read.

XVII

"After having been chased out of here as a fake invalid," said César Caseneuve, "I didn't know how to get in again. Desperate, mad with discouragement, I prowled around the house incessantly, going back and forth past the gate by day and night.

"The other evening, at midnight, when I was standing near the gate, I saw that fatal vehicle with which you're familiar going in...the sinister *tapissière*. Immediately, the idea occurred to me—why hadn't it occurred to me before?—of sneaking in by sliding unobtrusively behind it. I thought the idea triumphant, and immediately put it into execution, walking stealthily behind the two men who were following the vehicle, my shadow overlaid and hidden by theirs. I didn't get far. As soon as I was under the arch I was seen, identified, thrust back and expelled by I don't know whom, and the gate closed in my face, with its ironic grating sounds and all its iron bars. I was pushed back into the street. It was then, however, when all seem lost for me, that I conceived the plan that I'll tell you, and whose boldness will doubtless leave you incredulous at first, but which, in the final count, you'll be obliged to believe."

That project, I thought, *really is the one I attributed to him; what he's jut said confirms my opinion. Yes, that idea occurred to him in the street—the vehicle, the gate...so my anticipations were just...in order to get in here, he took the costume and the place of the driver of the tapissière.*

"First," César went on, "in order that no one would any longer pay any attention to me, I passed myself off as dead. Nothing is easier at present. I went to the Mairie myself, where no one knows me, to inscribe myself in the list of the deceased. Then, in order to put any enquiries off the track, although no one had any great interest in making any about me, I put on the uniform of a officer in the Garde Mobile, lent to me by a friend by whose side I fought against the insurgents last year at the Place du Panthéon and the Barrière d'Italie.

"By virtue of that uniform, still respected, I was able to circulate in the vicinity of the Val-du-Grâce, where you shall see how important it was for me to be, and it was easy for me to get into all the courtyards, in the guise of an officer from the nearby guard-post, charged with maintaining order in the quarter. Once that was done—that, alas, was not the difficult part—I thought of carrying out the plan in question, the idea that had lit up like a torch in my brain, like an inspiration, in front of the very gate of the sanitarium. It's time to tell you what it was.

"Paris has an organized service of special vehicles, which depart between ten and eleven o'clock in the evening, from various points of the barriers, to come to relieve the capital's hospices, over-full of a certain population—that which has definitively settled its accounts with life. My period of service at the Val-de-Grâce had informed me in detail of the itinerary followed each night by those necrological carriages. I knew, for example, that the one serving, among other establishments, the sanitarium in the Faubourg Saint-Denis, departs from Bicêtre at ten o'clock and goes to the Val-de-Grâce to take on its first cargo. That's where I waited the first time for eight hours. I saw it arriving cautiously from the Barrière Saint-Jacques. It came through the gate of the

Val-de-Grâce and stopped at the steps in the interior courtyard.

"It was at that moment that I had hoped to see, as usual, the driver and the two men charged with walking behind the vehicle by way of an escort go into the Val and leave me a free hand for a few minutes. My expectation was disappointed; instead of going into the monument, as usual, to help their comrades in their work, the three men stayed outside, two on guard behind the vehicle, at the very opening of the kind of double-batten door by means of which the phantom passengers are introduced horizontally, and which the two guards close thereafter with the aid of a strong iron crossbar. The other one, the driver, took up a position at the head of his horses, and did not budge.

"That change astonished me as much as it frustrated me. I could not restrain myself from asking the driver why it had been made. He told me that the previous evening, the horses, left to their own devices, had taken it into their heads to go out of the courtyard, go calmly back along the faubourg and go into the country by way of the Barrière Saint-Jacques, not stopping until they got home, to the village of Ivry where they had produced a rather disagreeable surprise by arriving, with their characteristic rig, into the midst of a local fête. Such was the explanation I received from the driver, which did not modify my situation at all. My hopes sank to the bottom, like a man falling into the sea with a lead weight attacked to his feet."

These statements by César no longer fit in with my initial supposition. It was not a matter of borrowing the cart-driver costume and taking his place. What, then, was the plan that he had formulated? What was the one he had put into execution? How had he got in?

237

"With its cargo loaded," César continued, "the long vehicle draws away from the Val-de-Grâce to complete it at other points. It resumes its route. It goes down the Faubourg Saint-Jacques, still making as little noise as possible, in order not to reveal its passing to the inhabitants, whose ears are pricked, kept alert by well-founded dread for themselves or their families. And I follow it, mechanically and pointlessly—pointlessly, because my plan seemed to have failed from the moment the three men could no longer leave their positions of surveillance around their depot.

"I knew that the long carriage was following that road to go to the Hôtel-Dieu, where it took on its second load. Now we're taken by surprise at the corner of the Rue Soufflot, directly opposite the Panthéon, by patriotic songs intoned in ferocious voices by drunken socialists, up late, who are emerging like a tempest from the famous club in the Rue de Grès. They're singing *Die for the Fatherland!* at the top of their voices. They come toward us, still singing, but while they're arriving from the Rue de Grès, other socialists, who reply to them with the acclamation: *Long live the democratic and social Republic!* are coming upon us from behind, from the Rue Saint-Hyacinthe. They're both interrupted, like two torrents that find a rock in their course, by the obstacle of the tapissière. As soon as they've recognized the moving destination, all of them, as if compressed by the effect of a spring, fall silent and open up a passage for us; we pass through the somber, murmuring, rippling, noisily silent swarm. I've never experienced such an immediate contrast in my life. They flow into the shadows in black waves, and we continue going down the old Parisian faubourg.

"Having arrived at the Quai Saint-Michel, the rig I'm following, still shaving the tortuous walls, takes the Petit-Pont and goes into the Rue Neuve-Notre-Dame, which leads, as you know, to the Hôtel-Dieu, into the Place du Parvis itself. There, I hesitate as to whether I should go back to my hotel in the Passage Dauphiné, where I've been living since being sacked from the Val-de-Grâce, or whether I should cross the bridges to exhaust myself further in impotent means with the illusory goal of getting into the sanitarium. I still don't go away, however, in the midst of that indecision, and in that I act very judiciously without knowing it, for I soon see the cart-driver say a few words in the ears of the two escorts placed behind the vehicle.

"Those few words having been said, they head toward a wine merchant's shop in the Rue des Trois-Canettes, where all three of them go in. I'm mistaken— the third one only goes half way in; he's the driver. Standing in the doorway, he stays on watch, his attention divided between his duty and his pleasure. He has one eye on the counter, the other on the tapissière, in order to be quite sure that the horses are behaving themselves, that they aren't going to the local fête at Ivry again, or any other fête. That accursed surveillance, so fundamentally praiseworthy, renders my plan as impossible to execute in the Place du Parvis as in the courtyard of the Val-de-Grâce. I'm beginning to despair again. How can that importunate eye be distracted?

"A young woman passes by, emerging from the hideous Rue des Trois-Canettes with a cracked and sniveling guitar under her arm. She's just been delighting the cut-throats of the local taverns with the delightful strains of her lyre. I call to her; she comes over. I tell her to go place herself in front of the wine merchant's shop and sing her most beautiful ballads there in her finest voice.

"'Sing them with gusto,' I tell her, 'so as to make the peasants gather round.'

"'I only know one,' she relies, but I know it, of course, in the finest perfection. It's *Black-eyed girl*.'

"'Here's thirty *sous* for you—go sing that one.'

"The young Sappho of the Trois-Canettes accepts, and runs to fulfill the conditions of our hasty bargain. She sings, she scrapes her strings, inspired by the money I've given her and a crowd assembles. My cart-driver already seems distracted. The distraction turns to delight; already, his redoubtable eye is no longer gazing at his horses; he leans over the young singer in a melancholy fashion and I see him give her something, doubtless an obol of admiration; Polyphemus is vanquished.

"I take advantage of the fine moment of generosity that has absorbed him, and slip into the vast tapissière, whose two battens have, as usual, remained open for the requirements of the service."

"You got into the tapissière!" exclaimed Marthe. "You shut yourself in with the corpses!"

I uttered the same cry inwardly, with an astonishment that rooted me to the spot, on hearing about that act of redoubtable temerity, of unparalleled imprudence, of unprecedented passion—an action whose folly of which, it must be admitted, only a vampire, in a fit or violent crisis, would be strong enough to carry through to the end.

You can imagine how, in listening to César, the ever-present idea of the vampire crossed the fanaticized mind of Madame Kanali, how the word *vampire* came to her agitated lips, and that I had had once again to beg her, tremulously, to restrain herself lest she give us away.

"Scarcely am I in the moving coffin," César continued, "the swaying, convulsive, ill-suspended grave, than I'm gripped by a nervous tremor, as if I'd fallen into a well of icy water. My hair stands on end with the chill; my chest contracts with the chill; I rebel, however; I want to struggle: a violent combat, ardent, then desperate, between the terror increasingly oppressing me, which is making my teeth clench and pushing me outside, and my love for you, Marthe, the love that makes me ashamed of my fear, which holds me in place and retains me. I don't know yet, at that moment, I confess, whether it is my love that will conclusively hold sway over my fear, or my fear over my love; but just when I am perhaps about to hurl myself, recklessly, outside the sinister cart, no longer being able to stand it, I hear someone open the door at the back.

"I only just have time to throw myself backwards and to imitate, by lying flat, the rigid immobility of the bodies that form, by their superimposition, a kind of wall on the side opposite the door that has just opened. Through that gap, I see the introduction, repeated several times, of objects similar to those I've just mentioned. The force of impulsion that shoves them from the outside to the inside pushes them up against me, but I dare not push them away for fear of giving myself away, although I'm fearful of their contact, of dying on the spot.

"The operation complete, the doors close again; the iron bar seals the entrance, and the carriage moves off again toward the Grève, via the Pont Notre-Dame. From the Grève it goes into the Rue Saint-Antoine, but quietly, moderating the rotations of its wheels on the roadway;

I've told you why; it's so as not to frighten the houses situated on its route.

"Can you imagine my situation, my dear Marthe? I was in complete darkness and only able to move with great difficulty in the midst of those and badly-stowed inert masses. I could hear the beating of my heart, as one hears the swinging of a pendulum by night. A sickening, stifling situation.

"Wanting, at any price, to see, to breathe, to live, I decided, with the aid of a knife that I was fortunate enough to have on me, to make a hole in the thin wall of the carriage. The task wouldn't have taken as long or been so difficult if I hadn't been restricted in my movements. However, after a few minutes, the opening was pierced, and I was then able to distinguish the reddish blinking of lights distributed here and there at the level of the shops we were passing by that were still open, and passers-by who were fleeing from us with signs of revulsion when they recognized the particular character of our conveyance.

"Toward the middle of the Rue Saint-Antoine, at the corner of the Rue Percée, it stopped, and I wondered why, knowing that we were still a long way from the Hôpital Saint-Antoine, which was probably our next stop. This was the reason—or, more accurately, the pretext—for that halt, which prolonged my intolerable sequestration so cruelly: I saw the driver confide the care of his horses to one of his companions and draw away in a casual and contented fashion; he went a little way along the Rue Percée and tapped on the window of a shop, which, from its grayish façade, I deduced must be that of a laundress. A young woman, sprightly and cheerful, appeared on the threshold in a white under-bodice, with a thousand creases in the sleeves and the

242

basques, with the fine figure of an eighteenth-century marquise, an intelligent forehead and an oval face, carved and creased by Coustou.[38]

"The muleteer went in unceremoniously, and the door remained ajar, which permitted me to see from my strange observatory that it was nothing less than an amorous assignation. What a well-chosen moment! As soon as they were in the shop, the gallant fellow took a large bouquet of wild flowers from beneath his smock, with a movement of his arm worthy of Céladon,[39] and handed it to his lady. That tribute appeared to obtain the highest approval for the one to whom it was addressed. The pretty laundress put the bouquet to her lips and kissed it for a long time, half-closing her eyes—a voluptuous sign of gratitude. I was, therefore, resolutely witness to an amorous episode: Charon quitting his ferry-boat to meet the laundresses of the Styx. Charming!

"Yes, but me, I was in the boat, waiting…still waiting…what a wait! I cursed that ill-timed love from the bottom of my soul. Had I really the right to do so, though? Was it not also love that had led me to my situation? And was it not thanks to the charioteer who was here that I was going to see you, Marthe, in a matter of minutes? No matter—the fellow irritated me. If I had dared, I would have shouted through my loophole, in a

---

[38] It is unclear whether the reference is to Nicolas Coustou (1658-1733), his brother Guillaume (1677-1746) or the latter's similarly-named son (1716-1777), all of whom were noted sculptors.

[39] The shepherd lover in Honoré d'Urfé's immensely long pastoral romance *L'Astrée* (1607-27), which was completed by other hands after the former's death. The love of Céladon and Astrée was cited by the utopian Charles Fourier as the spiritual ideal of the emotion.

manner to put a redoubtable end to his tenderness: 'Hey! When are we going?' I didn't do it, firstly because I no longer had any courage, any idea or any voice, and secondly because all my vital energy was concentrated in the gaze that I was directing at him, as if to pull him away from his laundress.

"My magnetism didn't work. The wretched muleteer sat down, and sat his lover down next to him; once they were both seated, he took a crumpled, blue-tinted piece of paper from inside his felt hat; then, putting his arm around the neck of his enchantress, he began reading the piece of paper with her. What was it? I couldn't guess. Ah! I was about to find out...two voices started singing. It was the ballad performed on the parvis of Notre-Dame, in front of the wine-merchant's, by the little Bohemian songstress of the Rue des Trois-Canettes: *Black-Eyed Girl.* All the verses went by; there was not a word of that abominable ballad that did not enter into the quick of my flesh like a red-hot nail.

"Finally, the sentimental scene came to an end; the funereal Lovelace, whose name was Fromentin—which I knew by virtue of the tender farewell addressed to him by the laundress from her doorway: 'Adieu, my Fromentin!'—rallied his two comrades, and, to compensate them for the tedium of a halt that had not had the same charm for them as for him, took them to the wine merchant's placed at the other corner of the Rue Percée! Always wine merchants!

"I would not have been able to witness that feast from the tortuous position that I occupied if the handsome Fromentin had not turned the heads of his horses toward the Place de la Bastille instead of leaving them immobile, as they had been in the Rue Percée for a good half hour. Great God, how all three of them took advantage of that infernal station, which added ten further minutes to the torture, the fire, the rack, the pincers—to all the tortures that I had already endured. What they drank in those ten minutes, what they swilled, is incalculable. If it had only been wine! But I saw all the shades of the rainbow mingled in their glasses, although the yellow returned most frequently. I concluded that cognac played a leading role in the party.

"In sum, they drank prodigiously. They drank too much, for, when we set off for the Bastille, in order to go into the Faubourg Saint-Antoine, they went from right to left, from side to side, as if they were being tossed by waves. The vehicle, left to its own devices, no longer following the good side of the road, also experienced that frightful pitching, and all of its human cargo poured over me. My arms were insufficient to ward off the avalanche. How is it that all my hair did not turn white? I say all, for the next day, the temple were blanched, for a long time, forever. You can see that, Marthe.

"However, by dint of gong right and left, and a little forwards, we reached the Place de la Bastille. There, the two men representing the reargaurd drew closer to Fromentin and said to him, without fear of being overheard in that vast space, where passers-by were becoming less numerous, and where, for reasons already deduced, they had little apprehension of their indiscreet contact: 'Fromentin, there's a superb coup to bring off if you wish, which would give us a good time for the rest of the night.'

"'What superb coup? Where's the superb coup?'

"'Don't shout!'

"'As if anyone were likely to hear us in this basket!'

"'All the same, keep your voice down!'

"'I'll keep my voice down—let's hear this coup, quickly!'

"The three men huddled together to the right of the shafts, almost edge to edge to the planks that separated me from them.

"'This is the coup. Well, instead of us killing the mood by going all the way to the Hospice Saint-Antoine, and from there to the Saint-Louis, then from there to the house in the faubourg, then from there to—damned if I know where—let's not go anywhere!'

"'What's that?' Fromentin interrupted. 'How do we do that?'

"'Let's go along the Canal Saint-Martin, which is right in front of us, close to the edge. We break the chain, that's all, and then throw all the merchandise— rat-a-tat!—into the water: goodnight all! Tomorrow we say that we were asleep, that the cabriolet tipped over. How does that suit you, Fromentin?' Choffar asked. Choffar was the name of the man who'd just finished talking.

"Continue to imagine, my dear Marthe, my new situation. Already the horses, avoiding the entrance to the Faubourg Saint-Antoine, were taking the road down to the Canal Saint-Martin, along the Rue de Charonne.

"The entire cargo was about to be tipped into the canal, and me with it."

XVIII

"The driver had consented, then?" Marthe asked.

"Perhaps it seems to you," César continued, "that nothing would have been easier than to cry out, to get out, to escape...but first of all, I couldn't get out; the iron bar was securing the two battens of the door. Cry out? It was half past eleven; no one would come to my aid; and after all those cries and all those movements, if I hadn't succeeded in getting myself out of it—and I wouldn't have got out of it—what would have happened? I'd have found myself in the presence of three vigorous fellows who would have roughed me up right away. They were drunk...one corpse more or less wouldn't have made much difference to them. I therefore had good reason to reflect profoundly on the originality of my situation.

"The cart was still going down, unsteadily, toward the canal. It wasn't until we were level with the Rue du Chemin-Vert that Fromentin appeared to hesitate, for his part, to carry out the abominable project of the mass drowning. Had love rendered him, that evening, better than his accomplices? I don't know...but I saw, through the fog of his drunkenness, a calculation of prudence glimmering.

"Afraid of opposing the opinion of his comrades, two muscular fellows who might well by-pass his assent if necessary, he told them that their plan pleased him enormously, and that he was all for it, but that it was still too early to carry it out without considerable risk. Plenty of people coming out of the theaters were still crossing the bridges to go home, either to the Barrières or the La Roquette and Ménilmontant quarters.

"It would be better, he went on, to go straight to the Hospice Saint-Antoine first, take on the usual cargo there, and then come back to the canal as if to go to the Hôpital Saint-Louis, one of their destinations, and to which, of course, they wouldn't go. That was what Fromentin said, in his semi-common sense. There might have been some resistance to his proposal, but, the fear he had put into them having weighed upon them, they took the Rue du Chemin-Vert and turned right by way of the Rue de Popincourt toward the Faubourg Saint-Antoine, in order to end up directly in front of the hospice.

"After a lot of jolting and pitching in the potholes of the atrocious Rue Popincourt, the most uneven of all the bad roads in Paris, a kind of communal route—which says enough about how rarely it is repaired—we reached the Faubourg Saint-Antoine.

"The concierge who came to open the gate of the hospice was astonished, and complained about the lateness of the vehicle. They were careful to keep quiet about the reason for the delay, but he deduced it easily from the unsteady gait and strongly alcoholic ambient atmosphere of the three men. Closing the two sides of the gate behind them, he muttered: 'It seems someone's been having a party this evening.' They made no reply, and followed him into the ground-floor rooms.

"In order to get the work done more rapidly when they came back, before leaving the tapissière they had removed the iron crossbar sealing the two battens of the door, so that the door was open and nothing as any longer preventing my escape. The facility was all the greater because the abominable somersaults of the Rue

Popincourt had upset the carriage's container to the point of opening gaps large enough to pass through by dragging oneself through with one's hands and knees.

"I therefore had the opportunity to escape, to put an end to the unspeakable tortures—and it is permissible to say 'unspeakable,' this time, with less banality—of one of the most frightful nights ever, and above all to spare myself the almost infallible chance of dying, drowned at the bottom of the muddy Canal Saint-Martin. I could doubtless have done that—but to give in to that idea would be to renounce forever penetrating into the sanitarium, seeing you again, my dear Marthe, who had been forewarned of my arrival.

"You were waiting for me, perhaps at the cost of great difficulties, for, with the aid of the owl, you had not left me in ignorance of the combined and coalesced sentiments of hatred and anger with which your father and mother had viewed my indefatigable obstinacy in returning to you in spite of their disapproval and prohibition. That you should expose to yourself to those risks while I...I might recoil before peril—any peril whatsoever! No! A thousand times no!"

"Then again, you see, Marthe I have proved that there is a fatality in passion. It is no longer you who acts when it is true, when it is strong; it is passion that leads you. It triumphs over everything, over the individual will, and that of others, over reason, self-interest, honor—often fear itself... yes, fear. I am the proof of it, and the example.

"To describe to you the black terrors, the mortal palpitations, the frights the horripilations, the superhuman swoons that I went through during that nocturnal expedition, without parallel, I believe, in human life, is impossible. I shall not try. To support myself, in order not to expire in place, I had but one means—that of thinking constantly of you, Marthe, of constantly pronouncing your name: Marthe; of saying to myself: *One more ordeal, and I shall be with Marthe! Behold the work of love!* That alone, I repeat, that alone, perhaps with maternal love, is capable of giving birth to that beautiful, rare and powerful miracle of determination over fear.

"My determination, therefore, defeated my nervous tremors. I stayed.

"The same reproaches that had greeted the three men, my companions, in the course of that night, so memorable for me, escorted them when they were on the point of setting off again, the loading operation having been completed. One of the hospital administrators had even joined the concierge at the gate, and threatened them with destitution if they took it into their heads to be late again.

"They left.

"I attributed the abandonment of their plan to go down to the Canal Saint-Martin, into which they had intended to unload the deposit entrusted to them, to those severe words on the part of the administrator. That salutary terror, to which I owe my life, made such an impact on their resolution that they avoided taking, in order to go the Hôpital Saint-Louis, the road they had taken in coming, in order—that as visible—not to expose themselves to the risk of changing their minds in the presence of the great temptation of the water.

"Taking the longer route, they climbed the Faubourg Saint-Antoine as far as the Rue Saint-Maur, which would take them to Saint-Louis without any deviation, for the Rue Saint-Maur, the most desperately extensive street in Paris, the dorsal spine of the mastodon, ends at the foundation of the pious king, whose name it has taken and preserved. I had, therefore, the right to count, after the various accents of the night, on a relative calm until the end of my journey.

"Vain hope! At a certain point of the Rue Saint-Maur, a difficult point to specify exactly, in view of the small number of poor disreputable lanterns placed out of pity on that immeasurable extent of terrain, but, to judge by the surroundings, somewhere between the Rue des Trois-Couronnes and the Rue de l'Orillon, in the dense obscurity in which I was curled up, in a space made even narrower by the addition made at the Hôpital Saint-Antoine, I felt a hand place itself on my jaw. A hand!"

"A hand? A hand, you say?"

"Yes, Marthe, a hand."

"Oh my God!"

Madame Kanali extended her head through the branches of the hedge of bushes that extended between the trees in places, listening with shivers of terror. I could hear her breath, noisy within her taut breast.

"That hand… it's distressing," said the doctor. "I've been through many situations in my life… but that one… oh, that one!"

"Yes, it's frightful," I said, "but let's listen."

"My blood," Caseneuve continued, "retreated *en masse* to my heart, which seemed to want to burst out of my breast, and rose into my throat. The cold of that hand entered into me like five talons of ice, so profoundly that I thought that one of those five terrible fingers had penetrate and was digging into my skull.

"Momentarily, the situation raised me to the vertiginous summit of madness. I saw red; I heard something akin to a monotonous sound of bells in both ears—that was the blood surging to my brain and erupting therein."

Marthe threw her arms around César's neck and looked at him, eye to eye and heart to soul, with the immense, indescribable interest that one feels for a beloved individual narrating a perilous ordeal—so perilous that it seems to be still present.

Another interest was combined with that one in Marthe's heart, that one very serious, very consoling, which gave birth to a conviction that she had now acquired forever: her mother was fanatically mistaken in classifying that poor young man, so brave by force of love, in the category of those who deceive the tomb in order to come to the earth to light to satisfy filthy appetites at the expense of the living. It was him, her beloved Caseneuve, who was threatened, at this point in his terrible poem, of becoming the victim of some brucolaque, of some vampire!

Hugging Marthe, entirely happy and shivering all over, to his bosom, César continued.

"What should have followed in servile fashion the chromatic scale of the old novels you read, my dear Marthe, is that I ought to have screamed at the icy contact of that hand. In fact, one does not scream in the situation in which I found myself trapped; on the contrary, the voice falls into the cavities of the breast, and the throat closes over it. One can no longer breathe; one can no longer see. My ears continued to run, to groan, to buzz around my head.

"However, as I did not want to die, I imparted a desperate, outré shock to myself, like that of a drowning man touching the bottom, and, raising myself up—for you will not have forgotten that I was still lying on my back—I pulled away the marble hand stuck to my cheek; I shoved it far away from me, with horror.

"But the hand immediately returned, this time applying itself to my breast, which it seized and dug into with a force at least equal to that I had put into shoving it away. Then, I passed my own arm beneath the arm that was gripping my clothing and my flesh, and seized the elbow that was compressing my breast.

"What a struggle! What a struggle in the darkness, in the suffocation, in the silence! With whom, then, was I contending in that darkness? A breath passed through my hair, ran over my face, preceding words that had the appearance of emerging from somewhere nearby I could not locate: 'Are you dead or alive?'

"I had the strength to reply: 'Alive!'

"'Good! I too am alive—but tell me, how the devil did you get into this gracious phaeton?

"'It's a long story,' I stammered, still asphyxiated by the unexpectedness of the occurrence.

"'You weren't put in here by mistake, I suppose...?'

"'No, not by mistake.'

"'It's just that in Paris at present,' my funereal interlocutor went on, 'there are kindly relatives and worthy heirs who are profiting from the rapidity with which people are exiting from life to make you exit a little sooner, in order to inherit more quickly. But in that case, why are you in this boudoir? Forgive me for my curiosity, but truly, when one doesn't have a motive like mine for cramming oneself in here... I don't know... I can't see any other motive...

"'Anyway, mine is... damn it, I can tell you. It's one young man to another, isn't it? For I divine from your voice that you're still a the fortunate age of billiards games, dominoes, card games, parties at Pinson's, idling, cigar in mouth, at the Brasserie du Luxembourg, balls at the Capucins and the Prado. Monsieur, I've just come out of the Prado—what about you?'

"'I haven't come out of it.'

"'Too bad! *It's a jolly place*, Monsieur Prudhomme[40] would say. *One drinks there between laughter and love*. So, I've come out of the Prado and I'm going back to the Hôpital Saint-Louis, where I'm an intern. You can see how I'm interned. This gracious vehicle is taking me back to my hôtel...Dieu. Joking apart, let's talk seriously. Who are you? One likes to know down here with whom one is traveling.'

"'I'm an intern like you,' I replied.

"'You're an intern! And to what royal establishment are you attached?'

"'I was most recently an intern at the Val-de-Grâce.'

"'I'm very glad to meet you! I'll go on then, I'll continue and conclude: at Saint-Louis, the interns only go out once a fortnight, and for myself, it's necessary that I get some air every evening. I have a sentiment in the Rue des Boucheries-Saint-Germain. How do I reconcile my duties as an intern with my tenderness as a lover? The amphitheater and the polka? This is how: I escape in the evening before the gates of the hospice are closed; I go down into Paris; I go to the café, the ballroom, as the mood takes me; finally, at eleven o'clock, to get back in...ah, but getting back in is a little more difficult—impossible, even. So what do I do?

---

[40] The archetype of self-satisfied banality in the work of Henry Monnier; the speaker must have encountered him in *Scènes populaires* (1830) rather than the definitive *Les Mémoires de Joseph Prudhomme* (1857).

"'Having observed that this jolly tapissière, before stopping at Saint-Louis, stopped, in its journey, at Saint-Antoine, and that during that stop it's entirely unmonitored for about six minutes, I acted in consequence of those fortunate observations. Taking advantage of the temporary absence of the three men commissioned to guard it, I climb in at the rear, lie down—and it takes me to Saint-Louis every night.

"'At Saint-Louis, I seize the moment when the three men are drinking in the wine merchant's shop located opposite the gate; I emerge from my brilliant carriage and climb up to my intern's bedroom, to descended therefrom at two hours after midnight and do my duty until dawn. That, my dear and admirable companion, is the cause of my absences and the reason for my presence among these shades.

"'Well,' I said, somewhat reassured by my young comrade and colleague, 'your story is much the same as mine.'

"'Impossible! Surely not!'

"'It's true,' I went on, 'except that you're making use of the vehicle to return from your amorous rendezvous and I'm making use of it to go to mine.'

"'Where is it, then?'

"'On the other side of the canal, at the sanitarium in the Faubourg Saint-Denis.'

"'I understand. Oh, admirable! So, we've both had the idea of having recourse to the same strange means, unprecedented since the world's beginning, to see our beloveds. O love and surgery!' After that exclamation, he resumed, with an adorable naivety: 'And who knows... perhaps there's a third young man with us in this space, so poorly designed to receive...'

255

"We did not have time to verify the fact; the necrological carriage went into the first courtyard of the Hôpital Saint-Louis, rolling over the poor gray sand and the sad yellow lawn that enamel the pavement there. What my joyful intern had told me was realized, to the letter.

"Once the carriage had stopped, the three men hastened, before any consignment of new passengers took their place, to go make their habitual maneuvers, belatedly, in the establishment of the wine merchant, whose shop was no longer open at that hour of the night save for once entrance, which was for them. While they were filling their glasses, my traveling companion bid me farewell; he shook my hand with the hand that fear had caused me to find icy, and he slid from shadow to shadow projected in the pavement by the old walls of the ancient establishment of Saint-Louis, all the way to a door, by means of which he went up quietly, as he had said, to this intern's bedroom, into which he slipped in such a manner as to let the house believe that he had never left the attics all night long.

"One other and final event marked my journey from the construction of the pious King Saint Louis. We crossed over the Canal Saint-Martin without the slightest accident reminding my three men of the intention they had manifested earlier in the evening of getting rid of their load in the black depths of those stagnant waters. In the old Rue des Récollets, however, between the Faubourg Saint-Martin and the Faubourg Saint-Denis, I almost lost within an instant, by my own fault, the fruit of my constancy, my firmness and, perhaps I have the right to say, my heroism, in spite of my mortal anxieties."

"What happened, then?" asked Marthe, who thought that she was emerging forever from a terrible dream.

"I have the habit," César concluded, "when I find myself in darkness and I want to know the time, of activating the chimes on my watch. That night, I did not reflect on the consequences of that action, so insignificant in other circumstances. I pushed the button of my watch, and at the third tinkling stroke sounded by the bell, the driver suddenly reined in his horses and I heard him say to his acolytes: 'Did you hear something?'

"'What? No.'

"'There's a repeating watch in there—a gold watch, for sure... people are in such a hurry nowadays... someone's forgotten to take his watch off. We're not going much further—let's take a look... it's worth the trouble...'

"'No, keep going,' said one of the two confidants to whom the carter was speaking. 'There's no more a watch in there than a pendulum clock.'

"'You're scared!'

"'No I'm not!'

"'Yes you are!'

"'Let's see—how many chimes did you hear sound?'

"'Three, I think.'

"'Well, that proves you were sleep and dreaming, because it's midnight. You'd have heard twelve strokes.'

"'That's true, damn it,' murmured Fromentin.

"'And then, think about it,' the other went on, 'repeating watches don't chime on their own hereabouts. If you heard one chimes inside, there'd have to be someone there inside...someone alive...'

"'That's true too, damn it'

"'You were dreaming a clock, that's all.'

"The dialogue stopped there—but I'd still run a terrible risk! If Fromentin had only heard three strokes out of twelve, it was because, realizing my silly imprudence, I'd put my watch into my mouth after the third stroke, in order to stifle the sound."

César paused momentary, and then went on: "I've told you, dear Marthe, about my first night with the shades; the four other nights that followed were marked by events that were scarcely calm, as you may suppose, but none was as tragically eventful as the first, which honesty obliged me to relate to you."

"What!" Marthe cried. "Five nights!" She put her hand over her eyes in order no longer to see, even in memory, the scenes of that narrative. Involuntarily, her pale lips murmured, repeatedly: "Five nights! Five nights!"

"Yes, five nights," César Caseneuve repeated in his turn, "on which I used the same means, the same ruse, to get in here, to see you, to tell you the sweetest thing in the world: *I love you*; and the best thing in the world: *I will love you all my life*; and finally, to say to you, this evening, that we shall never be parted again, never be parted again... Shh! Shh! Listen!"

"It's the quarter hour sounding," Marthe said.

"Then it's time to go," said Caseneuve, getting to his feet.

Marthe got up too.

"Do you have the courage," César said to her, "the immense courage, to be free? To be yourself, to be mine, to climb into that same... that same... thing that brought me here, and which is presently unguarded... oh, I've calculated my time well... and remain enclosed with me all the way to the barrière?"

Marthe was unsteady on her feet. Her hand, which was leaning on Caseneuve's shoulder, prevented her from falling over.

"At the barrière," César continued, "it stops one last time—and one last time, the three men escorting it go to drink at the tavern on the Butte Montmartre. It's left alone for a few minutes more on the exterior boulevard. We take advantage of that moment, we escape, we're free! Once free, you write to your father... but we don't have a minute, a second, to lose. We have to go. You have to go with me... it's now or never—will you? Oh, you're hesitating... well, don't hesitate, Marthe—do better. Refuse. It's a horrible means, it's horrible, a thousand times, horrible!"

"Let's go!" said Marthe, taking Caseneuve's arm. "Let's go!"

They went.

They did not get far.

Between the end of the pathway along which they were running and the gate of the house, the doctor, more on his guard this time that on the previous occasion, stopped the two young fugitives. They were caught.

But then, while Madame Kanali embraced Marthe, for whom she no longer had to fear the murderous affections of a vampire, the doctor told César, hugging him in his arms, that he would give him his daughter, since he had demonstrated, by his rare and sterling courage that he was worthy to be his son-in-law, and a physician like himself.

A few days later, all four of them left Paris and France to go to America, where Dr. Kanali intended, with a joy slightly colored by hatred of France, to embalm the President of the United States.

SF & FANTASY

Henri Allorge. *The Great Cataclysm*
Guy d'Armen. *Doc Ardan: The City of Gold and Lepers*
G.-J. Arnaud. *The Ice Company*
Charles Asselineau. *The Double Life*
Cyprien Bérard. *The Vampire Lord Ruthwen*
Aloysius Bertrand. *Gaspard de la Nuit*
Richard Bessière. *The Gardens of the Apocalypse*
Albert Bleunard. *Ever Smaller*
Félix Bodin. *The Novel of the Future*
Alphonse Brown. *City of Glass*
André Caroff. *The Terror of Madame Atomos; Miss Atomos; The Return of Madame Atomos; The Mistake of Madame Atomos; The Monsters of Madame Atomos; The Revenge of Madame Atomos*
Félicien Champsaur. *The Human Arrow; Ouha*
Didier de Chousy. *Ignis*
Captain Danrit. *Undersea Odyssey*
C. I. Defontenay. *Star (Psi Cassiopeia)*
Charles Derennes. *The People of the Pole*
Georges Dodds (anthologist). *The Missing Link*
Harry Dickson. *The Heir of Dracula*
Jules Dornay. *Lord Ruthven Begins*
Alfred Driou. *The Adventures of a Parisian Aeronaut*
Sâr Dubnotal *vs. Jack the Ripper*
Alexandre Dumas. *The Return of Lord Ruthven*
Renée Dunan. *Baal*
J.-C. Dunyach. *The Night Orchid; The Thieves of Silence*
Henri Duvernois. *The Man Who Found Himself*
Achille Eyraud. *Voyage to Venus*
Henri Falk. *The Age of Lead*
Paul Féval. *Anne of the Isles; Knightshade; Revenants; Vampire City; The Vampire Countess; The Wandering Jew's Daughter*
Paul Féval, *fils. Felifax, the Tiger-Man*
Charles de Fieux. *Lamékis*
Arnould Galopin. *Doctor Omega; Doctor Omega & The Shadowmen*
Léon Gozlan. *The Vampire of the Val-de-Grâce*
G.L. Gick. *Harry Dickson and the Werewolf of Rutherford Grange*
Edmond Haraucourt. *Illusions of Immortality*
Nathalie Henneberg. *The Green Gods*

V. Hugo, P. Foucher & P. Meurice. *The Hunchback of Notre-Dame*
Michel Jeury. *Chronolysis*
Gustave Kahn. *The Tale of Gold and Silence*
Gérard Klein. *The Mote in Time's Eye*
Jean de La Hire. *Enter the Nyctalope; The Nyctalope on Mars; The Nyctalope vs. Lucifer; The Nyctalope Steps In; Night of the Nyctalope*
Etienne-Léon de Lamothe-Langon. *The Virgin Vampire*
André Laurie. *Spiridon*
Gabriel de Lautrec. *The Vengeance of the Oval Portrait*
Alain le Drimeur. *The Future City*
Georges Le Faure & Henri de Graffigny. *The Extraordinary Adventures of a Russian Scientist Across the Solar System* (2 vols.)
Gustave Le Rouge. *The Vampires of Mars The Dominion of the World* (w/Gustave Guitton) (4 vols.)
Jules Lermina. *Mysteryville; Panic in Paris; To-Ho and the Gold Destroyers; The Secret of Zippelius*
Jean-Marc & Randy Lofficier. *Edgar Allan Poe on Mars; The Katrina Protocol; Pacifica; Robonocchio; Tales of the Shadowmen 1-8*
Xavier Mauméjean. *The League of Heroes*
Joseph Méry. *The Tower of Destiny*
Hippolyte Mettais. *The Year 5865*
Louise Michel. *The Human Microbes; The New World*
José Moselli. *Illa's End*
John-Antoine Nau. *Enemy Force*
Marie Nizet. *Captain Vampire*
C. Nodier, A. Beraud & Toussaint-Merle. *Frankenstein*
Henri de Parville. *An Inhabitant of the Planet Mars*
Gaston de Pawlowski. *Journey to the Land of the 4th Dimension*
Georges Pellerin. *The World in 2000 Years*
Ernest Pérochon. *The Frenetic People*
Pierre Pelot. *The Child Who Walked on the Sky*
J. Polidori, C. Nodier, E. Scribe. *Lord Ruthven the Vampire*
P.-A. Ponson du Terrail. *The Vampire and the Devil's Son*
Henri de Régnier. *A Surfeit of Mirrors*
Maurice Renard. *The Blue Peril; Doctor Lerne; The Doctored Man; A Man Among the Microbes; The Master of Light*
Jean Richepin. *The Wing*
Albert Robida. *The Adventures of Saturnin Farandoul; The Clock of the Centuries; Chalet in the Sky*

J.-H. Rosny Aîné. *Helgvor of the Blue River; The Givreuse Enigma; The Mysterious Force; The Navigators of Space; Vamireh; The World of the Variants; The Young Vampire*
Marcel Rouff. *Journey to the Inverted World*
Han Ryner. *The Superhumans*
Brian Stableford. *The New Faust at the Tragicomique;The Empire of the Necromancers (The Shadow of Frankenstein; Frankenstein and the Vampire Countess; Frankenstein in London); Sherlock Holmes & The Vampires of Eternity; The Stones of Camelot; The Wayward Muse.* (anthologist) *The Germans on Venus; News from the Moon; The Supreme Progress; The World Above the World; Nemoville; Investigations of the Future*
Jacques Spitz. *The Eye of Purgatory*
Kurt Steiner. *Ortog*
Eugène Thébault. *Radio-Terror*
C.-F. Tiphaigne de La Roche. *Amilec*
Théo Varlet. *The Xenobiotic Invasion; Timeslip Troopers* (w/André Blandin); *The Martian Epic* (w/Octave Joncquel)
Paul Vibert. *The Mysterious Fluid*
Villiers de l'Isle-Adam. *The Scaffold; The Vampire Soul*
Philippe Ward. *Artahe*
Philippe Ward & Sylvie Miller. *The Song of Montségur*

MYSTERIES & THRILLERS

M. Allain & P. Souvestre. *The Daughter of Fantômas*
A. Anicet-Bourgeois, Lucien Dabril. *Rocambole*
A. Bernède. *Belphegor*; *Judex* (w/Louis Feuillade)
A. Bisson & G. Livet. *Nick Carter vs. Fantômas*
V. Darlay & H. de Gorsse. *Lupin vs. Holmes: The Stage Play*
Paul Féval. *Gentlemen of the Night; John Devil; The Black Coats ('Salem Street; The Invisible Weapon; The Parisian Jungle; The Companions of the Treasure; Heart of Steel; The Cadet Gang; The Sword-Swallower)*
Emile Gaboriau. *Monsieur Lecoq*
Steve Leadley. *Sherlock Holmes: The Circle of Blood*
Maurice Leblanc. *Arsène Lupin vs. Countess Cagliostro; Lupin vs. Holmes (The Blonde Phantom; The Hollow Needle); The Many Faces of Arsène Lupin*
Gaston Leroux. *Chéri-Bibi; The Phantom of the Opera; Rouletabille & the Mystery of the Yellow Room*

Richard Marsh. *The Complete Adventures of Judith Lee*
William Patrick Maynard. *The Terror of Fu Manchu; The Destiny of Fu Manchu*
Frank J. Morlock. *Sherlock Holmes: The Grand Horizontals; Sherlock Holmes vs Jack the Ripper*
Antonin Reschal. *The Adventures of Miss Boston*
P. de Wattyne & Y. Walter. *Sherlock Holmes vs. Fantômas*
David White. *Fantômas in America*

SCREENPLAYS

Mike Baron. *The Iron Triangle*
Emma Bull & Will Shetterly. *Nightspeeder; War for the Oaks*
Gerry Conway & Roy Thomas. *Doc Dynamo*
Steve Englehart. *Majorca*
James Hudnall. *The Devastator*
Jean-Marc & Randy Lofficier. *Royal Flush*
J.-M. & R. Lofficier & Marc Agapit. *Despair*
J.-M. & R. Lofficier & Joël Houssin. *City*
Andrew Paquette. *Peripheral Vision*
Robert L. Robinson, Jr. *Judex*
R. Thomas, J. Hendler & L. Sprague de Camp. *Rivers of Time*

NON-FICTION

Stephen R. Bissette. *Blur 1-5. Green Mountain Cinema 1; Teen Angels*
Win Scott Eckert. *Crossovers* (2 vols.)
Jean-Marc & Randy Lofficier. *Shadowmen* (2 vols.)
Randy Lofficier. *Over Here*

HEXAGON COMICS

Franco Frescura & Luciano Bernasconi. *Wampus*
Franco Frescura & Giorgio Trevisan. *CLASH*
L. Bernasconi, J.-M. Lofficier & Juan Roncagliolo Berger. *Phenix*
Claude Legrand, J.-M. Lofficier & L. Bernasconi. *Kabur*
Franco Oneta. *Zembla*
L. Buffolente, Lofficier & J.-J. Dzialowski. *Strangers: Homicron*
Danilo Grossi. *Strangers: Jaydee*
Claude Legrand & Luciano Bernasconi. *Strangers: Starlock*